THE GLENCOE LITERATURE LIBRARY

Nectar in
a Sieve

and Related Readings

Glencoe
McGraw-Hill

New York, New York   Columbus, Ohio   Woodland Hills, California   Peoria, Illinois

Acknowledgments

Grateful acknowledgment is given authors, publishers, photographers, museums, and agents for permission to reprint the following copyrighted material. Every effort has been made to determine copyright owners. In case of any omissions, the Publisher will be pleased to make suitable acknowledgments in future editions.

NECTAR IN A SIEVE, by Karmala Markandaya. Copyright © 1954 by The John Day Company, copyright renewed © 1982 by Kamala Markandaya. This edition reprinted by arrangement with HarperCollins Publishers.

"Pictures of Marriage" from Personal History, Learning–I by Vad Mehta. Copyright © 1983 by Ved Mehta, first published by *The New Yorker*, reprinted with the permission of the Wylie Agency, Inc.

Letter to Lord Irwin and "About That Letter" from GANDHI IN INDIA: IN HIS OWN WORDS, edited by Martin Green, copyright © 1987, University Press of New England, pp. 113–121. Reprinted by permission.

"Rice" by Chemmanam Chacko reprinted by permission of Oxford University Press, New Dehli.

"In India, Marriages Made by Computer" by Sheila Tefft in *The Christian Science Monitor*, February 8, 1990, v82 n51 p14. Reprinted by permission.

Act I of A PASSAGE TO INDIA by Santha Rama Rau from the novel by E. M. Forster. Copyright © 1960 by Santha Rama Rau and Edward Morgan Forster. First American edition 1961. Published by Harcourt, Brace & World, New York. Reprinted by permission.

Cover Art: *Rice Fields, Goa, India*, 1997. Sophia Elliot. English. Oil on paper, 32 x 28 cm. Private Collection/Bridgeman Art Library.

Glencoe/McGraw-Hill

A Division of The *McGraw·Hill* Companies

Send all inquiries to:
Glencoe/McGraw-Hill
8787 Orion Place
Columbus, OH 43240

ISBN 0-02-817991-9
Printed in the United States of America
2 3 4 5 6 7 8 9 026 04 03 02 01 00

Contents

Nectar in a Sieve

Part One

Part Two

Continued

Contents *Continued*

Related Readings 143

Nectar in
a Sieve

Kamala Markandaya

Work without hope draws nectar in a sieve,
And hope without an object cannot live.

COLERIDGE

Part One

Chapter 1

SOMETIMES AT NIGHT I think that my husband is with me again, coming gently through the mists, and we are tranquil together. Then morning comes, the wavering grey turns to gold, there is a stirring within me as the sleepers awake, and he softly departs.

One by one they come out into the early morning sunshine, my son, my daughter, and Puli, the child I clung to who was not mine, and he no longer a child. Puli is with me because I tempted him, out of my desperation I lured him away from his soil to mine. Yet I have no fears now: what is done is done, there can be no repining. "Are you happy with me?" I said to him yesterday—being sure of the answer. He nodded, not hesitating, but a little impatient. An old woman's foibles. A need for comfort.

But I am comforted most when I look at his hands. He has no fingers, only stubs, since what has been taken can never be given back, but they are clean and sound. Where the sores were, there is now pink puckered flesh; his limbs are untouched. Kenny and Selvam between them have kept my promise to him.

In the distance when it is a fine day and my sight is not too dim, I can see the building where my son works. He and Kenny, the young and the old. A large building, spruce and white; not only money has built it but men's hopes and pity, as I know who have seen it grow brick by brick and year by year.

My three sisters were married long before I was. Shanta first, a big wedding which lasted for many days, plenty of gifts and feasts, diamond earrings, a gold necklace, as befitted the daughter of the village headman. Padmini next, and she too made a good match and was married fittingly, taking jewels and dowry with her; but when it came to Thangam, only relations from our own village came to the wedding and not from the surrounding districts as they had done before, and the only jewel she had was a diamond nose-screw.

"What for you," my mother would say, taking my face in her hands, "my last-born, my baby? Four dowries is too much for a man to bear." "I shall have a grand wedding," I would say. "Such that everybody will remember when all else is a dream forgotten." (I had heard this phrase in a storyteller's tale.) "For is not my father head of the village?" I knew this pleased my mother, for she would at once laugh, and lose her look of worry. Once when I repeated this, my eldest brother overheard me, and he said sharply, "Don't speak like a fool, the headman is no longer of consequence. There is the

Collector, who comes to these villages once a year, and to him is the power, and to those he appoints; not to the headman."

This was the first time I had ever heard that my father was of no consequence. It was as if a prop on which I leaned had been roughly kicked away, and I felt frightened and refused to believe him. But of course he was right, and by the time I came to womanhood even I had to acknowledge that his prestige was much diminished. Perhaps that was why they could not find me a rich husband, and married me to a tenant farmer who was poor in everything but in love and care for me, his wife, whom he took at the age of twelve. Our relatives, I know, murmured that the match was below me; my mother herself was not happy, but I was without beauty and without dowry and it was the best she could do. "A poor match," they said, and not always quietly. How little they knew, any of them!

A woman, they say, always remembers her wedding night. Well, maybe they do; but for me there are other nights I prefer to remember, sweeter, fuller, when I went to my husband matured in mind as well as in body, not as a pained and awkward child as I did on that first night. And when the religious ceremonies had been completed, we left, my husband and I. How well I remember the day, and the sudden sickness that overcame me when the moment for departure came! My mother in the doorway, no tears in her eyes but her face bloated with their weight. My father standing a little in front of her, waiting to see us safely on our way. My husband, seated already on the bullock cart with the tin trunk full of cooking vessels and my saris next to him. Somehow I found myself also sitting in the cart, in finery, with downcast eyes. Then the cart began to move, lurching as the bullocks got awkwardly into rhythm, and I was sick. Such a disgrace for me. . . . How shall I ever live it down? I remember thinking. I shall never forget. . . . I haven't forgotten, but the memory is not sour. My husband soothed and calmed me.

"It is a thing that might happen to anybody," he said. "Do not fret. Come, dry your eyes and sit up here beside me." So I did, and after a while I felt better, the tears left my eyes and dried on my lashes.

For six hours we rode on and on along the dusty road, passing several villages on the way to ours, which was a good distance away. Halfway there we stopped and ate a meal: boiled rice, dhal,[1] vegetables and curds. A whole coconut apiece too, in which my husband nicked a hole with his scythe for me so that I might drink the clear milk. Then he unyoked the bullocks and led them to the small pool of water near which we had stopped, giving them each a handful of hay. Poor beasts, they seemed glad of the water, for already their hides were dusty.

---

1. This and other Indian terms are defined in the glossary at the end of the novel, p. 142.

We rested a half-hour before resuming our journey. The animals, re-freshed, began stepping jauntily again, tossing their heads and jangling the bells that hung from their red-painted horns. The air was full of the sound of bells, and of birds, sparrows and bulbuls mainly, and sometimes the cry of an eagle, but when we passed a grove, green and leafy, I could hear mynahs and parrots. It was very warm, and, unused to so long a jolting, I fell asleep.

It was my husband who woke me—my husband, whom I will call here Nathan, for that was his name, although in all the years of our marriage I never called him that, for it is not meet for a woman to address her husband except as "husband."

"We are home," he cried. "Wake up! Look!"

I woke; I looked. A mud hut, thatched, small, set near a paddy field, with two or three similar huts nearby. Across the doorway a garland of mango leaves, symbol of happiness and good fortune, dry now and rattling in the breeze.

"This is our home," my husband said. "Come, I will show you."

I got out of the cart, stiff and with a cramp in one leg. We went in: two rooms, one a sort of storehouse for grain, the other for everything else. A third had been begun but was unfinished, the mud walls were not more than half a foot high.

"It will be better when it is finished," he said. I nodded; I wanted to cry. This mud hut, nothing but mud and thatch, was my home. My knees gave, first the cramped one, then the other, and I sank down. Nathan's face filled with concern as he came to hold me.

"It is nothing," I said. "I am tired—no more. I will be all right in a minute."

He said, "Perhaps you are frightened at living here alone—but in a few years we can move—maybe even buy a house such as your father's. You would like that?"

There was something in his voice, a pleading, a look on his face such as a dog has when you are about to kick it.

"No," I said, "I am not frightened. It suits me quite well to live here."

He did not reply at once but went into the granary and came out with a handful of paddy.

"Such harvests as this," he said, sliding the grains about in his hand, "and you shall not want for anything, beloved." Then he went out to get the tin trunk and after a while I followed.

Sometimes now I can see quite clearly: the veil is rent and for a few seconds I see blue skies and tender trees, then it closes on me again and once more I am back in a world of my own, which darkens a little with each pass-ing day. Yet not alone; for the faces of those I have loved, things that have been—shapes, forms, images—are always before me; and sometimes they are so vivid that truly I cannot say whether I see them or not, whether the veil is lifted to allow me the sight, or whether it is only my mind that sees. Today, for instance, I could see the brook that ran near our paddy field so clearly that I felt I had but to stoop to feel its water wet on my hands. Yet that brook belongs to a part of my life that is finished. I was a bride of only a week when I first followed it to look for a suitable place for my washing. I walked for nearly an hour before I found a wide stretch of water and a sandy beach, with boulders scattered about. I put my bundle down, untied it and put the clothes in. The water was clear but not swift running—the linen did not float too far or too quickly away from my hands. I tucked my sari up above my knees and stood in the river, scrubbing the clothes against a large flat stone and using just a little of the washing powder my mother had given me; good stuff, with a clean sweet smell and much power in it. When I had finished, I carried the clothes beyond the beach and laid them on the grassy bank to dry in the sun.

Just then I saw Kali, wife of our neighbour, coming towards me, and with her were two women I had not seen before. All carried bundles of washing on their heads, and two had children at their hips and the third was expecting. They called out when they saw me, and I came down, a little shy, since they seemed to know each other so well; but before long I came to know them well too, these three women who lived nearest to us, and whose lives were so closely woven with mine. Kali, big and plump, with ample hips and thrusting breasts, whose husband worked the next field to ours; Janaki, married to the village shopkeeper, with her homely face and sagging figure, for she had borne her husband several children; and Kunthi, youngest of the three, small and narrow, moving gracefully despite her burden.

"It is her first," said Kali, jovially, "but by no means her last, for as you see her husband has not wasted any time!" She laughed loudly. Janaki frowned at her. "Chup woman! Do you not see these are young girls?"

"And what of it? Are they not given in marriage? Kunthi is already bearing, and this newcomer—it will not be long. Men are all the same."

I saw Kunthi shrug with a slight disdain; Janaki was quiet. Perhaps they both knew the futility of trying to restrain Kali. She meanwhile was addressing herself to me.

"You are Rukmani, are you not? Wife of the farmer Nathan. The whole village has been curious about you—heaven knows why, one woman is like another. The fuss your husband made! Why, for weeks he was as brittle as a bamboo before it bursts into flame! He built your hut with his own hands—yes, he would not even have my husband to help."

"Built it?" I said. "I did not know—he did not tell me."

"Oh, yes! Every bit of it himself, and neglecting the land sometimes to do it, so that Sivaji had often to chide him, although he is a good man for a Zemindari agent."

He had made our home himself, and I had felt only fear to live in it. About a month later, when we were no longer strangers, I told him of what I had learnt.

"You built this for us," I said to him. "Why did you not tell me?"

"Who has been talking to you?" he asked, not answering my question.

"Kali. She told me a long time ago—when I first went to where the brook widens near the river."

"She is an old chatterbox and should have her mouth stitched."

"What for? I am glad she told me. Should I not be proud that you have built this house with your own hands?"

He considered. "You are not a child any more," he said at last. "You have grown fast since the day we were married, and that not so long ago."

While the sun shines on you and the fields are green and beautiful to the eye, and your husband sees beauty in you which no one has seen before, and you have a good store of grain laid away for hard times, a roof over you and a sweet stirring in your body, what more can a woman ask for? My heart sang and my feet were light as I went about my work, getting up at sunrise and going to sleep content. Peace and quiet were ours. How well I recall it, how grateful I am that not all the clamour which invaded our lives later could subdue the memory or still the longing for it. Rather, it has strengthened it: had there not been what has been, I might never have known how blessed we were. True, my husband did not own the land he tilled, as my father had done; yet the possibility was there that he might one day do so. We owned our own ploughing bullocks; we kept a milch goat. From each harvest we saved, and had gunny sacks full of the husked rice stored away in our small stone-lined granary. There was food in plenty for two people and we ate well: rice for morning and evening meals; dhal; sometimes a coconut grated fine and cooked in milk and sugar: sometimes a wheatcake, fried in butter and melting in the mouth.

Once or twice a week I would go to the village to buy sugar, ghee and vegetables, calling on the way home at Durgan the milkman's to get curds, for our goat was running dry and there was not always enough milk to make my own. I liked going to the village and meeting its people, for they were a friendly lot and most of them anxious to help if they could. I got to know them all very quickly: Old Granny, who lived on what she made by selling peanuts and guavas; Hanuman, the general merchant; Perumal, husband of Janaki, who kept the only shop; and Biswas, the money-lender. Sometimes Janaki or Kali would come to see how I was getting on, but not often, for they were kept busy looking after husband and children. As for Kunthi, very soon she was unable to do anything for herself, for she was a thin, slight girl, and we had to go in turns to buy her provisions and to help her with the work in the home. Kunthi was different from the other women, quieter, more reserved, and for all that we tried to be at ease with her there was a barrier which we could not surmount. Especially high against me it stood, strange and forbidding, although why this should be I could not think, finally putting it down to my imagination.

She had, everybody said, married beneath her. Perhaps they said that of me too, but I was plain and she was pretty, so it didn't make sense in her case. For myself, I am glad I married "beneath me," for a finer man no one could have had; but possibly she was not so lucky.

A man is indeed fortunate if he does not marry above him, for if he does he gets a wife who is no help to him whatsoever, only an ornament. I know, for I was ignorant of the simplest things, and no ornament either. Kali and Janaki between them had to show me how to milk the goat, how to plant seed, how to churn butter from milk, and how to mull rice. What patience indeed my husband must have had, to put up with me uncomplainingly during those early days of our married lives! Not one cross word or impatient look, and praise for whatever small success I achieved. I had planted, in the flat patch of ground behind the hut, a few pumpkin seeds. The soil here was rich, never having yielded before, and loose so that it did not require much digging. The seeds sprouted quickly, sending up delicate green shoots that I kept carefully watered, going several times to the well nearby for the purpose. Soon they were not delicate but sprawling vigorously over the earth, and pumpkins began to form, which, fattening on soil and sun and water, swelled daily larger and larger and ripened to yellow and red, until at last they were ready to eat, and I cut one and took it in. When Nathan saw it he was full of admiration, and made much of this one fruit— he who was used to harvesting a field at a time.

"One would have thought you had never seen a pumpkin before," I said, though pleased with him and myself, keeping my eyes down.

"Not from our land," said Nathan. "Therefore it is precious, and you, Ruku, are indeed a clever woman."

I tried not to show my pride. I tried to be offhand. I put the pumpkin away. But pleasure was making my pulse beat; the blood, unbidden, came hot and surging to my face.

After that, ten times more zealous, I planted beans and sweet potatoes, brinjals and chillies, and they all grew well under my hand, so that we ate even better than we had done before.

Chapter 2

Kunthi's child was born a few months before mine, a fine boy who nearly took his mother's life in exchange for his own. Janaki was ill and could not come, Kali was away, therefore I had to do what I could. Kunthi's husband went off to fetch the midwife, leaving me with the sweating girl. When she saw who I was—not at once, for she was half-crazed with pain—Kunthi cried out that she did not want me.

"You must go," she kept entreating.

"Why?" I said. "Do you dislike me so much, then?"

"No, no, but please go. I do not want you here."

"I cannot and will not. Besides, there is no one else."

"I shall be all right. The midwife will be here soon."

"And what will your husband say," I said, "if I leave you here alone?" and I took no more notice of her cries.

When she saw I would not go, she grew still and lay like a log, not a murmur from her, but the sweat forcing itself up in oily drops on her throat and temples.

Kunthi was lying in an exhausted sleep, with her baby beside her, before I went home. It was a whole day since I had left. Nathan was waiting for me and he said crossly: "You look like a corpse. Whatever possessed you to stay so long?"

"Blame the midwife," I said. "She could not be found. Or blame Kunthi's son. He took a long time."

I was tired and my voice was on edge.

"Well, so long as you don't forget you are pregnant," he said shortly and turned away. It was the first time I had seen him angry. Tears came pricking at my eyeballs.

I sat down to stop my head from spinning, and after a while the pain went. He means well, I thought. He is anxious only about our child. Better that he should worry than that he should not.

From then on, I began to take more care of myself, leaving more and more of the work to Nathan. Sowing time was at hand and there was plenty to be done in the fields: dams of clay to be built to ensure proper irrigation of the paddy terraces; the previous year's stubble to be lifted; rushes and weeds to be destroyed; then the transplanting. All this meant stooping, and Nathan would not hear of it.

With the leisure I now had I took up writing again. It was my father who taught me to read and write. People said he did it because he wanted his children to be one cut above the rest; perhaps so, but I am certain that he also knew that it would be a solace to me in affliction, a joy amid tranquillity. So he taught his six children, myself the youngest by ten years, with the patience he brought to all things. "Practise hard," he would say, watching me busy with slate and pencil. "For who knows what dowry there will be for you when you are ready!" And I, with only the thistledown of childish care upon me, would listen lightly and take up my pencil again.

"What use," my mother said, "that a girl should be learned! Much good will it do her when she has lusty sons and a husband to look after. Look at me, am I any worse that I cannot spell my name, so long as I know it? Is not my house clean and sweet, are not my children well fed and cared for?" My father laughed and said, "Indeed they are," and did not pursue the matter; nor did he give up his teaching.

When my child is ready, I thought now, I will teach him too; and I practised harder than ever lest my fingers should lose their skill. When Janaki, recovered from her sickness, came to see me, she marvelled that I could write; but Kali, who had come too, was scornful of the strange symbols which had no meaning for her and dismissed it as a foible of pregnancy.

"You will forget all about such nonsense when your child is born," she said. "Besides, there will be others and your hands will be full. Look at me, do I have one spare minute to myself?"

"How is it then," I asked, forgetting myself, "that you are here now—yes, and I have seen you in the village too—if you have so much to occupy you? As for my children, it is for them that I practise writing and reading, so that I can teach them when the time is ripe."

Kali sniffed, but she was good-natured and did not take offence.

Nathan used to come and sit beside me when I was writing. The first time he came to see what I was up to, he sat in silence with his brows drawn together and meeting; but after some watching he went away, and when he came back his face was clear.

"It is well," he said, stroking my hair. "You are clever, Ruku, as I have said before."

I think it cost him a good deal to say what he did, and he never varied his attitude once. That was typical of my husband: when he had worked things out for himself he would follow his conclusions at whatever cost to himself. I am sure it could not have been easy for him to see his wife more learned than he himself was, for Nathan could not even write his name; yet not once did he assert his rights and forbid me my pleasure, as lesser men might have done.

Now that I did not work in the fields I spent most of my time tending my small garden: the beans, the brinjals, the chillies and the pumpkin vine which had been the first to grow under my hand. And their growth to me was constant wonder—from the time the seed split and the first green shoots broke through, to the time when the young buds and fruit began to form. I was young and fanciful then, and it seemed to me not that they grew as I did, unconsciously, but that each of the dry, hard pellets I held in my palm had within it the very secret of life itself, curled tightly within, under leaf after protective leaf for safekeeping, fragile, vanishing with the first touch or sight. With each tender seedling that unfurled its small green leaf to my eager gaze, my excitement would rise and mount; winged, wondrous.

"You will get used to it," Nathan said. "After many sowings and harvestings you will not notice these things." There have been many sowings and harvestings, but the wonder has not departed.

I was tying the bean tendrils to the wire fence I had built when I saw a quiver in the leaves of the pumpkins. The fruit is ripening, I thought, the birds are already here. Or perhaps mice. Leaving the beans I went to look, stooping to part the leaves with my hand.

Why did not the snake strike at once?

Was the cobra surprised into stillness that a human should dare to touch it? My hands recoiled from the coldness of serpent flesh, my nails clawed at my palms, the leaves I had parted moved back to cover it. For a moment my legs remained stiffly planted beside the pumpkins, then the blood came racing to my limbs again, and I ran from the spot screeching with fear and not looking behind me.

Nathan came rushing to me, almost knocking me over, caught and shook me.

"What is it, what is it?" he shouted roughly.

"A snake," I whispered, bereft of voice and breath. "A cobra. I touched it."

He looked at me as if I were mad.

"Go in and stay there," he said. I wanted only to fall at his feet in my terror, to beg him not to leave me alone, but he was staring at me unrelenting. At last I went, cowed, but with the waters of panic receding.

"The snake had not stirred," Nathan said as he came back. He had cut it to pieces with his scythe and buried the remains so that I should not be upset.

"Yet you have lived long enough to learn to disregard them," he said. "Are they not found everywhere—tree snakes, water snakes and land snakes? You only need to be careful and they pass you by."

"True," I said, shamefaced yet rallying. "But it is one thing to see a snake and another to touch it. I have never touched one before."

"Nor again," Nathan said, grinning. "I have never seen you fly as fast as you did, child and all."

I lowered my eyes, abashed. I was getting very awkward in my movements. I realised I must have looked like a water buffalo, running in such a frenzy. "Never mind," said Nathan gently. "It will soon be over now."

He was right. Whether from fright, or the running, my baby was born a few days later, a month too soon but healthy for all that. Kali came as soon as she knew, and the midwife some hours later but in good time to deliver the child. They placed it in my arms when I had recovered a little from the birth, in silence. I uncovered the small form, beautiful, strong, but quite plain, a girl's body.

I turned away and, despite myself, the tears came, tears of weakness and disappointment; for what woman wants a girl for her first-born? They took the child from me.

Kali said: "Never mind. There will be many later on. You have plenty of time."

It is so easy to be comforting when your own wishes have come true. Kali had three sons already, she could afford to sympathise.

When I recall all the help Kali gave me with my first child, I am ashamed that I ever had such thoughts: my only excuse is that thoughts come of their own accord, although afterwards we can chase them away. As I had done for Kunthi, so Kali did for me—but much more: sweeping and cleaning, washing and cooking. She even took pains to water the garden, and one morning I saw her tending the pumpkin vine, which was overladen with blossom. In that moment a cold horror came on me again: my hands grew clammy, and I could feel once more the serpent's touch. I shrieked at her then, and she came running, her face frightened at the wildness in my voice.

"Whatever is wrong?" she gasped, running to my side. The baby had awakened and was crying loudly, so that she had to yell. I was so pleased to see her whole, I could not speak for relief. At last I told her, shakily, about the cobra, and, rather ashamed by now of making such a fuss, I exaggerated a little, making the snake enormous of its kind, and the danger more deadly than it had been.

Women can sometimes be more soothing than men: so now Kali. "Poor thing," she said. "No wonder you are terrified. Anyone would be. But it is a pity your husband killed the snake, since cobras are sacred."

"She is a fool," Nathan said contemptuously when I told him. "What would she have me do—worship it while it dug its fangs in my wife? Go now—forget it."

I think I did, although once or twice when I saw the thickness of the pumpkin vines I wondered nervously what might lie concealed there; and then I would take up knife and shovel to clear away the tangle; but when I drew near and saw the broad glossy leaves and curling green tendrils I could not bring myself to do it; and now I am glad I did not, for that same vine yielded to me richly, pumpkin after pumpkin of a size and colour that I never saw elsewhere.

We called our daughter Irawaddy, after one of the great rivers of Asia, for of all things water was most precious to us; but it was too long a name for the tiny little thing she was, and soon she became Ira. Nathan at first paid scant attention to her: he had wanted a son to continue his line and walk beside him on the land, not a puling infant who would take with her a dowry and leave nothing but a memory behind; but soon she stopped being a puling infant, and when at the age of ten months she called him "Apa," which means father, he began to take a lively interest in her.

She was a fair child, lovely and dimpled, with soft, gleaming hair. I do not know where she got her looks: not from me, nor from Nathan, but there it was; and not only we but other people noticed and remarked on it. I myself did not know how I could have produced so beautiful a child, and I was proud of her and glad, even when people pretended to disbelieve that I could be her mother. "Here is a marvel indeed," they would say, and make comparisons with ordinary parents who sometimes bore a child of matchless brilliance; or with a devout couple who had brought forth a wretch. I preferred to think the plain have their rewards, and this was mine.

"She is like you," Nathan would say to me as he surveyed her, but he was the only one who thought so.

Before long she was crawling all over the place, following her father into the fields, trailing me as I went about my work, and very soon she began to walk.

"You must not allow it so early," Kali said to me ominously, "or her legs will bend like hoops." And at first I listened to her and whenever I saw Ira trying to stand up or walk, I would rush forward and pick her up; but soon there was no stopping her. I should have been at it the whole time otherwise, and I had other things to do. Sowing time was at hand, and I was out all day with Nathan planting the paddy in the drained fields. Corn had to be sown too, the land was ready. My husband ploughed it, steadying the plough behind the two bullocks while I came behind, strewing the seed to either side and sprinkling the earth over from the basket at my hip.

When that was done, it was time for our hut to be thatched. It had stood up well to sun and wind, but after the monsoon rains several small patches showed wear and it was well to get things done in good time. Nathan cut fronds from the coconut palm that grew by our hut and dried them for me, together we twisted the fibre and bound the palms, shaping them to the roof and strengthening the whole with clay.

Ira was no trouble at all. She would sit happily playing by herself in the sun, chuckling at the birds or at anything else she could see, including her fond parents; or if it was hot and she grew fretful I would hang a cloth from a branch and put her in it, and she would go to sleep without any further bother. My mother, especially, grew very fond of her and came to see us often, although it meant travelling several hours in a bullock cart, which is very tiring when one is no longer young. Sometimes I would go to see my parents, but seldom, since there was so much to be done in my own home; and my mother, knowing this, did not reproach me for the long intervals between my visits.

Chapter 3

"Do NOT WORRY," they said. "You will be putting lines in your face." They still say it, but the lines are already there and they are silent about *that*. Kali said it, and I knew she was thinking of her own brood. Kunthi said it, and in her eyes lay the knowledge of her own children. Janaki said, morosely, she wished it could happen to her; a child each year was no fun. Only Nathan did not say it to me, for he was worried too, and knew better. We did not talk about it, it was always with us: a chill fear that Ira was to be our only child.

My mother, whenever I paid her a visit, would make me accompany her to a temple, and together we would pray and pray before the deity, imploring for help until we were giddy. But the Gods have other things to do: they cannot attend to the pleas of every supplicant who dares to raise his cares to heaven. And so the years rolled by and we still had only one child, and that a daughter.

When Ira was nearing six, my mother was afflicted with consumption, and was soon so feeble that she could not rise from her bed. Yet in the midst of her pain she could still think of me, and one day she beckoned me near and placed in my hand a small stone lingam, symbol of fertility.

"Wear it," she said. "You will yet bear many sons. I see them, and what the dying see will come to pass . . . be assured, this is no illusion."

"Rest easy," I said. "You will recover."

She did not—no one expected she would—but she lingered for a long time. In her last months my father sent for the new doctor who had settled in the village. Nobody knew where he came from or who paid him, but there he was, and people spoke well of him, though he was a foreigner. As for my father, he would have called in the Devil himself to spare my mother any suffering. So it was in a house of sorrow that I first met Kennington, whom people called Kenny. He was tall and gaunt, with a pale skin and sunken eyes the colour of a kingfisher's wing, neither blue or green. I had never seen a white man so close before, and so I looked my fill.

"When you have done with staring," he said coldly, "perhaps you will take me to your mother."

I started, for I had not realised I was goggling at him. Startled, too, that he should have spoken in our tongue.

"I will show you," I said, stumbling in my confusion.

My mother knew no man could save her and she did not expect miracles.

Between her and this man, young though he was, lay mutual understanding and respect, one for the other. He told her no lies, and she trusted him. He came often, sometimes even when he was not summoned; and his presence, as much as the powders and pills he made her take, gave my mother her ease. When she died it was in the same way, without a struggle, so that although we grieved for her our hearts were not torn by her suffering.

Before I left for my village, I told him that for what he had done there could be no repayment. "Remember only," I said, "that my home is yours, and all in it."

He thanked me gravely, and as I turned to go he raised a hand to stop me.

"There is a look about you," he said. "It lies in your eyes and the mark is on your face. What is it?"

"Would you not grieve too," I said, "if the woman who gave you birth was no more than a handful of dust?"

"It is not that alone. The hurt is of longer standing. Why do you lie?"

I looked up and his eyes were on me. Surely, I thought, my mother has told him, for he knows; but as if he guessed my thoughts he shook his head. "No, I do not know. Tell me."

I held back. He was a foreigner, and although I no longer stood in awe of him, still the secret had been long locked up in my breast and would not come out easily.

"I have no sons," I said at last, heavily. "Only one child, a girl."

Once I had started the words flowed, I could not stop myself. "Why should it be?" I cried. "What have we done that we must be punished? Am I not clean and healthy? Have I not borne a girl so fair, people turn to gaze when she passes?"

"That does not seem to help you much," he said shortly. I waited. If he wishes to help me he can, I thought, so much faith had I in him. My heart was thumping out a prayer.

"Come and see me," he said at last. "It is possible I may be able to do something. . . . Remember, I do not promise."

My fears came crowding upon me again. I had never been to this kind of doctor; he suddenly became terrifying.

"You are an ignorant fool," he said roughly. "I will not harm you."

I slunk away, frightened of I know not what. I placed even more faith in the charm my mother had given me, wearing it constantly between my breasts. Nothing happened. At last I went again to him, begging him to do what he could. He did not even remind me of the past.

Ira was seven when my first son was born, and she took a great interest in the newcomer. Poor child, it must have been lonely for her all those years. Kali's and Janaki's children were much older, and as for Kunthi, she preferred to keep aloof. Her son was a sturdy youngster and would have been a good playmate for my child; but, as the years went by, her visits to our house grew less and less frequent until at last we were meeting as strangers.

My husband was overjoyed at the arrival of a son; not less so, my father. He came, an old man, all those miles by cart from our village, to hold his grandson.

"Your mother would have been glad," he said. "She was always praying for you."

"She knew," I told him. "She said I would have many sons."

As for Nathan, nothing would do but that the whole village should know—as if they didn't already. On the tenth day from the birth he invited everybody to feast and rejoice with us in our good fortune. Kali and Janaki both came to help me prepare the food, and even Kunthi's reserve crumbled a little as she held up my son to show him to our visitors. Between us we prepared mounds of rice, tinting it with saffron and frying it in butter; made hot curries from chillies and dhal; mixed sweet, spicy dishes of jaggery and fruit; broiled fish; roasted nuts over the fire; filled ten gourds with coconut milk; and cut plantain leaves on which to serve the food. When all was ready we spread the leaves under the gaudy marriage pandal Nathan had borrowed for the occasion and ate and drank for long, merry hours. Afterwards Kunthi was persuaded to play for us on her bulbul tara, which she did skilfully, plucking at the strings on her slender fingers and singing in a low, clear voice which people strained to hear, so that it was very quiet.

The baby, who had slept through all the clamour, woke up now in the sudden hush and began squalling. Kunthi stopped her thrumming. People crowded around me, trying to pat the baby who had caused all this excitement—although he was no beauty, with puckered face and mouth opened wide to emit shriek after shriek.

"Such a furore," Kali said. "One would think the child had wings, at the very least."

"Seven years we have waited," said Nathan, his eyes glinting, "wings or no wings."

The one person I had wanted most to see at our feast was not there. I had gone to seek him, but he was not to be found. "He goes and comes," they told me. "Nobody knows where or why." So I had to be content without him; but contentment cannot be forced, and Nathan noticed my preoccupation.

"What now?" he said. "Are you not happy? Would you have the moon too, as Kali would have wings?"

"Indeed no," I said, "it is just that I would have liked to see Kenny under our roof. He did so much for my mother." And for us, I thought, but could not say it; for at the beginning I had not wished my husband to know that I was putting myself in the hands of a foreigner, for I knew not what his reaction would be. I had consoled myself that it would be time enough to tell him if a child was born; and now I found I could not do it, because he would surely ask why I had not told him before . . . What harm, I thought, if he does not know; I have not lied to him, there has just been this silence.

In our sort of family it is well to be the first-born: what resources there are, have later to be shared out in smaller and smaller portions. Ira had been fed well on milk and butter and rice; Arjun too, for he was the first boy. But for those who came after, there was less and less. Four more sons I bore in as many years—Thambi, Murugan, Raja and Selvam. It was as if all the pent-up desires of my childless days were now bearing fruit. I was very fortunate, for they were, without exception, healthy; and in their infancy and childhood my daughter looked after them almost as much as I did. She was a great one for babies, handling them better than many a grown woman while she was still a child.

How quickly children grow! They are infants—you look away a minute and in that time they have left their babyhood behind. Our little girl ran about in the sun bare and beautiful as she grew, with no clothes to hamper her limbs or confine her movements. Then one day when she was five— long before Arjun was born—Nathan pointed her out to me as she played in the fields.

"Cover her," he said. "It is time."

I wanted to cry out that she was a baby still, but of course Nathan was right; she had left infancy forever. And so I made a skirt for her, weaving bright colours into the white cotton that she might like it, and so she did for a time, wearing it gladly, twirling it about her as she spun round and round; but when the novelty had worn off, she became fractious and wanted to tear it from her. It was nearly a month before she resigned herself to it.

With six children to feed we could no longer afford to eat all the vegetables we grew. Once a week I would cut and pack our garden produce, selecting the best and leaving the spoilt or bruised vegetables for ourselves, cover the basket with leaves and set off for the village. Old Granny was always glad to buy from me, and at first I would make straight for the corner of the street where she sat with her gunny sack spread before her. The old lady would pick out the purple brinjals and yellow pumpkins, the shiny green and red chillies, feeling them with her wrinkled fingers and complimenting me on their size.

"None like yours," she would say. "Such colour, such a bloom on them!" Perhaps she said it to everyone who came to her, but I would feel absurdly pleased and go away with my insides smiling. Then one day Biswas, the moneylender, stopped me in the street. I would have passed after a brief salutation, for among us there is a dislike of the moneylending class, but he stood squarely in my path.

"Ah, Rukmani," he said, "in a hurry as usual, I see."

"My children are not of age to be left alone for long," said I, speaking civilly.

"Yet surely you have time for a little business with me?"

"If you will tell me what business?"

"Buying and selling," he said, cackling, "which is your business, as lending is mine."

"If you will make yourself clear," I said, "I will stay and hear; otherwise I must be on my way."

"Those vegetables," he said, "that Old Granny buys from you. What price does she pay you?"

"A fair price," I said, "and no haggling."

"I will pay you four annas a dozen for brinjals, and six annas each for pumpkins, if they are large." He was offering almost double what Old Granny paid.

I went away. The following week I sold almost my whole basket to him, keeping only a little for Old Granny. I did not like selling to him, although he paid me a better price. It was business and nothing else with him, never a word of chaff or a smile—or perhaps it was the flattery I missed—and I would much rather have had it the other way; but there you are, you cannot choose.

To my surprise Old Granny made no comment, beyond smiling reassuringly when I muttered guiltily that our needs at home were growing. In the beginning she may not have known, but when I sold her, week after week, one small pumpkin or half a dozen brinjals she must have guessed the truth. But she said nothing, nor did I, for we both knew she could not pay me more, and I could not afford to sell for less. As it was, we were going short of many things. We no longer had milk in the house, except for the youngest child; curds and butter were beyond our means except on rare occasions. But we never went hungry as some of the families were doing. We grew our own plantains and coconuts, the harvests were good and there was always food in the house—at least a bagful of rice, a little dhal, if no more. Then when the rice terraces were drained, there was the fish, spawned among the paddy, and what we could not eat, we dried and salted away. And every month I put away a rupee or two against the time Ira would be married. So we still could not grumble.

Chapter 4

CHANGE I HAD KNOWN BEFORE, and it had been gradual. My father had been a headman once, a person of consequence in our village: I had lived to see him relinquish this importance, but the alteration was so slow that we hardly knew when it came. I had seen both my parents sink into old age and death, and here too there was no violence. But the change that now came into my life, into all our lives, blasting its way into our village, seemed wrought in the twinkling of an eye.

Arjun came running to us with the news. He had run all the way from the village and we had to wait while he gulped in fresh air. "Hundreds of men," he gasped. "They are pulling down houses around the maidan and there is a long line of bullock carts carrying bricks."

The other children clustered round him, their eyes popping. Arjun swelled with importance. "I am going back," he announced. "There is a lot to be seen."

Nathan looked up from the grain he was measuring into the gunny bag for storing. "It is the new tannery they are building," he said. "I had heard rumours."

Arjun, torn between a desire to dash back and a craving to hear more from his father, teetered anxiously to and fro on his heels; but Nathan said no more. He put the grain away carefully in the granary, then he rose. "Come," he said. "We will see."

All the families were out: the news had spread quickly. Kali and her husband, Kunthi and her boys, Janaki, surrounded by her numerous family, even Old Granny, had come out to see. Children were everywhere, dodging in and out of the crowd and crying out to each other in shrill excited voices. Startled pi-dogs added to the din. We formed a circle about the first arrivals, some fifty men or so, who were unloading bricks from the bullock carts. They spoke in our language, but with an intonation which made it difficult for us to understand them.

"Townspeople," Kali whispered to me. "They say they have travelled more than a hundred miles to get here." She was prone to exaggerate, and also believed whatever was told her.

In charge of the men was an overseer who looked and spoke like the men, but who was dressed in a shirt and trousers, and he had a hat on his head such as I had only seen Kenny wear before: a topee the colour of thatch. The others wore loincloths and turbans and a few wore shirts; but as the day wore on they doffed their shirts, one by one, until all were as our men.

The men worked well and quickly, with many a sidelong glance at us; they seemed to enjoy having created such a stir and lured such a big audience. As for the overseer, he made much play of his authority, directing them with loud voice and many gestures but doing not a stroke of work himself. Still, it must have been hot for him standing there waving his arms about, for the shirt he wore was sticking to his back. Now and then he would lift his hat as if to allow the wind to cool his scalp.

Until at last there was a commotion about the edges of the circle of which we were the inner ring. The crowd was parting, and as the movement spread to us we gave way too, to let a tall white man through. He had on a white topee, and was accompanied by three or four men dressed like him in shorts. The overseer now came forward, bowing and scraping, and the red-faced one spoke to him rapidly but so low that we could not hear what he was saying. The overseer listened respectfully and then began telling us to go, not to disturb the men, although for so long he had been glad of many watchers. In our maidan, in our village he stood, telling us to go.

"As if he owned us," muttered Kannan the chakkli. I think that already he foresaw his livelihood being wrested from him, for he salted and tanned his own skins, making them into chaplis for those in the village who wore them. So he stood his ground, glaring at the overseer and refusing to move, as did a few others who resented the haughty orders that poured from the man's lips; but most of us went, having our own concerns to mind.

Every day for two months the line of bullock carts came in laden with bricks and stones and cement, sheets of tin and corrugated iron, coils of rope and hemp. The kilns in the neighbouring villages were kept busy firing the bricks, but their output was insufficient, and the carts had to go further afield, returning dusty and brick-filled. Day and night women twisted rope, since they could sell as much as they made, and traders waxed prosperous selling their goods to the workmen. They were very well paid, these men, some of them earning two rupees in a single day, whereas even in good times we seldom earned as much, and they bought lavishly: rice and vegetables and dhal, sweetmeats and fruit. Around the maidan they built their huts, for there was no other place for them, and into these brought their wives and children, making a community of their own. At night we saw their fires and by day we heard their noise, loud, ceaseless, clangour and din, chatter, sometimes a chanting to help them get a heavy beam into position, or hoist a load of tin sheeting to the roof.

Then one day the building was completed. The workers departed, taking with them their goods and chattels, leaving only the empty huts behind. There was a silence. In the unwonted quiet we all wondered apprehensively what would happen next. A week went by and another. Losing our awe we entered the building, poking into its holes and corners, looking into the great vats and drums that had been installed; then, curiosity slaked, we set about our old tasks on the land and in our homes.

There were some among the traders—those who had put up their prices and made their money—who regretted their going. Not I. They had invaded our village with clatter and din, had taken from us the maidan where our children played, and had made the bazaar prices too high for us. I was not sorry to see them go.

"They will be back," said Nathan my husband, "or others will take their place. And did you not benefit from their stay, selling your pumpkins and plantains for better prices than you did before?"

"Yes," said I, for I had, "but what could I buy with the money with prices so high everywhere? No sugar or dhal or ghee have we tasted since they came, and should have had none so long as they remained."

"Nevertheless," said Nathan, "they will be back; for you may be sure they did not take so much trouble only to leave a shell in our midst. Therefore it is well to accept these things."

"Never, never," I cried. "They may live in our midst but I can never accept them, for they lay their hands upon us and we are all turned from tilling to barter, and hoard our silver since we cannot spend it, and see our children go without the food that their children gorge, and it is only in the hope that one day things will be as they were that we have done these things. Now that they have gone let us forget them and return to our ways."

"Foolish woman," Nathan said. "There is no going back. Bend like the grass, that you do not break."

Our children had not seen us so serious, so vehement, before. Three of my sons huddled together in a corner staring at us with wide eyes; the two youngest lay asleep, one in Ira's arms, the other leaning heavily against her; and she herself sagged against the wall with their weight as she sat there on the floor. There was a look on her lovely soft face that pierced me.

"Ah well," I said, dissembling, "perhaps I exaggerate. If they return we shall have a fine dowry for our daughter, and that is indeed a good thing."

The lost look went from Ira's face. She was a child still, despite the ripeness of her thirteen years, and no doubt fancied a grand wedding even as I had done.

They came back. Not the same men who went, but others, and not all at once but slowly. The red-faced white man came back with a foreman, and took charge of everything. He did not live in the village but came and went, while his men took over the huts that had lain empty, the ones who came last settling beside the river, bringing their wives and children with them, or dotting the maidan even more thickly with the huts they built for themselves and their families.

I went back to my home, thankful that a fair distance still lay between them and us, that although the smell of their brews and liquors hung permanently in the sickened air, still their noise came to us from afar.

"You are a queer being," Kunthi said, her brows flaring away from her eyes. "Are you not glad that our village is no longer a clump of huts but a small town? Soon there will be shops and tea stalls, and even a bioscope, such as I have been to before I was married. You will see."

"No doubt I will," I said. "It will not gladden me. Already my children hold their noses when they go by, and all is shouting and disturbance and crowds wherever you go. Even the birds have forgotten to sing, or else their calls are lost to us."

"You are a village girl," said Kunthi, and there were shadows of contempt moving behind her eyes. "You do not understand."

If I was a village girl, Kali and Janaki were too, and had no taste for the intruders; but after awhile Janaki confessed that at least she now knew what to do with her sons, for the land could not take them all; and as for Kali, well, she had always been fond of an audience for her stories. So they were reconciled and threw the past away with both hands that they might be the readier to grasp the present, while I stood by in pain, envying such easy reconciliation and clutching in my own two hands the memory of the past, and accounting it a treasure.

I think the end of my daughter's carefree days began with the tannery. She had been used to come and go with her brothers, and they went whither they wished. Then one day, with many a meaningful wink, Kali told us that it was time we looked to our daughter.

"She is maturing fast," she said. "Do you not see the eyes of the young men lighting on her? If you are not careful you will not find it easy to get her a husband."

"My daughter is no wanton," Nathan replied. "Not only men but women look at her, for she is beautiful."

"She is that," Kali said handsomely. "Therefore look to her even more closely." There was no subduing Kali, as I well knew.

Thereafter, although we did not admit it to each other, we were more careful of Ira. Poor child, she was bewildered by the many injunctions we laid upon her, and the curtailing of her freedom tried her sorely, though not a word of complaint came from her.

Chapter 5

In all the years of our tenancy we never saw the Zemindar who owned our land. Sivaji acted for him, and being a kindly, humane man we counted ourselves lucky. Unlike some, he did not extract payment in kind to the last grain; he allowed us to keep the gleanings; he did not demand from us bribes of food or money; nor did he claim for himself the dung from the fields, which he might easily have done, stipulating only that Kali and I should gather our share on different days to avoid arguments. This way we got fairly equal quantities and there was no bad blood between us.

One morning, so early that the dew still jewelled the grass and the clamour of the tannery had not yet begun, I went out on my errand. It was as well to go out early, otherwise you could never tell how much had already been taken by urchins, for dung was easy to sell and commanded a good price. Several times before, I had seen boys on the land and had chased them from it, but without succeeding in getting hold of their loot.

That morning there were a lot of pickings; I soon filled the small basket I had with me. As I bent down for the last handful I became aware that someone was watching me.

It was Kenny, thinner than when I had last seen him, but how could I ever forget him? Leaving my basket, I ran to him, dirty hands and all, with a glad welcoming heart.

"My lord, my benefactor," I cried. "Many a time I have longed to see you. Now at last you come," and I bent down to kiss his feet, shod as they were in leather shoes. He withdrew them quickly and told me to get up.

"I am not a benefactor," he said, "nor a lord. What ails you?"

"You *are* my benefactor," I said stoutly. "Have I not five sons to prove it?"

"Am I to blame for your excesses?" said he, grimacing, but his eyes were alight with laughter, no doubt at my crestfallen face.

"Come with me," I said, recovering myself. "You shall see them, excesses or not."

"For a few minutes only, I am busy," he replied, and as I picked up my basket he peered in. "I see you collect dung and take it with you. Is it not for the land?"

"Indeed no. Dung is too useful in our homes to be given to the land, for it is fuel to us and protection against damp and heat and even ants and mice. Did you not know?"

"Too well," he answered shortly. "I have seen your women forever making dung cakes and burning them and smearing their huts. Yet I thought you would know better, who live by the land yet think of taking from it without giving."

"What substitute then?" I said quietly.

He made no reply but came after me. All the children were awake, waiting for their morning meal of rice water. Nathan was working in the fields, and I sent one of the boys to call him in. For Kenny I spread a mat and he sat down while we grouped ourselves about him, but I could see he was not accustomed to sitting crosslegged on the floor, for his knees instead of resting on the mat sprang up aslant like the horns of a bull, and I was uncomfortable for him, and distressed that I had nothing else to offer.

Ira strained the rice water into wooden bowls for us—the rice itself we kept for our midday meal—but to one bowl she added a handful of the cooked rice and a little salt, which we could not afford for ourselves, and this she handed to Kenny, stooping low and keeping her eyes down.

"My daughter Irawaddy," I said, proud that she should know her duties to a guest.

Kenny took the bowl from her with a smile.

"You are a good cook for one so young," he said, laying his hand for a moment on her head. She did not raise her eyes, but her face kindled, and I was pleased too that he should notice my child. He spoke to each of the others in turn until Murugan, my third son, came bouncing in leading his father by the hand.

"You have heard me tell of Kenny often enough," I said. "This is he, friend to my father's house." So much I said, and left the other unsaid.

My husband made namaskar.

"I have," he replied formally, "and I am happy that he should honour our poor household by his presence."

"Yet not so poor," the other replied politely, "for the women of your house do you credit, and you have begotten five healthy sons."

My heart quailed at his words for fear he should betray me, yet no betrayal, since how could he guess my husband did not know I had gone to him for treatment? Why had I, stupidest of women, not told him? I waited, gnawing my lip, but he said no more.

Kenny came often to our house thereafter. Of himself he did not speak, of wife or children or parents or home. I held my tongue, for I felt to ask would be to offend him. Yet he had a love for children; mine were always eager to see him, making great fuss of him when he came, and he for his part would suffer them patiently, often bringing with him half a coconut, or ladus made of nuts and rolled into balls with jaggery, which the children loved. Once he came when I was suckling Selvam, my youngest son, who had turned three, and saw that my breasts were sore where the child's mouth had been.

"The boy is long past weaning," he said frowning. "Why do you force it?"

"We had to sell our goat," I said. "I can no longer afford to buy milk, but while my son is young and needs it I will give it to him."

Thereafter he brought me a little cow's milk when he could, or sent it with one of the children from the village, who were always glad to help him, for he had a way of attracting children; there was ever a troop following him about.

As before, he came and went mysteriously. I knew little beyond the fact that he worked among the people of the tannery, treating and healing their bodies during long hours and then going to his lone dwelling; but when he left the village, for days or years at a time, nobody knew where he went or what he did, and when he returned he was more taciturn than ever and none dared ask.

Chapter 6

I KEPT IRA as long as I could but when she was past fourteen her marriage could be delayed no longer, for it is well known with what speed eligible young men are snapped up; as it was, most girls of her age were already married or at least betrothed. The choice of go-between was not easy to make: Kali was the nearest to hand and the obvious one, but she was garrulous and self-opinionated: rejection of the young man she selected would involve a tedious squabble. Besides, she had sons of her own and might well consider them suitable husbands, which I certainly could not, for they owned no land. Old Granny, on the other hand, would be the ideal go-between: she was old and experienced, knew very well what to look for and never lacked patience; but for some years now I had not traded with her and she might with every justification refuse to act for me. But in the end it was to her I went.

"A dowry of one hundred rupees," I said. "A maiden like a flower. Do your best for me and I shall be ever in your debt. This I ask you," I said, looking straight at her, "although Biswas takes my produce and for you there has been nothing."

"I bear you no grudge, Rukmani," she replied. "Times are hard and we must do what we can for ourselves and our children. I will do my best."

Thereafter never a week went by but she brought news of this boy or that, and she and I and Nathan spent long hours trying to assess their relative merits. At last we found one who seemed to fulfill our requirements: he was young and well favoured, the only son of his father from whom he would one day inherit a good portion of land.

"They will expect a large dowry," I said regretfully. "One hundred rupees will not win such a husband, we have no more."

"She is endowed with beauty," Old Granny said. "It will make up for a small dowry—in this case."

She was right. Within a month the preliminaries were completed, the day was fixed. Ira accepted our choice with her usual docility; if she fretted at the thought of leaving us and her brothers she showed no sign. Only once she asked a little wistfully how frequently I would be able to visit her, and, although I knew such trips would have to be very rare since her future home lay some ten villages away, I assured her not a year would pass without my going to see her two or three times.

"Besides, you will not want me so often," I said. "This home, your brothers, are all you have known so far, but when you have your own home and your own children you will not miss these. . . ."

She nodded slightly, making no comment, yet I knew how bruised she must be by the imminent parting. My spirit ached with pity for her, I longed to be able to comfort her, to convince her that in a few months' time her new home would be the most significant part of her life, the rest only a preparation . . . but before this joy must come the stress of parting, the loneliness of beginning a new life among strangers, the strain of the early days of marriage; and because I knew this the words would not come. . . .

Wedding day. Women from the village came to assist. Janaki, Kali, many I hardly knew. We went with Ira to the river and, when she was freshly bathed, put on her the red sari I had worn at my own wedding. Its rich heavy folds made her look more slender than she was, made her look a child. . . . I darkened her eyes with kohl and the years fell away more; she was so pitifully young I could hardly believe she was to be married, today.

The bridegroom arrived; his parents, his relatives, our friends, the priests. The drummer arrived and squatted outside awaiting permission to begin; the fiddler joined him. There should have been other musicians—a flautist, a harmonium player, but we could not afford these. Nathan would have nothing we could not pay for. No debts, he insisted, no debts. But I grudged Ira nothing: had I not saved from the day of her birth so that she should marry well? Now I brought out the stores I had put by month after month— rice and dhal and ghee, jars of oil, betel leaf, areca nuts, chewing tobacco and copra.

"I didn't know you had so much," said Nathan in amazement.

"And if you had there would be little enough," I said with a wink at the women, "for men are like children and must grab what they see."

I did not wait for his retort, hearing only the laughter that greeted his sally, but went out to speak to the drummer. Arjun, my eldest son, was sitting next to the man, cautiously tapping the drum with three fingers as he had been shown.

"There is plenty of food inside," I said to him. "Go and eat while there is still some left."

"I can eat no more," he replied. "I have been feasting all day."

Nevertheless he had made provision for the morrow: I saw in his lap a bundle bulging with food; sugar syrup and butter had soaked through the cloth patchily.

"Join your brothers," I said, hoisting him up. "The drummer is going to be busy."

He ran off, clinging tightly to his bundle. The wedding music began. Bride and groom were sitting uneasily side by side, Ira stiff in the heavy embroidered sari, white flowers in her hair, very pale. They did not look at each other. About them were packed some fourteen or fifteen people—the hut could hold no more. The remainder sat outside on palm leaves the boys had collected.

"What a good match," everybody said. "Such a fine boy, such a beautiful girl, too good to be true." It was indeed. Old Granny went about beaming: it was she who had brought the two parties together; her reputation as a matchmaker would be higher than ever. We none of us could look into the future.

So they were married. As the light faded two youths appeared bearing a palanquin for the newly married couple, lowered it at the entrance to the hut for them to step into. Now that it was time to go, Ira looked scared, she hesitated a little before entering: but already a dozen willing hands had lifted her in. The crowd, full of good feeling, replete with food and drunk with the music, vicariously excited, pressed round, eagerly thrusting over their heads garland after garland of flowers; the earth was spattered with petals. In the midst of the crush Nathan and I, Nathan holding out his hands to Ira in blessing, she with dark head bent low to receive it. Then the palanquin was lifted up, the torchbearers closed in, the musicians took their places. We followed on foot behind, relatives, friends, well-wishers and hangers-on. Several children had added themselves to the company; they came after, jigging about in high glee, noisy and excited: a long, ragged tail-end to the procession.

Past the fields, through the winding streets of the village we went, the bobbing palanquin ahead of us. Until we came at last to where, at a decorous distance, the bullock cart waited to take them away.

Then it was all over, the bustle, the laughter, the noise. The wedding guests departed. The throng melted. After a while we walked back together to our hut. Our sons, tired out, were humped together asleep, the youngest clutching a sugary confection in one sticky fist. Bits of food lay everywhere. I swept the floor clean and strewed it with leaves. The walls showed cracks, and clods of mud had fallen where people had bumped against them, but these I left for patching in the morning. The used plaintain leaves I stacked in one heap—they would do for the bullocks. The stars were pale in the greying night before I lay down beside my husband. Not to sleep but to think. For the first time since her birth, Ira no longer slept under our roof.

Chapter 7

NATURE IS LIKE A WILD ANIMAL that you have trained to work for you. So long as you are vigilant and walk warily with thought and care, so long will it give you its aid; but look away for an instant, be heedless or forgetful, and it has you by the throat.

Ira had been given in marriage in the month of June, which is the propitious season for weddings, and what with the preparing for it, and the listlessness that took hold of me in the first days after her departure, nothing was done to make our hut weatherproof or to secure the land from flooding. That year the monsoon broke early with an evil intensity such as none could remember before.

It rained so hard, so long and so incessantly that the thought of a period of no rain provoked a mild wonder. It was as if nothing had ever been but rain, and the water pitilessly found every hole in the thatched roof to come in, dripping onto the already damp floor. If we had not built on high ground the very walls would have melted in that moisture. I brought out as many pots and pans as I had and we laid them about to catch the drips, but soon there were more leaks than we had vessels. . . . Fortunately, I had laid in a stock of firewood for Ira's wedding, and the few sticks that remained served at least to cook our rice, and while the fire burnt, hissing at the water in the wood, we huddled round trying to get dry. At first the children were cheerful enough—they had not known such things before, and the lakes and rivulets that formed outside gave them endless delight; but Nathan and I watched with heavy hearts while the waters rose and rose and the tender green of the paddy field sank under and was lost.

"It is a bad season," Nathan said sombrely. "The rains have destroyed much of our work; there will be little eating done this year."

At his words, Arjun broke into doleful sobs and his brother, Thambi, followed suit. They were old enough to understand, but the others, who weren't, burst into tears too, for by now they were cramped and out of humour with sitting crouched on the damp floor; and hungry since there was little to eat, for most of the food had gone to make the wedding feast, and the new season's harvesting lay outside ungathered and rotting. I hushed them as best I could, throwing a reproachful glance at my husband for his careless words, but he was unnoticing, sunk in hatred and helplessness.

As night came on—the eighth night of the monsoon—the winds increased, whining and howling around our hut as if seeking to pluck it from the earth. Indoors it was dark—the wick, burning in its shallow saucer of oil, threw only a dim wavering light—but outside the land glimmered, sometimes pale and sometimes vivid, in the flicker of lightning. Towards midnight the storm was at its worst. Lightning kept clawing at the sky almost continuously, thunder shook the earth. I shivered as I looked— for I could not sleep, and even a prayer came with difficulty.

"It cannot last," Nathan said. "The storm will abate by the morning."

Even as he spoke a streak of lightning threw itself down at the earth, there was a tremendous clap of thunder, and when I uncovered my shrinking eyes I saw that our coconut palm had been struck. That, too, the storm had claimed for its own.

In the morning everything was calm. Even the rain had stopped. After the fury of the night before, an unnatural stillness lay on the land. I went out to see if anything could be saved of the vegetables, but the shoots and vines were battered and broken, torn from their supports and bruised; they did not show much sign of surviving. The corn field was lost. Our paddy field lay beneath a placid lake on which the children were already sailing bits of wood.

Many of our neighbours fared much worse than we had. Several were homeless, and of a group of men who sheltered under a tree when the storm began six had been killed by lightning.

Kali's hut had been completely destroyed in the last final fury of the storm. The roof had been blown away bodily, the mud walls had crumbled.

"At least it stood until the worst was over," said Kali to me, "and by God's grace we were all spared." She looked worn out; in the many years I had known her I had never seen her so deflated. She had come to ask for some palm leaves to thatch the new hut her husband was building; but I could only point to the blackened tree, its head bitten off and hanging by a few fibres from the withered stump.

"We must thatch our roof before the night," I said. "The rains may come again. We need rice too."

Nathan nodded. "We may be able to buy palm leaves in the village— also rice."

He went to the granary in a corner of which the small cloth bundle of our savings lay buried. It had been heavy once, when we were newly married: now the faded rag in which it was tied was too big and the ends flapped loosely over the knot. Nathan untied it and counted out twelve rupees.

"One will be enough," I said. "Let us go."

"I will take two. We can always put it back."

In the village the storm had left disaster and desolation worse than on our own doorstep. Uprooted trees sprawled their branches in ghastly fashion over streets and houses, flattening them and the bodies of men and women indiscriminately. Sticks and stones lay scattered wildly in angry confusion. The tannery stood, its bricks and cement had held it together despite the raging winds; but the workers' huts, of more flimsy construction, had been demolished. The thatch had been ripped from some, where others stood there was now only a heap of mud with their owners' possessions studding them in a kind of pitiless decoration. The corrugated-iron shacks in which some of the men lived were no more: here and there we could see the iron sheets in unexpected places—suspended from tree tops, or blown and embedded on to the walls of houses still left standing. There was water everywhere, the gutters were overflowing into the streets. Dead dogs, cats and rats cluttered the roadside, or floated starkly on the waters with blown distended bellies.

People were moving about amid this destruction, picking out a rag here, a bundle there, hugging those things that they thought to be theirs, moving haltingly and with a kind of despair about them. People we knew came and spoke to us in low voices, gesturing hopelessly.

"Let us go," I said. "It is no good; we will come back later."

We turned back, the two rupees unspent. Our children came running out to meet us, their faces bright with hope.

"The shops are closed or destroyed," I said. "Go inside. I will get you some gruel presently."

Their faces faded; the two younger ones began crying listlessly from hunger and disappointment. I had no words to comfort them.

At dusk the drums of calamity began; their grave, throbbing rhythm came clearly through the night, throughout the night, each beat, each tattoo, echoing the mighty impotence of our human endeavour. I listened. I could not sleep. In the sound of the drums I understood a vast pervading doom; but in the expectant silences between, my own disaster loomed larger, more consequent and more hurtful.

We ventured out again when the waters had subsided a little, taking with us as before two rupees. This time things were somewhat better; the streets were clear, huts were going up everywhere. My spirits rose.

"To Hanuman first for rice," said Nathan, excited. "The gruel we have been swallowing has been almost plain water these last few days."

I quickened my steps: my stomach began heaving at the thought of food.

Hanuman was standing in the doorway of his shop. He shook his head when he saw us. "You have come for rice," he said. "They all come for rice. I have none to sell, only enough for my wife and children."

"And yet you are a merchant who deals in rice?"

"And what if so? Are you not growers of it? Why then do you come to me? If I have rice I do not choose to sell it now; but I have told you, I have none."

"We ask for only a little. We will pay for what we have—see, here is the money."

"No, no rice, but—wait . . . they say Biswas is selling . . . you can try. . . ."

To Biswas. "We come for rice. Look, here is our money."

"Two rupees? How much do you think you can buy with two rupees?"

"We thought—"

"Never mind what you thought! Is this not a time of scarcity? Can you buy rice anywhere else? Am I not entitled to charge more for that? Two ollocks I will let you have and that is charity."

"It is very little for two rupees—"

"Take it or leave it. I can get double that sum from the tanners, but because I know you—"

We take it, we give up the silver coins. Now there is nothing left for the thatching, unless we use a rupee or two from the ten that remain in the granary.

I put the rice in my sari, tuck the precious load securely in at the waist. We turn back. On the outskirts of the village there is Kenny. His face is grim and long, his eyes are burning in his pallid face. He sees us and comes up.

"You too are starving, I suppose."

I tap the roll at my waist—the grains give at my touch.

"We have a little rice—it will last us until times are better."

"Times are better, times are better," he shouts. "Times will not be better for many months. Meanwhile you will suffer and die, you meek suffering fools. Why do you keep this ghastly silence? Why do you not demand—cry out for help—do something? There is nothing in this country, oh God, there is nothing!"

We shrink from his violence. What can we do—what can he mean? The man is raving. We go on our way.

The paddy was completely destroyed; there would be no rice until the next harvesting. Meanwhile, we lived on what remained of our salted fish, roots and leaves, the fruit of the prickly pear, and on the plantains from our tree. At last the time came for the rice terraces to be drained and got ready for the next sowing. Nathan told me of it with cheer in his voice and I told the children, pleasurably, for the fields were full of fish that would feed us for many a day. Then we waited, spirits lifting, eyes sparkling, bellies painful with anticipation.

At last the day. Nathan went to break the dams and I with him and with me our children, sunken-eyed, noisy as they had not been for many days at the thought of the feast, carrying nets and baskets. First one hole then another, no bigger than a finger's width, until the water eroded the sides and the outlets grew large enough for two fists to go through. Against them we held our nets, feet firm and braced in the mud while the water rushed away, and the fish came tumbling into them. When the water was all gone, there they were caught in the meshes and among the paddy, shoals of them leaping madly, wet and silver and good to look upon. We gathered them with flying fingers and greedy hearts and bore them away in triumph, with a glow at least as bright as the sun on those shining scales. Then we came and gathered up what remained of the paddy and took it away to thresh and winnow.

Late that night we were still at work, cleaning the fish, hulling the rice, separating the grain from the husk. When we had done, the rice yield was meagre—no more than two measures—all that was left of the year's harvest and the year's labour.

We ate, finding it difficult to believe we did so. The good food lay rich, if uneasy, in our starved bellies. Already the children were looking better, and at the sight of their faces, still pinched but content, a great weight lifted from me. Today we would eat and tomorrow, and for many weeks while the grain lasted. Then there was the fish, cleaned, dried and salted away, and before that was gone we should earn some more money; I would plant more vegetables . . . such dreams, delightful, orderly, satisfying, but of the stuff of dreams, wraithlike. And sleep, such sleep . . . deep and sweet and sound as I had not known for many nights; it claimed me even as I sat amid the rice husks and fish scales and drying salt.

Chapter 8

KUNTHI'S TWO ELDEST SONS were among the first in the village to start work at the tannery, and between them they brought home more than a man's wages.

"You see," said Kunthi. "The tannery is a boon to us. Have I not said so since it began? We are no longer a village either, but a growing town. Does it not do you good just to think of it?"

"Indeed no," said I, "for it is even as I said, and our money buys less and less. As for living in a town—if town this is—why, there is nothing I would fly from sooner if I could go back to the sweet quiet of village life. Now it is all noise and crowds everywhere, and rude young hooligans idling in the street and dirty bazaars and uncouth behaviour, and no man thinks of another but schemes only for his money."

"Words and words," said Kunthi. "Stupid words. No wonder they call us senseless peasant women; but I am not and never will be. There is no earth in my breeding."

"If there were you would be the better for it," said I wrathfully, "for then your values would be true."

Kunthi only shrugged her delicate shoulders and left us. She spent a lot of her time making unnecessary journeys into the town where, with her good looks and provocative body, she could be sure of admiration, and more, from the young men. At first the women said it and the men said they were jealous; then men too began to notice and remark on it and wonder why her husband did nothing. "Now if *I* were in his place," they said . . . but they had ordinary wives, not a woman with fire and beauty in her and the skill to use them: besides which, he was a quiet, dull man.

"Let her be," said Janaki. "She is a trollop, and is anxious only that there should be a supply of men."

Her voice held both anger and a bitter hopelessness: for a long time now her husband's shop had been doing badly. He was unable to compete with the other bigger shopkeepers whom the easy money to be had from the tanners had drawn to the new town.

A few days after our conversation the shop finally closed down. Nobody asked: "Where do you go from here?" *They* did not say, "What is to become of us?" We waited, and one day they came to bid us farewell, carrying their possessions, with their children trailing behind, all but the eldest, whom the tannery had claimed. Then they were gone, and the shopkeepers were glad that there was less competition, and the worker who moved into their hut was pleased to have a roof over his head, and we remembered them for a while and then took up our lives again.

It was a great sprawling growth, this tannery. It grew and flourished and spread. Not a month went by but somebody's land was swallowed up, another building appeared. Day and night the tanning went on. A never-ending line of carts brought the raw material in—thousands of skins, goat, calf, lizard and snake skins—and took them away again tanned, dyed and finished. It seemed impossible that markets could be found for such quantities—or that so many animals existed—but so it was, incredibly.

The officials of the tannery had increased as well. Apart from the white man we had first seen—who owned the tannery and lived by himself—there were some nine or ten Muslims under him. They formed a little colony of their own, living midway between the town and open county in brick cottages with whitewashed walls and red-tiled roofs. The men worked hard, some of them until late at night, the women—well, they were a queer lot, and their way of life was quite different from ours. What they did in their houses I do not know, for they employed servants to do the work; but they stayed mostly indoors, or if they went out at all they went veiled in bourkas. It was their religion, I was told: they would not appear before any man but their husband. Sometimes, when I caught sight of a figure in voluminous draperies swishing through the streets under a blazing sun, or of a face peering through a window or shutter, I felt desperately sorry for them, deprived of the ordinary pleasures of knowing warm sun and cool breeze upon their flesh, of walking out light and free, or of mixing with men and working beside them.

"They have their compensations," Kali said drily. "It is an easy life, with no worry for the next meal and plenty always at hand. I would gladly wear a bourka and walk veiled for the rest of my life if I, too, could be sure of such things."

"For a year perhaps," I said, "not forever. Who could endure such a filtering of sunlight and fresh air as they do?"

"You chatter like a pair of monkeys," said Kali's husband, "with less sense. What use to talk of 'exchange' and so forth? Their life is theirs and yours is yours; neither change nor exchange is possible."

Once, and once only, I actually saw one of those women, close. I was taking a few vegetables to market when I saw her beckoning me to come indoors. I did so, and as soon as the door was closed the woman threw off her veil the better to select what she wanted. Her face was very pale, the bones small and fine. Her eyes were pale too, a curious light brown matching her silky hair. She took what she wanted and paid me. Her fingers, fair and slender, were laden with jewelled rings, any one of which would have fed us for a year. She smiled at me as I went out, then quickly lowered the veil again about her face. I never went there again. There was something about those closed doors and shuttered windows that struck coldly at me, used as I was to open fields and the sky and the unfettered sight of the sun.

Chapter 9

ONE MORNING I WAS POUNDING some red chillies into powder. *Chochup!* went the pestle into the mortar, crushing the brittle chillies and the seeds in them. Each time it fell, a fine red dust rose up, spreading a rich, acrid smell in the air. A pleasant smell, hot and pungent, which made my nostrils water and squirted the tears into my eyes, so that every few minutes I had to stop to wipe them. It was a fine, peaceful morning, not a sound from the tannery, which for one blessed day in the week closed down completely. Each time I paused I could hear sparrows twittering, and the thin, clear note of a mynah.

Into view on the horizon came two figures, moving very slowly. I went on with my pounding. The figures grew larger every time I looked up, and then when they were still a fair distance away I recognised my daughter. I had seen her only once since her marriage, and since then a year had passed. Excited, I gathered up the chilli powder and put it away, rinsed my eyes, washed my face and came out. On the doorstep I traced out a colam, a pattern in white rice flour to welcome them.

They approached slowly, as if their feet were somehow weighted, not with the lightness which should have brought them quickly to my side. Something is wrong, I thought. Young people should not walk thus. And when I saw their faces the words of welcome I had ready died unuttered.

In silence Ira knelt at my feet. I raised her up quietly, with hammering heart. "Let us go in," I said. "You must be tired."

Ira entered obediently. Her husband stood stiffly outside. "Come," I said again, "sit and rest for a while. You have travelled a long way."

"Mother-in-law," he said, "I intend no discourtesy, but this is no ordinary visit. You gave me your daughter in marriage. I have brought her back to you. She is a barren woman."

"You have not been married long," I said with dry lips. "She may be as I was, she may yet conceive."

"I have waited five years," he replied. "She has not borne in her first blooming, who can say she will conceive later? I need sons."

I summoned Nathan from the fields. The tale was repeated, our son-in-law departed.

"I do not blame him," Nathan said. "He is justified, for a man needs children. He has been patient."

"Not patient enough," I said. "Not patient like you, beloved."

Ira was sitting with her face in her arms. She looked up as her father and I came in and her mouth moved a little, loosely, as if she had no control over her lips. She was lovely still, but strain and hopelessness had shadowed her eyes and lined her forehead. She seemed almost to back away as I went to her.

"Leave me alone, Mother. I have seen this coming for a long time. The reality is much easier to bear than the imaginings. At least now there is no more fear, no more necessity for lies and concealment."

"There should never have been," I said. "Are we not your parents? Did you think we would blame you for what is not your fault?"

"There are others," she replied. "Neighbours, women . . . and I a failure, a woman who cannot even bear a child."

All this I had gone through—the torment, the anxiety. Now the whole dreadful story was repeating itself, and it was my daughter this time.

"Hush," I said. "We are all in God's hands, and He is merciful."

My thoughts went to Kenny. He can help, I thought; surely he can do something. My crushed spirit revived a little.

About this time Arjun was in his early teens. He was tall for his age and older than his years. I had taught him the little I knew of reading and writing; now he could have taught me and most other people in the town. I do not know how he did it, for we could not afford to send him to school or to buy him books. Yet he always had a book or two by him, about which he grew vague if I asked questions, and spent many hours writing on scraps of paper he collected, or even, when he had none, on the bare earth. Secretly I was glad, for I saw my father in him, although sometimes my husband worried that he showed no inclination for the land; but when one day he told me he was going to work in the tannery I was acutely dismayed. It seemed it was going to be neither the one thing nor the other, neither land nor letters, which was to claim him.

"You are young," I attempted to dissuade him. "Besides, you are not of the caste of tanners. What will our relations say?"

"I do not know," he said. "I do not care. The important thing is to eat."

How heartless are the young! One would have thought from his words we had purposely starved him, when in fact of what there was he always got the biggest share after my husband.

"So," I said, "we do not do enough for you. These are fine words from an eldest son. They do not make good hearing."

"You do everything you can," he said. "It is not enough. I am tired of hunger and I am tired of seeing my brothers hungry. There is never enough, especially since Ira came to live with us."

"You would grudge your own sister a mouthful," I cried, "who eats half what I give her so that you boys can have the more!"

"The more reason for me to earn," rejoined Arjun. "I do not grudge food to her or to you. I am only concerned that there is so little."

He was right, of course. The harvests had been very poor, shop prices were higher than ever.

"Well," I said. "Go if you must. You speak like a man although you are a child still. But I do not know whether you can obtain work at the tannery. People say they have all the labour they want."

"Kunthi's son will help me," he replied. "He has promised."

I did not want to be indebted to Kunthi, or to her son. She was so different from us, sly and secretive, with a faintly contemptuous air about her which in her son was turned almost to insolence. He had inherited her looks too, and the knowledge of it lay in his bold eyes. A handsome, swaggering youth, not for my son.

"There is no need to go through him," I said with determination. "I will ask Kenny to help you. White men have power."

"Indeed they have," he said bitterly. "Over men, and events, and especially over women."

"What do you mean?" I said to him. "Speak with a plain tongue or not at all."

He looked at me obliquely with darkening eyes, but would say no more.

A few days later he began working at the tannery, and before long Thambi, my second son, had joined him. The two of them had been very close to each other from their earliest years, and it was not strange that Thambi should follow his brother. Nathan and I both tried to dissuade him, but without avail. My husband especially had been looking forward to the day when they would join him in working on the land; but Thambi only shook his head.

"If it were your land, or mine," he said, "I would work with you gladly. But what profit to labour for another and get so little in return? Far better to turn away from such injustice."

Nathan said not a word. There was a crushed look about him which spoke of the deep hurt he had suffered more than any words could have done. He had always wanted to own his own land, through the years there had been the hope, growing fainter with each year, each child, that one day he would be able to call a small portion of land his own. Now even his sons knew it would never be. Like his brother before him, Thambi had found the cruelest words of any.

Yet they were good sons, considerate of us, patient with others, always giving us a fair share of their earnings. With their money we began once again to live well. In the granary, unused for so long, I stored away half a bag of rice, two measures of dhal and nearly a pound of chillies. Hitherto, almost all we grew had been sold to pay the rent of the land; now we were enabled to keep some of our own produce. I was especially pleased that I had not been forced to sell all the chillies, for these are useful to us; when the tongue rebels against plain boiled rice, desiring ghee and salt and spices which one cannot afford, the sharp bite of a chillie renders even plain rice palatable. I was able at last to thatch our hut again, substantially, with two or three bindings of leaves. For the first time in years I bought clothes for the older children, a sari for myself, and although he protested I bought for my husband a dhoti which he badly needed, since the other was in rags and barely covered his loins. Both he and I had the garments we had worn at our daughter's marriage, but these we never thought of wearing: whatever hardships our day-to-day living might have, we were determined not to disgrace our sons on the day of their weddings.

Chapter 10

Deepavali, the Festival of Lights, approached. It is a festival mainly for the children, but of course everyone who can takes part. I twisted cotton into wicks, soaked them in oil and placed them in mud saucers ready to be lit at night. To the children I handed out two annas apiece, to be spent on fireworks. I had never been able to do so before—in previous years we had contented ourselves with watching other people's fireworks, or with going down to the bonfire in the village, and even now I felt qualms about wasting money on such quickly spent pleasures; but their rapturous faces overcame my misgivings. It is only once, I thought, a memory.

As it grew dark we lit the tapers and wicks and encircled our dwelling with light. A feathery breeze was stirring, setting the flames leaping and dancing, their reflections in the black glistening oil cavorting too. In the town and in the houses nearby, hundreds of small beacons were beginning to flash; now and then a rocket would tear into the sky, break and pour out its riches like precious jewels into the darkness. As the night went on, the crackle and spit of exploding fireworks increased. The children had bought boxes of coloured matches and strings of patt-has and a few pice worth of crackers, like small nuts, which split in two with a loud bang amid a shower of sparks when lit. The last were the most popular—the boys pranced round shrieking with laughter and throwing the crackers about everywhere, yet they were nimble enough to skip out of harm's way. All except Selvam, the youngest. He stood a safe distance away, legs apart and obviously ready to run, holding a stick of sugar cane nearly as tall as himself, which he had bought instead of fireworks.

"Go and play," I said to him. "Deepavali comes but once a year and this is the first time we have bought fireworks. Do not lose the opportunity."

"I am afraid," he said frankly, his small face serious.

After we had eaten, and rather well, and there were no crackers left, and the oil in the saucers had run dry, we walked to the town. Selvam refused to come. He was a stubborn child; I knew it was useless to try to persuade him. Ira stayed behind too, saying she preferred to stay with him. I think she was glad of the excuse he provided, for since her return she had not cared to be seen about, and of course there would be a large crowd in the town. Villagers from all round, like us, were converging towards the bonfire to be lit there; already smoke wisps were curling towards the clouds, torches were beginning to flare. The smell of oil was everywhere, heavy and pungent, exciting the senses. Our steps quickened. Quicker and quicker, greedy, wanting to encompass everything, to miss not one iota of pleasure. Then as happens even in the brightest moment, I remembered Janaki. Last year she had come with us, she and her children. This year who knew—or cared? The black thought momentarily doused the glow within me; then, angered and indignant, I thrust the intruder away, chasing it, banishing it . . . tired of gloom, reaching desperately for perfection of delight, which can surely never be.

There was a great noise everywhere. Men, women and children from the tannery and the fields had come out, many of them in new clothes such as we too had donned, the girls and women with flowers in their hair and glass bangles at their wrists and silver rings on their toes; and those who could afford it wore silver golsu clasped round their ankles and studded belts around their waists.

In the centre of the town the bonfire was beginning to smoulder. For many weeks the children had been collecting firewood, rags, leaves and brushwood, and the result was a huge pile like an enormous ant hill, into which the flames ate fiercely, hissing and crackling and rearing up as they fed on the bits of camphor and oil-soaked rags that people threw in.

In the throng I lost Nathan and the boys, or perhaps they lost me—at any rate we got separated—I pushed my way through the crush, this way and that, nobody giving an inch, in my efforts to find them; and in the end I had to give up. Before long, in the heat and excitement, I forgot them. Drums had begun to beat, the fire was blazing fiercely, great long orange tongues consuming the fuel and thrusting upwards and sometimes outwards as if to engulf the watchers. As each searching flame licked round, the crowd leaned away from its grasp, straightening as the wind and the flames changed direction; so that there was a constant swaying movement like the waving of river grasses. The heat was intense—faces gleamed ruddy in the firelight, one or two women had drawn their saris across their eyes.

Leaping, roaring to climax, then the strength taken from fury, a quietening. Slowly, one by one, the flames gave up their colour and dropped, until at last there were none left—only a glowing heap, ashen-edged. The drumbeats died to a murmur. The scent of jasmine flowers mingled with the fumes of camphor and oil, and a new smell, that of toddy, which several of the men had been drinking—many to excess, for they were lurching about loud-mouthed and more than ordinarily merry. I looked about for my family and at last saw my husband. He seemed to have gone mad. He had one son seated on his shoulders and one son at each hip, and was bounding about on the fringes of the crowd to the peril of my children and the amusement of the people. I fought my way to him. "Have you taken leave of your senses?" I cried out above the din.

"No; only of my cares," he shouted gaily, capering about with the children clinging delightedly to him. "Do you not feel joy in the air?"

He sounded so light of heart I could not help smiling.

"I feel nothing," I said, going up to him. "Perhaps it is the toddy that makes the feeling."

"Not a drop," he said coming up to me. "Smell!"

"You are too tall—I cannot," I replied.

"Lift her up," somebody yelled, and a dozen voices repeated the cry: "Lift her up, lift her up!"

My husband looked at me solemnly. "I will," he said, and dropping his sons he seized me and swung me high up, in front of all those people. Several of the women were laughing at him indulgently, the children were twittering with pleasure.

"Whatever will they say," I said, my face burning as he let me down again. "At our age too! You ought to be ashamed!"

"That I am not," he said, winking, to the vast delight of the onlookers. "I am happy because life is good and the children are good, and you are the best of all."

What more could I say after that?

Nathan sang loudly all the way back. He was in high spirits. The children, tired out, clumped along in silence, the youngest with frequent pleas to be carried; and when we took no notice he began snuffling.

It was a very hot night—Selvam and Ira were sleeping out in the open, in the small square in front of our hut which I had swept and washed with dung that morning. The others stretched themselves out and were asleep almost as they lay down. Nathan had lost none of his good humour. He seemed very wide awake. I stretched myself out beside him, close to him in the darkness, and as we touched he turned abruptly towards me. Words died away, the listening air was very still, the black night waited. In the straining darkness I felt his body moving with desire, his hands on me were trembling, and I felt my senses opening like a flower to his urgency. I closed my eyes and waited, waited in the darkness while my being filled with a wild, ecstatic fluttering, waited for him to come to me.

Chapter 11

ONE OF MY HUSBAND'S male relatives had died and he had to attend the funeral. When he had gone I took the opportunity of going to see Kenny. I had not done so before because I was sure Nathan would not like his wife or his daughter going to a white man, a foreigner. My father had been different—but Nathan, I felt, would not approve. And if he did not, the one chance Ira had would be lost, and this made it the more important that he should not know. I explained this to Ira cautiously, and she nodded listlessly and said yes, it was a necessary precaution, but she did not look at me and she showed no enthusiasm. I was getting more and more worried about her: she moped about, dull of hair and eye, as if the sweetness of life had departed—as indeed it has for a woman who is abandoned by her husband.

Kenny was working in the small building they had put up near the tannery. I could see him whenever the door opened to let someone out. There was a long line of men waiting; I squatted some distance away. The day wore on. The sun had set, the glow of twilight was touched with darkness, before he came out. He looked grim and tired, for his eyes were burning, there was an air of such impersonal cruelty about him that despite myself I shivered.

"No more tonight," he said briefly to the assembled men, and stepping down from the verandah he strode away. I waited till the crowd dispersed, then I followed. He was walking quickly with long strides, I had to run to catch up. He stopped at last when he heard my footsteps and waited for me to come up, frowning so that I began to feel afraid.

"I said no more tonight. Did you not hear me? Do you think I am made of iron?"

"I waited all day," I gasped. "I must see you. My husband will be back soon and then I cannot come."

His frown deepened. He said coldly, "You people will never learn. It is pitiful to see your foolishness."

"It is for my daughter I come," I said. "She cannot bear; she is as I was."

"You will be a mother even before she is," he replied with a glimmer of a smile, "for it seems you have no difficulty."

"It is so," I said. "I would it were otherwise and she in my condition, for she is much afflicted since her husband has no use for her."

"Why did she not come then," he said, "since it is her need? It would have been more sensible."

There was an edge to his voice, and his mouth twisted as if in exasperation.

"Forgive me," I whispered, quaking, "I was not sure—"

To my surprise, he put both hands on my shoulders, forcing me to look at him, and I saw he was laughing.

"I am sorry I frightened you," he said. "You should not act like a timid calf at your age. As for your daughter, I will do what I can—but remember, no promises."

He turned and was gone. I sat down to think, and to collect my wits. When at last I rose to go, a full moon was shining, golden and enormous, very low in the sky. Bats went swooping silently by. I kept to the narrow footpath, clear and white in the moonlight, walking swiftly and absorbed in my thoughts.

I heard no footsteps, only a voice calling my name from the shadows. I stopped, my heart hitting out wildly at my breast, and then I saw it was Kunthi, standing where the path forked with the moonlight streaming down on her.

"You startled me," I said, "I did not expect—"

"That I can see," she said coolly, coming towards me. "You keep late hours, Rukmani."

"No later than yours," I replied, not liking her tone. "I have my reasons."

"Of course," she said softly, derision in her voice. "We all have reasons."

"Mine are not the same as yours," I said with contempt, surveying her. She came very close, so close that I smelt the rose petals in her hair, saw the paint on her mouth.

"Meaning?"

"That we live differently. It is charitable to say no more. Let me pass."

She stood squarely in my path. "I would not have thought it," she said slowly, "had I not seen for myself."

"Thought what," I said. "Seen what?"

"That you have so much passion in your body," she said insolently, "that you seek assuagement thus. Your husband would give much to know where you have been tonight."

I saw her mouth forming these words, her eyes half-hooded and mocking, then I saw her face suddenly close to mine and did not realise I had thrown myself at her until I felt her body in my grip. An overwhelming rage possessed me. I kept shaking her furiously, I could not stop. Her slender body was no match for mine. I saw her head fall back, the thin sari she wore slipped from her shoulders. Then I saw that it was not tied at the waist but below the navel, like a strumpet's, and that she was naked below. Sandalwood paste smeared her swelling hips, under her breasts were dark painted shadows which gave them sensuous depth, the nipples were tipped with red.

I released her. She stood there before me panting, with her hair shaken loose and coiling about her shoulders.

"Guard your tongue," I said, "or it will be the worse for you."

She said nothing for a moment, while she rearranged her garments, recovering herself a little; then once again that maddening, insulting half-smile curved her lips.

"And for you," she said, with knives in her voice, "and for your precious husband."

With that she was gone.

I went alone to summon my daughter's husband.

"Take her back," I said. "There is nothing wrong with her now, she will bear you many sons yet."

"I would," he replied, with a hint of sorrow in his eyes, "for she was a good wife to me, and a comely one, but I have waited long and now I have taken another woman."

I went away. Ira was waiting, eagerness shining from her.

"You must not blame him," I said. "He has taken another woman."

She said not a word. I repeated what I had said, for she seemed not to understand, but she only looked at me with stony eyes.

Thereafter her ways became even more strange. She spent long hours out in the country by herself, spoke little, withdrew completely into herself and went about her tasks with a chill hopelessness that daunted me. No one could see in her now the warm lovely creature she had been, except sometimes when Selvam came to her, perching on her lap and coaxing a smile from her, for she always had a special love for him. As my pregnancy advanced she turned completely away from me. Sometimes I saw her looking at me with brooding, resentful eyes, and despite myself I could not help wondering if hatred lay behind her glance.

Then at last my child was born, a nicely formed boy, smaller than the others had been, but of course I was older now. We nicknamed him Kuti, which means tiny, and being a happy, untroublesome baby everybody took pleasure in his arrival. None more so than Ira: the transformation in her was astonishing as it was inexplicable. I had feared she might dislike the child, but now it was as if he were her own. She lost her dreary air, her face became animated, the bloom of youth came back to her.

"Our daughter is herself again," said Nathan to me. "I have heard her carolling like a bird."

"She is happy with the child," I replied, "but I do not know what is to become of her in the future."

"Always worrying," he chided. "It is not a mercy that she is young again, should one not be grateful?"

He was a man and did not understand. How could I stop worrying? We had no money to leave her. Who would look after her when we were gone and the boys were married with families of their own? With a dowry it was perhaps possible she might marry again; without it no man would look at her, no longer a virgin and reputedly barren.

No one had been more upset about the outcome of Ira's marriage than Old Granny. It was she who had arranged the match, and though failing in health she thought it her duty to come to me. She had aged considerably since the last time I had seen her. She walked slowly, pausing before each step to gather strength for the next; her hands kept up a slight, shuddering movement like the nervous flutter of a bee on a flower.

"No fault of yours, or the girl's or her husband's," I told her. "It is Fate. Nevertheless, I do not like to think of the future."

"Why fear?" said the old lady. "Am I not alone, and do I not manage?"

I thought of her sitting in the street all day long with the gunny sacking in front of her piled with a few annas' worth of nuts and vegetables; and I thought of Ira doing the same thing, and I was silent.

"It is not unbearable," said she, watching me with her shrewd eyes. "One gets used to it."

It is true, one gets used to anything. I had got used to the noise and the smell of the tannery; they no longer affected me. I had seen the slow, calm beauty of our village wilt in the blast from town, and I grieved no more; so now I accepted the future and Ira's lot in it, and thrust it from me; only sometimes when I was weak, or in sleep while my will lay dormant, I found myself rebellious, protesting, rejecting, and no longer calm.

Chapter 12

ONE DAY IN EACH WEEK, when the tannery stopped work, Arjun and Thambi would help their father on the land, and this gave Nathan great pleasure. He liked to see his sons beside him, to teach them the ways of the earth: how to sow; to transplant; to reap; to know the wholesome from the rotten, the unwelcome reed from the paddy; and how to irrigate or drain the terraces. In all these matters he had no master, and I think it helped him to know he could impart knowledge to his sons, more skilled though they were in other things, and able to read and write better than any in the town.

The rest of the week they worked at the tannery, going there soon after daybreak and not coming back until it was dark. By the time they had entered their late teens they were earning good wages: a rupee for each day's work, and without fail they would hand me their earnings, keeping nothing back for gaming or whoring as many of the lads did. Each morning I cooked rice for them, sometimes dhal or vegetables as well, which they took with them to eat at midday; and when they came home I gave them rice water and dried fish, sometimes a little buttermilk or perhaps even a few plantains I had kept from selling. But from what they gave me I had also to buy clothes for them, for they were expected to put on shirts over their loincloths, and red turbans on their heads, so that although we had full bellies and were well clothed, there was not much left over, and the hope I secretly cherished of putting by some money for Ira soon withered; and when it finally died I recovered my peace of mind and was happy enough.

If there was nothing to be done in the fields Nathan would accompany me when I went to market. This happened so seldom that it was always an occasion, and to round it off we would go to the tannery to see our sons. They invariably came out at midday for their meal, and we would sit with them for a few minutes, talking while they ate their rice and enjoying the rest. Then one day—a bright, soft morning with a whisper of rain in it—we got there to find the gates closed and guards posted along the iron railings that encircled the compound.

Midday, mid-afternoon, still no sign of the workers. At last I pluck up courage to enquire of the guards—it needs courage, for they are in uniform, and have lathis strapped to their wrists.

The first one is surly. "Begone! I have no time for idle women!"

The next swings his lathi jauntily; he does not know anything, he will not say.

So to the next. He is a big, hefty fellow, and he looks down at me and says there has been trouble—the workers will not be out today—no, not even to eat.

My knees turn to water. "What trouble?" I stammer. "Are my sons in it?" He shakes his head, he does not know.

My husband is behind me. He supports me a little with his arm and we go home. And wait. At last they come, long after dusk, with the faces of angered men, though neither is yet twenty.

"What has happened?" we ask with trepidation. They are still our sons, but suddenly they have outgrown us.

"Trouble," they say. "We asked for more money and they took from us our eating time."

I bring out some dried fish and rice cakes. They are ravenous. "More money?" I say, "What for? Do they not pay you well already?" "What for?" one echoes. "Why, to eat our fill, and to marry, and for the sons we shall beget." And the other says, "No, it is not enough."

I do not know what reply to make—these men are strangers. Nathan says we do not understand, we must not interfere: he takes my hand and draws me away. To his sons he is gentle.

Into the calm lake of our lives the first stone has been tossed.

Looking back now, I wonder how it came to pass that not until that fateful day did we realise the trouble that had been brewing. No gossip, not a whisper, had come to us of the meetings the men had held at which my sons had been spokesmen; nor of the agitation that followed; nor of the threats by the owners—there were now four—of the tannery. All this we heard only later.

Then one day they did not go to work.

"We shall not go back until our demands are met," Thambi said. "All the workers have stopped. We do not ask for charity, but for that which is our due."

"How can you force them?" I said. "Are they not the masters? For every one of you who is out, there are three waiting to step into your place."

"We will see," he replied in a hard voice, and I dared say no more.

When a whole week had passed thus, the tannery officials called a meeting to announce that those who did not return to work would be replaced. My sons came home from that meeting even more silent, if possible, than they had been in the past. This was the test, and it failed. The next morning the tannery had its full complement again, most of them workers who had gone back, the remainder men who were only too glad to obtain employment.

For so long hope and the heat of battle had sustained Arjun and Thambi. Now there was only bitterness.

"The people will never learn," Arjun said savagely. "They will rot before they do."

People will never learn! Kenny had said it, and I had not understood, now here were my own sons saying the same thing, and still I did not understand. What was it we had to learn? To fight against tremendous odds? What was the use? One only lost the little one had. Of what use to fight when the conclusion is known? I asked myself, and got no answer. I went to my husband and he was perplexed twice over.

Of course ours was not the only family involved. There were several others, among them Kali's, and she came to bemoan the result.

"Two more mouths to feed," she complained. "Only one of my three sons had the sense to go back. I do not know what is to become of us, for the land cannot sustain us all. So much for reading and writing," she said, accusing me with eye and finger. "Did I not say no good would come of it? Now look into what mess your sons have led us."

"Ay, and out of it to better things," said Thambi, with flint in his voice, "but for spawn like yours who have sold themselves cheaper than dirt."

"You will speak with respect," I cried, "or else—"

Then Nathan interrupted, so violently that I started.

"Enough!" he shouted. "More than enough has been said. Our children must act as they choose to, not for our benefit. Is it not enough that they suffer?"

The veins on his forehead were bulging. I had never seen him so angry before. Kali went away. Then the men went too, father and sons, leaving me alone who had no understanding.

Once more Nathan was sole provider for us, and we forgot the good living we had known. The reserves of grain I had put by began to dwindle despite my care. Fortunately, harvest time was near, and I consoled myself with the thought of it.

Arjun and Thambi began to frequent the town more and more, coming and going at all hours with no word as to what they did, and I suffered it in silence, for I knew they had no money to lead them to harm, and I had no cure for the restlessness that afflicted them.

One morning I was laying out some clothes to dry in the sun when Selvam came running in, his face hot and excited.

"Tom-toms are beating," he announced breathlessly. "The town is full of drummers, they are calling for men."

I stopped my work and gazed at him, and all at once my heart turned over. It was as if a scene long past were occurring again—this was not Selvam but Arjun, and he was telling me not of drummers but of bullock carts bringing the tannery to us brick by brick. I passed my hand over my eyes, feeling slightly giddy.

"Come and see, come quickly," the boy was saying, eager and unnoticing. The others crowded round and he repeated his story with relish. He had roused his brothers' interest and I was forgotten.

When they had gone—a triumphant Selvam in the van—and the place was quiet, I did indeed hear the drums, muffled and distant, insistently calling. Well, I thought, if it concerns me I shall hear soon enough, and if not I shall have saved myself a walk. . . . So with ordinary things I sought to still my qualms.

"They are calling for labourers," Arjun said, not looking up. "It would be a good opportunity for us."

Only Arjun and Thambi, who had stayed in the town until nightfall, and my husband and I, were up. The others were long asleep.

"They are paying well," Arjun resumed. "It would be good for us to work again. It is not fitting that men should corrupt themselves in hunger and idleness."

"I have heard," said Nathan, "that labour is required of you not here, but in the island of Ceylon."

"Yes. It is work in the tea plantations of Ceylon."

"You may not have the knowledge for such work."

"They will teach us—they have said so."

"Who will pay for the journey—is it not one of many hundreds of miles?"

"True. They will arrange everything, and everything will be paid for."

So Nathan was silenced, for he saw they were men and had made their decisions, but how could I let them go, who were my own flesh and blood, without a fight?

"Promises," I said. "Fair words. Who is to see if they are honoured? What is to happen if they are broken?"

"They need labour," Arjun said drily. "Self-interest alone will keep these promises."

"What is it that calls you?" I said. "Is it gold? Although we have none, remember that money is not everything."

"It is an important part of living," he answered me patiently, "and work is another. There is nothing for us here, for we have neither the means to buy land nor to rent it. Would you have us wasting our youth chafing against things we cannot change?"

"Indeed no," I said. "But Ceylon is a distant land, its people are not ours. How will you fare?"

"No worse than here," they replied. "No worse than here."

The wick was sputtering in the oil. There were only a few drops left in the coconut shell, but there was none to replenish it. We sat on in the darkness. Then at last I made one more effort.

"If you go you will never come back," I cried. "The journey costs hundreds of rupees, you will never have so much."

The tears came, hot and bitter, flowing and flowing as if the very springs of sorrow had been touched in my body. They spoke soothingly—of how much they would earn, and how one day they would return—as one does to a child; and I listened to them; and it was all a sham, a poor shabby pretence to mask our tortured feelings.

They left at first daylight, each carrying a bundle with food in it, and each before he went kissed Nathan's feet, then mine, and we laid our hands on them in blessing. I knew we would never see them again.

"They are growing up," Nathan said. "Would you have them forever at your breast?"

"Ah, no," I said wearily. "They must go their way. Only it seems to me their way lies far from here. Two sons have gone, now the third is going—and not to the land, which is in his blood, but to be a servant, which he has never been. What does he know of such work?"

"He will learn," said Nathan. "He is quick and has an agile brain. Should you not be thankful that he goes no further than two days' journeying, and that it is a good house that takes him? Kenny himself has assured you of that—you should be grateful that he has recommended our son."

"I am indeed," I said, flat and dispirited. "He has done much for us."

"You brood too much," Nathan said, "and think only of your trials, not of the joys that are still with us. Look at our land—is it not beautiful? The fields are green and the grain is ripening. It will be a good harvest year, there will be plenty."

He coaxed me out into the sunlight and we sat down together on the brown earth that was part of us, and we gazed at the paddy fields spreading rich and green before us, and they were indeed beautiful. The air was cool and still, yet the paddy caught what little movement there was, leaning slightly one way and the next with soft whispering. At one time there had been kingfishers here, flashing between the young shoots for our fish; and paddy birds; and sometimes, in the shallower reaches of the river, flamingoes, striding with ungainly precision among the water reeds, with plumage of a glory not of this earth. Now birds came no more, for the tannery lay close—except crows and kites and such scavenging birds, eager for the town's offal, or sometimes a pal-pitta, skimming past with raucous cry but never stopping, perhaps dropping a blue-black feather in flight to delight the children.

Nathan went and plucked a few green stems and brought them to me. "See how firm and strong they are—no sign of disease at all. Look, the grain is already forming."

I took the paddy from him and parted the grass and there within its protective husk lay the rice-grain, just big enough to see, white, perfect, and holding in itself our lives.

"It promises a good harvest," he repeated eagerly. "We shall be able to pay the landlord, and eat, and perhaps even put by a little. We may even make enough to visit our son—would not that be good?"

Thus he sought to comfort me, and after a time I was with him, thinking pleasurably of harvesting, and of plucking the pumpkins swelling on the vine, and visiting our son—and so we made our plans.

Before long Kenny brought me news of my third son. He was doing well, he said. His employer was well pleased with his work, he would be well looked after and I had no cause for his anxiety. The boy would soon be writing to me himself.

"It is very kind of you to tell me," I said. "You have done much for me and mine."

"It is nothing," he said. "You ask little."

I glanced at him, sitting there in our hut with long, haggard face and eyes like a kingfisher's wing, living among us who were not his people, in a country not his own, and of a sudden I was moved to ask him if he was indeed alone.

"Alone?" he said. "I am never alone. Do you not see the crowds always at my door? Have you ever known me to lack a following?"

"I did not mean that," I said, quietly waiting.

He did not reply at once. His face had shrivelled. I have offended him, I thought, panic overcoming me. Why did I have to speak? . . . The silence deepened. Then at last he looked up. "I am surprised you have not asked me before," he said. "It is many years since I saw you in your mother's house."

Well, I thought, if I have not asked, it is because I have not dared; there is a look about you that is quelling, and your manner forbids such talk.

I said awkwardly, "I have thought about it more than once . . . but it is not my place to ask questions. You come and go, and it is your own concern. I do not know what made me ask you now."

"Yet, since you have asked, I will tell you," he said. "I have the usual encumbrances that men have—wife, children, home—that would have put chains about me, but I resisted, and so I am alone. As for coming and going, I do as I please, for am I not my own master? I work among you when my spirit wills it. . . . I go when I am tired of your follies and stupidities, your eternal, shameful poverty. I can only take you people," he said, "in small doses."

I was silent, taking no offence. Barbed words, but what matter from one so gentle? Harsh talk from one in whom the springs of tenderness gushed abundant, as I knew.

"I told you what I did, in a moment of lunacy," he said. "I do not want it repeated."

"I am not cursed with a gossip's tongue," I said, annoyed. "I would not repeat what you have said."

"Never. Understand?"

"I understand."

He rose to his feet and without another word was gone, walking with long, quick strides and stooping a little as always. A strange nature, only partly within my understanding. A man half in shadow, half in light, defying knowledge.

Chapter 13

THAT YEAR THE RAINS FAILED. A week went by, two. We stared at the cruel sky, calm, blue, indifferent to our need. We threw ourselves on the earth and we prayed. I took a pumpkin and a few grains of rice to my Goddess, and I wept at her feet. I thought she looked at me with compassion and I went away comforted, but no rain came.

"Perhaps tomorrow," my husband said. "It is not too late."

We went out and scanned the heavens, clear and beautiful, deadly beautiful, not one cloud to mar its serenity. Others did so too, coming out, as we did, to gaze at the sky and murmur, "Perhaps tomorrow."

Tomorrows came and went and there was no rain. Nathan no longer said perhaps; only a faint spark of hope, obstinately refusing to die, brought him out each dawn to scour the heavens for a sign.

Each day the level of the water dropped and the heads of the paddy hung lower. The river had shrunk to a trickle, the well was as dry as a bone. Before long the shoots of the paddy were tipped with brown; even as we watched, the stain spread like some terrible disease, choking out the green that meant life to us.

Harvesting time, and nothing to reap. The paddy had taken all our labour and lay now before us in faded, useless heaps.

Sivaji came to collect his master's dues and his face fell when he saw how much was lost, for he was a good man and he felt for us.

"There is nothing this year," Nathan said to him. "Not even gleanings, for the grain was but little advanced."

"You have had the land," Sivaji said, "for which you have contracted to pay: so much money, so much rice. These are just dues, I must have them. Would you have me return empty-handed?"

Nathan's shoulders sagged. He looked tired and dispirited. I came and stood beside him, Ira and the boys crouched near us, defensively.

"There is nothing," Nathan repeated. "Do you not see the crops are dead? There has been no rain and the river is dry."

"Yet such was the contract, else the land would not have been rented to you."

"What would you have me do? The last harvest was meagre; we have nothing saved."

Sivaji looked away. "I do not know. It is your concern. I must do as I am bid."

"What then?"

"The land is to be given to another if you cannot make payment."

"Go from the land after all these years? Where would we go? How would we live?"

"It is your concern. I have my orders and must obey them."

Nathan stood there sweating and trembling.

"Give me time," he said at last humbly, "until the next crop. I will pay then, somehow."

"Pay half now," Sivaji said, "and I will try and do as you wish." He spoke quickly, as if to give himself no time to repent of his offer, and hurried away even before my husband had assented.

"No easy job for him," I said. "He is answerable, even as we are."

"That is why he and his kind are employed," Nathan said bitterly. "To protect their overlords from such unpleasant tasks. Now the landlord can wring from us his moneys and care not for the misery he evokes, for indeed it would be difficult for any man to see another starve and his wife and children as well; or to enjoy the profits born of such travail."

He went into the hut and I followed. A few mud pots and two brass vessels, the tin trunk I had brought with me as a bride, the two shirts my eldest sons had left behind, two ollocks of dhal and a handful of dried chillies left over from better times: these we put together to sell.

"Rather these should go," said Nathan, "than that the land should be taken from us; we can do without these, but if the land is gone our livelihood is gone, and we must thenceforth wander like jackals." He stared awhile at what we had to sell, and made an effort to say something and tried again and at last he said, choking. "The bullocks must go. Otherwise we shall not have enough."

But when we had added them and reckoned and re-reckoned, there was still not enough. "There are the saris left," I said. "Good ones and hardly worn, and these we must sell."

I brought out the red sari that had served for both my wedding and my daughter's, and the sari and dhoti I had bought when Thambi worked at the tannery, made a parcel of them and set out.

"Ah, Rukmani," said Biswas with false welcome. "What brings you here? I have not seen you for a long time, nor had any of your succulent fruit. Would that be what you bear with you?"

"No indeed," I answered shortly, his voice grating on me as always. "For the earth is parched to dust and all that I grew is dead. The rains failed, as you know."

"Yes, yes, yes," he said, looking at me with his cunning eyes. "These are hard times for us."

Not for you, I thought. You thrive on others' misfortunes.

"We need money for the land," I said. "I have brought the two shirts my sons no longer need, being away, two saris I never wear and my husband's dhoti to sell to you. The saris are very finely worked, and worn but a few times." I took them out and laid them before him.

He fingered the rich stuff, and measured the borders between outstretched thumb and little finger, and lifted up the silver threads to examine them the closer, and held up the shirts to the light for sign of wear.

"How much do you want for these?"

"It is for you to make the offer."

"Tell me first how much you want and I will see what I can do."

"Enough to pay the land dues."

"How much is that?"

"It is my business."

He was silent for a while, and I said to him exasperated, "Tell me if you are not prepared to buy and I will go elsewhere."

"Always in haste," he rebuked me in that gentle, oily voice of his. "Yet I think this time you will have to await my pleasure, Rukmani."

"What do you mean?" I said, ruffled. "There are many who would be pleased to buy such good material."

"I think not," he said. "I think not. For, you see, the wives of other men have come to me, even as you have, and have gone away as you threaten, yet they have to come back to me because nobody else can afford to buy in these hard times."

"As no doubt you can," I said with contempt, and then an inspiration came to me and I went on: "Unless you pay a fair price I shall take these saris elsewhere. There is the Muslim wife of a tannery official whom I know, and she will buy from me as she has done before."

"Indeed," he said, a little disconcerted. "Well, Rukmani, since we have done business for a long time, and because you are a woman of spirit whom I have long admired, I will give you thirty rupees. Nobody could be fairer."

"Fairer by far," I retorted. "I will not take one pie under seventy-five rupees. Take it or not as you please."

I put the clothes away, making a pretence of going to the door. I hoped he would call me back, for in truth I did not know where else to turn, but if not—well, thirty rupees was too far from our needs to be of use, and if I did not get what I asked I might as well keep the saris.

As I got to the door he called to me. "Very well, Rukmani. I will pay you what you ask, since it will help you."

I waited. He disappeared into another room and came back in a few minutes with a sour face and a small leather pouch full of money. He pulled the drawstrings and took from it notes and silver, counting them twice over to make sure.

"A very rare price," he said, handing me the money. "Remember always the good turn I have done you."

I tucked the money away, making no reply, and I went back with a lighter step than I had come out.

Nathan had returned too, having sold the pots and pans, the food and the bullocks. We pooled the money and counted it, and there was in all one hundred and twenty-five rupees, not even the half we had to pay.

"There is still the seed," Nathan said. "We must sell that."

"What of the next crop?" I said. "If we sell the seed we may as well give up the land too, for how shall we raise a new crop?"

"It is better to be without the seed than bereft of the land in which to plant it. Seed is cheap, it can be bought. I can earn a few rupees, or perhaps my sons . . ."

How? I cried to myself. How? Is not my son every day at the tannery, and no one will look at him because of his brothers! And you, my husband, what chance have you when so many young men are festering in idleness!

"It will mean only a few rupees," I said. "Let us not sacrifice the future to our immediate need."

"What is the alternative?" he shouted. "Do you think I am blind and do not see, or so stupid as to believe that crops are raised without seed? Do you take me for a fool that—"

He was not shouting at me but at the terrible choice forced upon us; this I knew, yet could not prevent my throat contracting, or force the tears back into their wells.

"Let us only try," I said with the sobs coming fast. "Let us keep our hope for a next harvest."

"Very well, very well," Nathan exclaimed. "Let us try by all means. We may be kicked for our pains, but what of that! Anything to stop your wailing. Now go, do not cross me further."

He is worried, I thought, smothering my sobs. He is distracted and does not mean to be harsh.

I went inside and lay down, with the money tied to my body, and at last dozed off into a troubled sleep.

In the morning Sivaji came, and my husband took the money and counted it out in front of him.

"One hundred and twenty-five rupees," he said. "Not half what we owe, but the best we can do without selling the seed for the next sowing."

"It would raise only a few rupees," I pleaded. "Let us but keep it, and we will repay you twofold."

"It is not for me," Sivaji answered. "You make payment to another. What shall I say to him that I bring so little? You made promise of half."

"Give us a little grace," Nathan said, dragging the words out. "We will make full repayment and over after the next harvesting."

So we stood and argued and begged, and in the end Sivaji agreed to wait. He took the money and turned to go, then he hesitated and said, a little wistfully: "What I do I must, for I must think of my own. . . . I do not wish to be hard. May you prosper."

"May you prosper too," I whispered, hardly able to speak, for his words had left me defenceless. "May the Gods give you their blessing." And so he departed.

The drought continued until we lost count of the time. Day after day the pitiless sun blazed down, scorching whatever still struggled to grow and baking the earth hard until at last it split and great irregular fissures gaped in the land. Plants died and the grasses rotted, cattle and sheep crept to the river that was no more and perished there for lack of water, lizards and squirrels lay prone and gasping in the blistering sunlight.

In the town a water reservoir had been built for the tannery workers and their families, but now others were allowed a limited quantity as well. So thither I journeyed every morning, and, when I said how many we were, perhaps half a mud pot would be doled out, sometimes a little more, depending upon who was in charge. Then some of the women in their greed began to claim to have more children than they had, and non-existent relatives, and there were jealousies and spite and bitter argument. Until at last it was decreed that each person must come in his own right only, not for others, even children and old men, and this put an end to the cheating and quarrelling; but it was hard for many who had not their full strength.

Then, after the heat had endured for days and days, and our hopes had shrivelled with the paddy—too late to do any good—then we saw the storm clouds gathering, and before long the rain came lashing down, making up in fury for the long drought and giving the grateful land as much as it could suck and more. But in us there was nothing left—no joy, no call for joy. It had come too late.

Chapter 14

A s SOON AS THE RAINS were over, and the cracks in the earth had healed, and the land was moist and ready, we took our seed to our Goddess and placed it at her feet to receive her blessing, and then we bore it away and made our sowing.

When a few weeks had gone by, the seed sprouted; tender shoots appeared, thrusting upwards with increasing strength, and soon we were able to transplant the seedlings one by one, and at first they stood out singly, slender, tremulous spires with spaces between: but grew and grew and soon were merged into one thick green field of rustling paddy. In that field, in the grain which had not yet begun to form, lay our future and our hope.

Hope, and fear. Twin forces that tugged at us first in one direction and then in another, and which was the stronger no one could say. Of the latter we never spoke, but it was always with us. Fear, constant companion of the peasant. Hunger, ever at hand to jog his elbow should he relax. Despair, ready to engulf him should he falter. Fear; fear of the dark future; fear of the sharpness of hunger; fear of the blackness of death.

Long before the paddy ripened we came to the end of our dried-fish stocks. There was no money left—every pie had gone to pay the land dues. Nothing left to sell. Nothing to be had from my efforts, for the vines and vegetables had withered in the long weeks of drought.

At last no option but to draw upon my secret hoard: a small stock of rice, ten ollocks in all, shielded from every temptation to sell or barter, kept even when the need to hold our land had squeezed us dry of everything else. Now I brought it out and measured it again, ten ollocks exactly. Then I divided it into several equal portions, each of the portions as little as would suffice for one day, and counted the portions, of which there were twenty-four, so that for nearly a month we would not starve. For a long time I hesitated, wondering whether we could do with less, thus making thirty divisions, but finally I decided against it, for Kuti was already ailing, and we needed to preserve our strength for the harvest.

For at least twenty-four days we shall eat, I thought. At the end of that time—well, we are in God's hands. He will not fail us. Sometimes I thought that, and at other times I was seized with trembling and was frightened, not knowing where to turn.

The nights were always the worst, and not for me alone. Peace then seemed to forsake our hut and I could hear my husband and children moving restlessly in their sleep and muttering, whether from hunger or fear I do not know. Once Nathan cried out loudly and sprang up in his sleep. I went to him, and he woke then and clung to me.

"Only a dream," I said. "Sleep, my dear one."

"A nightmare," he said sweating. "I saw the paddy turned to straw, the grain lost. . . . Oh God, all was lost."

His voice was stark, bereft of the power of dissembling which full consciousness brings.

"Never fear," I said with a false courage lest panic should swoop down on us. "All will be well."

He composed himself for sleep again.

"You are a good wife," he murmured. "I would not have any other."

I drifted at last into uneasy sleep, and dreamt many evil dreams, and in one I saw a shadowy figure with no face creeping into our hut and bearing away the ten ollocks of rice. I knew it was but the result of an overburdened spirit, but the following night I had the same dream. As the days passed I found myself growing increasingly suspicious. Except for my family, I trusted no one. Only at night when there were no passers-by, did I feel completely safe. Then I would bring out the rice, and measure it, and run the grain through my fingers for sheer love of it, fondling it like a simpleton. When I had taken out the allotted portion for the next day I would bury the remainder: one half, tied in a white cloth, in a hole I dug some distance from our hut, the other half in our granary.

Several times I thought of going to Kenny, and twice I did go. He would have helped us, of that I am sure, but each time I was told he had gone away . . . the townsfolk had not seen him for many weeks. I would have gone again and again, but I had not my full strength; it was no longer easy to walk to the town and back. We might have borrowed from Biswas, but there was nothing left to pledge; in any event, we would not have been able even to pay the interest he demanded.

Seven days went by and seven precious portions of rice were eaten. On the eighth day Kunthi came as I was cooking the rice water.

I had not set eyes on her for a considerable time—not since the day I had seen her in her nakedness; and she had changed so much I scarcely recognised her. I gazed at her hardly believing. The skin of her face was stiff and shiny as if from overstretching, elsewhere it showed folds and wrinkles. Under her faded sari her breasts hung loose; gone was the tense suppleness that had been her pride and her power. Of her former beauty not a vestige remained. Well, I thought. All women come to it sooner or later: she has come off perhaps worse than most.

"Sit and rest awhile," I said. "What brings you hither?"

She made no answer, but walked to the pot on the fire and looked in. "You eat well," she said. "Better than most."

"Not well. We eat, that is all."

"You still have your husband?"

"Why, yes," I said staring at her, not quite taking her meaning. "Why do you ask?"

She shrugged. "I have lost mine. I wondered how you had fared."

Poor thing, I thought. She has suffered. I looked at her pityingly.

"I do not want your pity," she said savagely, "nor does my husband. He is alive and well—he is living with another."

I thought of her husband, slow, sturdy, dependable, rather like an ox, and I could not believe it of him; then I thought of Kunthi as I had once seen her, with painted mouth and scented thighs that had held so many men, and I wondered if after all these years he had not at last found out about her. Perhaps the truth has been forced upon him, I thought, looking at her with suspicion, and I gazed again upon that ravaged beauty.

"Stare your fill," she said scornfully. "You always lacked graces, Rukmani."

I averted my eyes hastily. I hardly knew what to say.

"I have come," she continued, "not to be seen, or to see you, but for a meal. I have not eaten for a long time."

I went to the pot and stirred it, scooped out a little, placed it in a bowl, handed it to her. She swallowed it quickly and put the bowl down.

"I must have some rice too. I cannot come every day . . . as it is I have waited a long time to make sure you were alone."

"There is no rice to be given away," I said. "I must think of my husband and children. These are not times of plenty."

"Nevertheless," she replied, "I will have some. The damage will never be repaired while I hunger. There is no life for me until I am whole again."

She is mad, I thought. She believes what she says; does not realise there is no going back for her.

"Listen," I said, "there is none, or very little. Drink our rice water, come here daily, but do not ask for rice. I have a daughter and sons, even as you have, to consider. What I have belongs to us all. Can you not go to your sons?"

"My sons," she said, looking at me speculatively, "are not mine alone." Seeing my bewilderment she added, "They have wives. I would never approach them now."

"What are sons for—" I began.

"Not to beg from," she interrupted with a flicker of contempt. "I can look after myself; but first the bloom must come back."

I was mute: I had said all there was to say and now there was nothing more.

"Well," she said, breaking the silence, and with an edge to her voice. "How much longer have I to wait?"

She came close to me and put her face near mine. I saw the grey, drawn flesh and the hooded eyes, deep sunken in their sockets, and I made to turn away but she held me.

"I have not so much patience," she said. "I will have the rice now or your husband shall hear that his wife is not as virtuous as he believes—or she pretends."

"He believes what is true," I said with anger. "I do not pretend."

"Perhaps he has not seen what I have seen," she said, and there was menace in her voice and threat in the words. "Comings and goings in the twilight, and soft speech, and gifts of milk and honey such as men make to the women they have known."

"Stop," I howled at her, and put my hands to my ears. Thoughts kept hurtling through my head like frenzied squirrels in a new-forged cage. With sudden clarity I recalled my daughter's looks that far-off day when I had gone to Kenny; my son's words: "Such men have power, especially over women"; remembered my own foolish silences. I closed my eyes and sank down. She came and sat beside me.

"Which is it to be? Which is it to be? . . ."

Her words were hammering at my brain, the horrible syllables were beating the air around me, the whole place was full of their sound.

I need you, I cried to myself, Nathan, my husband. I cannot take the risk, because there is a risk since she is clever and I am not. In your anger or your jealousy, or even because you are not yourself after these long strained months, you may believe what she says and what she means. Because I have deceived you and cannot deny all she proclaims, you may believe the more. I will kill her first, I thought, and the desire was strong. I felt myself shaking. I raised my hands to my eyes and there was a quivering redness there. Then I heard a cry, whether of bird or child or my own tortured self I do not know, and the redness cleared. I felt the water oozing through my closed eyes, through my closed fingers. I took my hands away, and there was Kunthi waiting by my side with the patience of one who knows what power she wields, patient, like a vulture.

The ration of seven days to Kunthi, and eight already eaten. There is still enough for nine days, I thought, not with comfort but with desolation, and hatred came welling up again for her who had deprived me of the grain, and contempt for myself who had relinquished it.

I waited a long time that night before going out, for fear that Kunthi might be watching. There is nothing she would not do, I thought, lying there in the darkness. I must wait, and walk with care, and return unseen. I will match my wits against hers, I thought cunningly, lying and listening to uneasy slumber about me, and I will yet win; clever though she is, she shall not have all. . . . I rose at last and went out softly, and looked about me, and went quickly to the hole I had dug, and clawed away the earth until I saw the bundle, white under the starlight. I squatted down, crooning silently, untied it, ran my fingers through the grain; and I knew then there was no more than a handful left—a day's supply, no more, not the nine days' supply I had looked to find.

My stomach lurched, blood came pounding to my head, I felt myself going dizzy. Who could have known, who had done this to me? I heard a voice moaning and it was mine and the sound was terrifying, for I had not meant to speak. I looked about me wildly, seeking to see even in that darkness. Nothing in sight, not a sound except my own loud heartbeats. I dug my nails into my palms, striving for calm, trying to think. Who could have done this? Kunthi?—but she only knew of the granary, not this other hiding place. My own family? No, I thought with despair, thrusting aside the small core of suspicion each time it formed. Surely not. Who else? Who?

A long time passed; when at last I rose, my limbs were stiff and prickling, and darkness had given way to the first grey beginnings of dawn.

Nathan was not in the hut when I went back: I saw him sitting beside the paddy fields as he often did when he could not sleep. The boys were still asleep, the two older ones side by side, Kuti squeezed close to Ira and she with her arm thrown across him. I shook her by the shoulder, and Kuti woke first and began to cry. I picked him up and took him outside and left him there, and when I went back the others were awake. I looked at the three faces and I thought bitterly. One of them has done this to me. . . . Which one? Which one? I thought, questioning, looking at the three faces as if to read their thoughts; but there was nothing to see save alarm; they shrank a little from my vehemence.

"I must know," I shouted. "I must know who has done this thing."

They looked at me as if I had lost my senses. Ira said timidly, "We would not take what belonged to us all."

"Tell me I am imagining the loss," I stormed at her, "or that I myself have eaten it."

They stared at me in silence, amazed. Outside Kuti was bawling. Attracted by his cries, Nathan had come up, now he called to me.

"See to the child," he said frowning. "Can you not hear him? He will choke."

"So much the better," I said. "It will be one mouth less to feed."

"You are ill," he said. "You do not know what you are saying." He picked up the child, soothing him in his arms, and then gave him to Ira.

"My heart is sick," I said. "I have been robbed, and by one of my own children, of rice, which above all things is most precious."

"Is that what you have said to them?"

I nodded. I saw his face wither.

"I took it," he said at last.

"You? My husband? I do not believe it!"

"It is true."

Silence fell like a shroud. I listened to it locked in my own brooding bitterness. Then it was rent by a sound so raw, so painful, that my nerves began screaming in response. I looked up and it was Nathan. His face was working, from his throat came those dry hideous sobs.

"Not for myself," he was muttering, trying to control his treacherous voice, "for another. I took it for another. There was no other way. I hoped you would not notice. I had to do it."

I went to him. I did not want to know any more why he had done it or for whom, it was no longer important; but he was still speaking: it was as if he could not stop.

"Kunthi took it all, I swear it. She forced me, I did not want you to know."

Presently he was quiet.

"She has a strange power, this woman," I said, half to myself.

"Not strange," Nathan said. "I am the father of her sons. She would have told you, and I was weak."

Disbelief first; disillusionment; anger, reproach, pain. To find out, after so many years, in such a cruel way. Kali's words: "She has fire in her body, men burn before and after." My husband was of those men. He had known her not once but twice; he had gone back to give her a second son. And between, how many times, I thought, bleak of spirit, while her husband in his impotence and I in my innocence did nothing.

"It was a long time ago," Nathan said. "I was very young, and she a skilful woman."

"The first time was before our marriage," he said.

"One did not see the evil for the beauty," he said.

At last I made an effort and roused myself.

"It is as you say a long time ago," I said wearily. "That she is evil and powerful I know myself. Let it rest."

It became possible for me to speak as well. I told him of her earlier visit and the grain she had extorted from me also; and it seemed to me that a new peace came to us then, freed at last from the necessity for lies and concealment and deceit, with the fear of betrayal lifted from us, and with the power we ourselves had given her wrested finally from Kunthi.

Now that the last of the rice was gone it was in a sense a relief: no amount of scheming and paring would make it go any further; the last grain had been eaten.

Thereafter we fed on whatever we could find: the soft ripe fruit of the prickly pear; a sweet potato or two, blackened and half-rotten, thrown away by some more prosperous hand; sometimes a crab that Nathan managed to catch near the river. Early and late my sons roamed the countryside, returning with a few bamboo shoots, a stick of sugar cane left in some deserted field, or a piece of coconut picked from the gutter in the town. For these they must have ranged widely, for other farmers and their families, in like plight to ourselves, were also out searching for food; and for every edible plant or root there was a struggle—a desperate competition that made enemies of friends and put an end to humanity.

It was not enough. Sometimes from sheer rebellion we ate grass, although it always resulted in stomach cramps and violent retching. For hunger is a curious thing: at first it is with you all the time, waking and sleeping and in your dreams, and your belly cries out insistently, and there is a gnawing and a pain as if your very vitals were being devoured, and you must stop it at any cost, and you buy a moment's respite even while you know and fear the sequel. Then the pain is no longer sharp but dull, and this too is with you always, so that you think of food many times a day and each time a terrible sickness assails you, and because you know this you try to avoid the thought, but you cannot, it is with you. Then that too is gone, all pain, all desire, only a great emptiness is left, like the sky, like a well in drought, and it is now that the strength drains from your limbs, and you try to rise and find you cannot, or to swallow water and your throat is powerless, and both the swallow and the effort of retaining the liquid tax you to the uttermost.

"It will not be long before the harvest," Nathan would murmur, and I would agree with him, stifling the query whether our strength would last till then, saying, "Ah yes, not long now; only a little time before the grain is ripe."

It happened to me too, but I could not see myself, only what happened to others: saw their flesh melt away and their skin sag and sink between their jutting bones, saw their eyes retreat into their skulls, saw their ribs curve out from under the skin; and what withered the young bore doubly hard on the old and they were emaciated twice over.

But of us all Kuti suffered the most. He had never been a healthy child; now he was constantly ailing. At first he asked for rice water and cried because there was none, but later he gave up asking and merely cried. Even in his sleep he whimpered, twisting and turning endlessly, permitting no one to rest. Ira was gentlest with him, and tirelessly patient, nursing him in her skinny arms and giving him most of what came to her. But more often than not he turned away, unable to take the rough food we offered, and then she would hold him against her and give him her breast, and he would pull at the parched teat and be soothed, and for a while his thin wailing would die away.

Chapter 15

ONE DAY RAJA WENT OUT as usual and did not come back. At dusk they brought his body home slung between two men, one at the head and one at the feet. There was a small trickle of blood running from his mouth, fresh and still bright red, and more blood from a cut in his head, dark and congealed here and matting his hair.

They laid him on the ground. They bowed their heads and shuffled their feet and spoke in low voices and then they went away. It was real; yet it seemed a nightmare, it could not be true that my son lay dead before me. Thus my thoughts, dazed and confused, injecting pain where there was numbness; and my mind, furtively touching the edges of realisation, then fleeing from it in terror.

He had been caught, they said; something about money. What had my son to do with money, who had not a pie of his own! He was not very strong, they told me. They merely laid hands on him, and he fell. As if I did not know how thin and brittle he had grown! But why should others lay hands on him? They told me, but the sense of their words escaped. They told me, but I could not remember. They repeated themselves again and again, but I kept forgetting. I heard Ira begin to sing a low dirge; she was rocking gently back and forth, and she was crying.

"What are you crying for?" I said. "You have little enough strength, without dissolving it in tears."

She looked at me stupidly, and away, and down at her brother. Her sorrow flowed to me; the numbness began to clear. I tried frantically to keep it—I might as well have tried to imprison a cloud.

For this I have given you birth, my son, that you should lie in the end at my feet with ashes in your face and coldness in your limbs and yourself departed without trace, leaving this huddle of bones and flesh without meaning.

Already I think, the eyes must be closed, though death has glazed them, and I do so; the jaw must be tied, for it is sagging, I put a bandage about it; the body must be washed and I wash it; and Ira comes to help and cleanses the mouth which I have forgotten to do. These things were you, now there is no connection whatever; the sorrow within me is not for this body which has suffered and in suffering has let slip the spirit, but for you, my son.

Nathan prepares the bier, I see him lifting the body on to it. Then he goes out, walking towards the town. At dawn the funeral drums begin, and soon after our friends and neighbours come. Granny first, though hardly able to walk; then Durgan; Kannan with his wife, bearing a few jasmine buds; and Kali, bringing with her a muslin cloth to cover the bier. They pay their respects in silence, and when the sun has risen, the men pick up the bier and depart; but the women stay behind, for this is the custom. All that morning the sound of the drums comes faintly to us, rising and falling, rising and falling with the wind; until at last a final beat comes quivering through the air and we strain our ears for the next, but this, this sound which has already gone, is the last.

Now not even a heap of bones: only a few ashes to show that once a man has lived.

Raja had not been dead three full days when two officials from the tannery came to see us, and the one who was tall and burly with long mustaches did all the talking, and the other who was thin and insignificant stepped timidly in his shadow and agreed with what he said.

"The watchmen were only doing their duty," the tall one began. "They are engaged to protect our property, you understand?"

"I understand."

"No violence was used," he said. "Only enough to stop him. You agree, it was necessary."

"He was doing nothing."

"On the contrary. He was seen in the yard, where he had no business to be, and when the chowkidars caught him they found he had stolen a calfskin."

"I do not believe it," I said. "What use had he for such a thing?"

"Not in itself maybe," he replied in a strained voice, as if struggling to keep his temper, "but of course he could have sold it—sold it anywhere. We have had a lot of losses recently."

"You cannot blame my son," I said wearily. "We live from hand to mouth, as you can see . . . there is no wealth here, such as your goods might have brought."

"I am not blaming your son alone," he said carefully, "but of course it is well known your sons have been troublemakers. Now we do not want any trouble from you, you understand. The lad was caught in the act of stealing— maybe, as you say, for the first time and in a moment of weakness—still, he was caught, and for the consequences that followed, no one was to blame except himself. He should not have struggled. In these circumstances you naturally have no claim on us."

"Claim?" I said. "I have made no claim. I do not understand you."

He made a gesture of impatience.

"You may think of it later, and try to get compensation. I warn you, it will not work."

Compensation, I thought. What compensation is there for death? I felt confused, I did not understand what he was getting at. There was a pause. The timid man said kindly: "He was not brutally treated or anything, you know. They merely tapped him with a lathi, as he was trying to escape, and he fell. He must have been very weak or something."

"He was," I said. "He worked hard, and ate little."

"Naturally, it must have been a blow for you," said the timid one. "It is hard to lose—that is—" He tailed off incoherently, seeing his companion's glance fixed on him.

"The point is," the other said, and he thumped on the floor to emphasize his point, "that no fault attaches to us. Absolutely none. Of course, as my friend has said, it is your loss. But not, remember, our responsibility. Perhaps," he went on, "you may even be the better off. . . . You have many mouths to feed, and—"

The thinner man raised his hand to check him, appalled by the words, yet scared by his own daring. Poor little mouse, that gesture must have taken all his courage, he had none left for speech. His aggressive companion stopped short; the look of surprise spreading over his face was quickly re-placed by displeasure. He turned to me.

"I did not intend to wound you. But sometimes the truth must be stated, unpalatable as it is."

I nodded. There was no sense in agreeing or disagreeing, the gulf be-tween us was too wide; it was no use at all flinging our words at each other across that gaping chasm.

"So you agree," he insisted. "No responsibility attaches to us."

"Yes," I said, my lips felt stiff.

"I am glad everything is settled then. An unpleasant matter, but amicably settled." He drew his lips back, imitating a smile, and turned triumphantly to his companion.

"Did I not tell you there would be no trouble? You always fear the worst. I told you they would be reasonable."

The other did not look triumphant: if anything, he seemed to have shrunk a little, he avoided looking at me altogether; but as they went out together he glanced at me quickly, once, and in that brief moment I saw that his eyes were grieving.

"You should not care," I said very softly to him alone. "It does not matter."

He heard me and half-turned, his eyes clearing a little.

"I am very sorry for you," he said in a low voice. "May you find peace."

He went, his face overlaid with shame and misery.

Chapter 16

"THERE IS THE REAPING," I said, "and the threshing and winnowing. How shall we manage when the time comes?"

"When the time comes," Nathan said with a gleam in his eye, "the strength will be forthcoming, never fear."

I looked at him doubtfully: thin and drawn, with thighs and arms so puny that no muscle showed even when he flexed them. The rice would have to be lifted plant by plant, and the grain separated from the husk, and the husk beaten for the last few grains . . . it meant working long hours in the flooded fields with bent back, and much labouring thereafter converting the paddy into rice. It was no task for weakened bodies.

"You will see," he said with confidence. "We will find our strength. One look at the swelling grain will be enough to renew our vigour."

Indeed, it did our hearts good to see the paddy ripen. We watched it as a dog watches a bone, jealously, lest it be snatched away; or as a mother her child, with pride and affection. And most of all with fear.

As we sat there Irawaddy came to us, stepping softly.

"It is hot within," she said forlornly. "I could not rest."

She went and picked a head of paddy before sitting down beside us. I saw her fingers parting the husk, feeling for the grain within.

"How much longer?"

The same question, the answer to which she already knew, who had lived on the land since birth.

"Three weeks," Nathan's reply, grave, sincere, absolutely honest where another might have been tempted to easier words.

"It is not long to wait," I said, trying to hearten her. "And if the Gods are kind it may even be sooner."

That was what we prayed for—that it might not be too late. The tears that brightened Ira's eyes, the silences of my husband, the twitching face of Selvam, all came from one thing, the thought, imprisoned in the brain but incapable of utterance, that Kuti might not live to see the harvesting. The rest of us might struggle on, our endurance was greater; but he was only a child, not yet five, who had already waited a long time and who had suffered more than any of us. Whether from the unsuitable food, or from the constant restless movement of his body, he had developed a thick, irritating rash which he kept scratching; and where his nails caught, sores and blisters began, destroying whatever little peace he might have had. Sometimes after moaning for hours at a stretch he would fall into an exhausted daze—it could not be called sleep, it was nothing so sweet—and I would go to him with beating heart to see if the fight was ended; but again and again he struggled back to consciousness, took up again his tormented living; almost I wished it otherwise.

Some two or three days later I noticed a change in Kuti: his eyes lost their dullness and the whimpering that had been so harrowing to listen to lessened and stopped. I thought it was the end—a brief rallying, a frothing up of the last reserves of strength when there is no longer any need to hold back, like the sudden brilliant glow of an expiring taper—since we gave him nothing, there being nothing to give, that might account for the change. The following day, however, the improvement continued, and that night he slept peacefully. I gazed at the small tired face, soothed by sleep as it had not been for many nights, and even as I puzzled about the change, profound gratitude flooded through me, and it seemed to me that the Gods were not remote, not unheedful, since they had heard his cries and stilled them as it were by a miracle. Irawaddy crept up to me as I watched, and smiled at me and the child; and I whispered, "He is better," but there was no need as she, of all people, knew.

Through relief and exhaustion I slept well that night, waking refreshed before daybreak with a renewed hopefulness. Soon all will be well, I thought. We shall eat and the strength will come back to us, and there will be no more fear. This has been a bad time but it is passing as all things must, and now it is not joy, which passes in a trice, but sorrow, which is slower in the going, and so one must be patient. A few more days' waiting, a few more days' anxiety—it is not beyond enduring, it is not too much to ask. This I thought as I lay there, listening to the sounds of sleep and lost in my own imaginings.

The darkness was lifting when I heard the sound of footsteps, wary, soft, less heard than felt as a slight tremor of the ground. If it had been a reverberating gong, that sound could not have had more violent effect. My fancies fled headlong from me; in their place a cloud of black and grey arose, revolving before my eyes and assuming fantastic shapes and forms until at last one stood out clearly away from the swirling mists and with a face to it. Kunthi. No one but Kunthi, coming stealthily by night to thieve from us what little we had, unashamed as she was and always had been.

The footsteps were coming nearer: I raised myself on my elbow the better to listen, trying to still the thudding in my eardrums which impeded my hearing. Nearer and nearer. I stood up, bracing myself for the encounter, and stepped from the familiar darkness of the hut into the greying night outside. The figure was there, soft and blurred in outline, but a woman's. I threw myself at it, pinioning the arms savagely; thrust at it and beat it to the ground; fell on it with fury; felt the weak struggles of the body beneath mine like the feeble fluttering of a trapped bird, and exulted. The air was full of harsh sounds, but whether they issued from my throat or hers, or existed only in my imagination, I do not know. The being that was me was no longer in possession: it had been consumed in the flames of anger and hatred that raged through me in those few minutes; what took its place I do not know.

Then I heard a thin, shrill scream. "Mother! *Mother!*" Hands were dragging me away. I felt myself pulled and thrown to one side. "Fiend! Madwoman!" Nathan was shrieking. "Accursed mother!" He was bending over the form, doing something to it. I saw he was quite naked and wondered at it, forgetting he had come straight from sleep. He turned to me.

"Are you out of your mind? Your own daughter, you have killed her. Murderess!"

He and Selvam carried her in. I slunk after them, disbelieving. It could not be Irawaddy. It was some monstrous mistake they had made, not I. I crept to her side and saw it was Irawaddy. Her face was puffed and bore horrible marks, one lip was bleeding where her tooth had bitten down. I closed my eyes. Red circles opened out before them, receding into an endless blackness. I shook myself clear of them and went to aid my husband. He had a pot of water beside him and was wiping the blood from her body. Her sari was stained with blood. I took the cloth from him.

"I will see to her."

He thrust me aside. "Get away; you have done enough harm. You are not fit."

"I thought it was Kunthi," I whispered.

He moved a little, making room for me, but remained near, not wholly trusting.

She had been badly cut. A long jagged gash showed in her left side, there was a similar one on her left wrist.

"These wounds," I said. "I did not make them." I did not expect him to believe me.

"I know. The bangles broke."

Bangles? How could she have bangles, who had not a pie of her own? I stared at him, not knowing amid these unreal happenings whether those were his words or only what I had heard. He pointed.

"Do you not see the glass—there and there. She was wearing bangles."

They had broken against her body, which had protected me from injury. I began to swab. The cuts were full of glass, some of it in splinters, some of it in powder like shining sand. When I had cleaned them I bound the two largest gashes. For the rest there was nothing I could use, but these were smaller and mercifully soon stopped bleeding. The sari I had taken from her was soaked with blood and grimy where dust clung to the wet cloth. I took it down to the river intending to wash it, shook it clear of dust and broken glass. As I did so, something dropped from the folds, fell in the muddy water, sank and was lost; but not before I had seen that it was a rupee.

I went on with my work, scrubbing the bloodstains, rinsing the cloth, laying it on the grass to dry: then I came back, swept and cleaned the hut, cleared the courtyard, removed all signs of the struggle that had been. The sun was moving to midday by the time I had finished. Now that there was nothing more to do, the thoughts I had so far avoided came crowding in on me in agitated turmoil. Who had given her the money? Why? Had she stolen it, and if so how and who from? Why did she have to walk by night wearing glass bangles? I kept very still, not to waken my sleeping daughter, while the thoughts went galloping through my head, and question after question, unanswered.

Kuti, lying in a corner of the hut, began to moan. Ira heard and opened her eyes, gesturing vaguely towards him. I went to her first.

"Lie still; the cut will open again."

She looked at me sombrely: "Feed him; he is hungry. Take the rupee you will find in my sari."

I knew then that it was she who had been responsible for the improvement in Kuti, not I, not my prayers.

Nathan was about to say something, to question her perhaps. I gripped his arm, forcing him to silence. Ira was struggling to rise. I went to her.

"Lie still," I said again, laying restraining hands on her. "I will see to him."

I picked up the moaning child and took him outside, trying to quieten him. It was useless. Ira had fed him and freed him from hunger, the taste was with him still and he would not be quietened. I walked away from the hut with him in my arms, and at length his sharp cries sank into soft whimpering and finally into silence.

The lips of her wounds had hardly drawn together when Ira was on her feet again.

"Where do you go?" I said to her. "Rest a little longer; the marks are still livid."

"Rest!" she said contemptuously. "How can I rest or anyone rest? Can you not hear the child?"

"Where do you go?" I repeated. "Tell me only where you go."

"Do not ask," she said. "It is better that you should not know."

She was combing her hair, letting it fall away from her neck, first one way, then another, until the whole, head and hair, was sleek and shining. She had not troubled so much since she was a bride.

I saw her go out in the dusk, sari tightly wrapped about her. Saw her walk to the town, along the narrow lane which ran past the tannery, following it to where it broadened with beedi shops along one side and tawdry stalls on the other, where men with bold eyes lounged smoking or drinking from frothing toddy pots. She moved jauntily, stepping with outrageous fastidiousness amid the litter of the street, the chewed sugar cane, the trampled sweetmeats, the red betel-nut spittle; jauntily, a half-smile on her lips answering the jeers and calls that were thrown at her, eyes darting quickly round searching, then retreating behind half-drawn lids. At each turning leading from the street—and there were many of these, dim lanes and alleys—she paused, and advanced a little along it, and waited, lost in the shadows.

"I must know," I said imploring. "It is better that I should know than that I should imagine."

Ira gave me a sidelong glance: "Your imagination would not travel that far."

"You do not know me," I said, troubled. "And I no longer understand you."

"The truth is unpalatable," she replied.

I pondered awhile, searching my memory: then it came to me: the man who had called after Raja's death. He had said the same thing. The truth is unpalatable.

Nathan came in from the fields at sundown as Ira was setting forth. He had been clearing the irrigation channels and strengthening the dams, the fork he carried was caked with soil and water. He thrust it into the earth and leaned on it.

"Where do you go at this hour?"

"It is better not to speak."

"I will have an answer."

"I can give you none."

Nathan's brows drew together: she had never before spoken to him in this manner. Looking at her, it seemed to me that almost overnight she had changed; she had been tender and modest and obedient, now she had relinquished every one of these qualities; it was difficult to believe she had ever been their possessor.

Nathan was groping for words, stumbling a little over them.

"I will not have it said—I will not have you parading at night—"

"Tonight and tomorrow and every night, so long as there is need. I will not hunger anymore."

"Like a harlot," he said. "A common strumpet."

The veins in his forehead were standing out, on each temple a pulse throbbed fiercely. Ira stood defiant before him, uttering no denial, fingers plucking at the fringe of her sari. I closed my eyes, I could not bear to see them thus.

"These are but words," she said at last. "There are others, kinder ones, which for decency's sake—"

"Decency!" he spat at her. "Do not speak of decency!"

She was quiet for a moment, and he said with deliberate cruelty, "No man will look at you, defaced as you are."

"The cuts will heal," she retorted. "Men do not seek my face."

I think he laid a restraining hand on her: for I heard her say, "Let me pass," and there was a slight rustling sound as she withdrew from his grasp.

Well, we let her go. We had tried everything in our power, there was nothing more we could do. She was no longer a child, to be cowed or forced into submission, but a grown woman with a definite purpose and an invincible determination. We had for so long accepted her obedience to our will that when it ceased to be given naturally, it came as a considerable shock; yet there was no option but to accept the change, strange and bewildering as it was, for obedience cannot be extorted. It was as simple as that: we forbade, she insisted, we lost. So we got used to her comings and goings, as we had got used to so much else.

With her earnings Irawaddy was able to buy rice and salt, and milk for the child, who was too weak for anything else. After the roots and leavings we had existed on, I was grateful enough for the food, but of what she bought Nathan would not touch a morsel. Day after day he went out as before, delving and scraping for food, as thin and dry as a hollow bamboo stick.

"What is done is done," I said, urging him to eat. "There is no stricture on you, for you have tried."

"I will not touch it," he said, eyeing me steadily. What bitterness was behind this I do not know, or what condemnation of his powerlessness to feed his children; but this I do know: his spirit was very strong, and he was an upright man.

For the first few days after Ira resumed feeding Kuti with milk, he seemed to grow better, but the improvement—if improvement it had been: I do not know, for he ceased to cry and we took this for improvement—did not continue. Soon it became clear that he was sinking. His eyes grew larger in his pinched face, there was a brightness in their soft brown as if all that was left of life was concentrated there; and indeed they seemed to be the only active part of him. From his corner, when he was no longer capable of any other movement, his eyes constantly followed us, seeming never to tire in their restless wandering. Otherwise he lay quiet like a bruised fledgling, with the dry, parched lips of exhaustion and a body which could struggle no more.

Only once I heard him call: a slight whisper that barely reached me.

"Ama?"

"Yes, dear?"

"I cannot see you—I cannot see anything."

"I am here my son, very near you."

There was a feeble movement of his arms, and I knelt beside him and clasped them round my neck, holding them there, for he was too weak.

"Sleep, dearest. Soon you will be better, and then you will be able to see again. I promise you, you will see again."

He seemed content; he accepted the lies I told him and sighed a little— perhaps in relief, for who knows what fears tormented his child's mind? Soon I felt him relax and loosing his hands gently drew away from him. A little later I heard a slight sound and turning saw that he had opened his eyes and was gazing at Ira, staring at her unwinking. I went to him and saw that his eyes were sightless; already a thin film was over-spreading them. I picked him up and held him to me; his limp, emaciated body, so light I might have been holding a handful of leaves, not a child, sagged lifeless against mine. I crooned to him, forgetting he was dead, until the cold came creeping through his limbs and he began to stiffen; then at last I laid him down, closing his eyes and pushing back the fronds of hair that clung damply to his brow. He looked tired but very calm, with the signs of suffering taken from his countenance. Nathan came and knelt beside him with harsh sorrowing face and bitter eyes. Our last child, conceived in happiness at a time when the river of our lives ran gently, had been taken from us; I knew too well what he felt. Yet, although I grieved, it was not for my son: for in my heart I could not have wished it otherwise. The strife had lasted too long and had been too painful for me to call him back to continue it.

Chapter 17

WHEN KUTI WAS GONE—with a bland indifference that mocked our loss—the abundant grain grew ripe. It was the second crop of the year, sown on ground which had not been allowed to lie fallow, and so we did not think it would be other than meagre; but contrary to our expectations it was a very good harvest. Every husk was filled, the paddy stood firm and healthy, showing no breaks in their ranks. We worked through the days and in the twilight getting in the rice, and then we worked three more days draining the fields and clearing them, and then three more nights sifting and win-nowing. Even so, a heap of unhusked paddy lay in our granary, waiting until the marketing should be done.

"It is as I said," Nathan exclaimed. "Strength has been given to us. Else how could so much have been achieved by such as we?" He looked around triumphantly, pointing to the neat white hills of rice and the husks in a rustling brown heap. We looked at each other, streaked with sweat, thin and bony like scarecrows and as ugly, and suddenly what he had said seemed very funny; and first Selvam and then Ira began to laugh, helpless, speech-less, with tears running down their cheeks, until we older people slowly joined them—could not help but join in their laughter—and the spectre of what had been tweaked at our memories in vain. There we were, the four of us, hysterical, released, rocking with laughter and gasping for breath which ran out as fast as we sucked it in. The hollow cheeks and bulging stomachs, the grotesque, jutting bones, became matter for laughter; already, though they were still with us, in our minds they belonged to the past—to the painful past that we thrust from us with all our force; and the laughter was in some measure born of relief that we could do so.

Nathan especially was in exuberant mood. He kept slapping his thigh and shaking his head as if he could not believe in so much good fortune; in his palm he held a few grains of rice, rubbing them together to produce a dry rustle which seemed to delight him, for he kept repeating the movement. Perhaps it was to reassure himself that they were real and not part of his desperate imaginings.

"There will be enough to pay what we owe," he exclaimed, "and to keep what we want. We can stock the fields with fish as well—"

"And plant vegetables," I said. "I shall need to buy bean seeds and chilli seeds, and perhaps a few young pumpkin vines . . . sweet potatoes of course . . . I have made a lot from my vegetables before."

"Indeed yes," he said eagerly. "There will be money enough for all this, you will see. God has given us another chance in His mercy."

"First the marketing," I said smiling, for who would not at such optimism, "then the plans."

Then and there, in a fever of impatience, we got out the gunny bags and the tall brass measure, and set to calculating quantities and prices.

The sowing of seed disciplines the body and the sprouting of the seed uplifts the spirit, but there is nothing to equal the rich satisfaction of a gathered harvest, when the grain is set before you in shining mounds and your hands are whitened with the dust of the good rice; or the very act of measuring—of filling the measure, and topping it with a peak, careless of its height because you can afford to be, and also because you know in your prudence that the grains will see to it that you are not too generous, and slip and tumble down the sides of the measure if that peak be too tall. So many handfuls to one measure, so many measures to one sack; one after the other the sacks are filled and put away, with rejoicing and thankfulness.

Later we go to offer prayers, bearing camphor and kumkum, paddy and oil. Our hearts are very grateful.

Chapter 18

I WENT TO MARKET laden with smooth-skinned brinjals and pumpkins, round and fleshed like young women. The earth had yielded richly: there were, besides, beans and potatoes, melons and chillies, and I was well pleased with them and with the silver coins I had received in exchange. I no longer sold to Biswas; there were several other shops in the town now where I was paid better, and where I did not have to endure the sly, spiteful observations he made. Increasing years had added more grease to his bulk, more flesh to his paunch; they had not sweetened his nature or endowed him with more kindliness. Confounding the curses that came his way—and there were many, for his usury was harsh beyond necessity—he continued to prosper, squeezing the life from those hapless creatures who were driven to borrow from him, and gaining his strength from their weakness.

Seeing me pass, he came and stood in his doorway and called. "Rukmani! I have news for you. Stop a minute!"

"What is it?"

"Kenny is back. I have seen him."

"So," I said warily. "That is good news for everybody."

"Especially for you," he said, keeping his eye on me.

"For everybody," I repeated, "for he is a good doctor. Many people are in his debt."

"He is also a man," he said. "They say he is a good friend to you."

"To me and mine," I said with rising temper. "He has done much for us."

"For you particularly," he insisted, his flabby lips twitching with innuendo. "I have heard from Kunthi that this is so."

"A whore's tale," I said contemptuously, "as suspect as her body."

He thrust his face up to mine.

"Yet not for that reason dismissed," he said, leering.

I wanted to strike him, I wanted to ram his words back into his throat. I held myself still with an effort.

"Foul-mouthed pig!" I said. "Carrion crow!"

He only smiled, being used to harsh words.

"As hot headed as ever, Rukmani," he said. "Where will you turn when you next need money?"

He was so slippery, so worthless, that my anger died. Not even the malignant power of Kunthi could rouse me: I felt too remote.

I hung about for a while, unable to make up my mind whether to try to seek him in the town, or whether to go home in prudence and await his coming, as I felt sure he would. Then it struck me as ludicrous that at this late stage I should walk with caution, and I went therefore to the white-washed cottage on the fringes of the town, expectant, carrying a garland of roses and jasmine to welcome him, and a lime for good luck.

The cottage was bare—it always had been—and chill and lifeless from long disuse. Dust lay thick on the floor, there were neat hillocks of chipped cement and the earth where bandicoots, for some obscure reason of their own, had dug. So much I saw from the broken front window, then I pushed open the door to enter.

Kenny was standing in the smaller room that led off the main one. He turned when he heard me come in, I saw him frown.

"How did you know I was here?"

Accustomed though I was to him, the brusque words, his short manner, dashed the welcome from my lips.

"Biswas told me," I said. "I came at once."

There was a silence. The garland I was holding became an encumbrance, I felt I had been stupid to buy it. Even the lime seemed unnecessary. I tried to hide them behind my back. He noticed at once.

"What have you got there?"

"A few things—I have just been to market," I began lamely.

"A garland, is it not?"

"Yes," I said sheepishly. "I bought it for you. You guess well."

He drew me to the window and pointed. Outside lay a heap of garlands, roses, lilies, chrysanthemums; evidently others had been before me.

"Not a guess," he said gravely, "a certainty. You were not the first."

"Well-intentioned for all that—" I was beginning hotly when he began to laugh, grinning widely so that the lines of his face were somehow lost in the creases of laughter, making him look young and amiable. I felt better at once; the strangeness vanished.

"You have been away a long time," I said. "Too long; we have missed you."

"Why? " he said. "More trouble?"

I was in two minds as to what to say and looked covertly at him. His face had become very serious, almost grim, with every trace of laughter taken from it. After so many years he was as unpredictable as ever.

"We have had our troubles," I said cautiously. "Yet it was not only on that account we missed you. It was—" I stopped, not knowing how to finish. He would have helped us in our need with food and money and skill, yet it was something more than this that he offered us, and I could not find words for it.

"Your presence," I said haltingly, "means a lot to us. There is a rare gentleness in you, the sweeter for its brief appearances."

I do not know what emboldened me—perhaps it was his silence. He seemed to be hardly listening. He was still standing, looking out of the window, biting his nails.

"Troubles," he said. "We all have them. I suppose the crops failed and you starved."

"It was a bad time," I answered him. "We lost two sons. Raja died by an accident. The child was too tender for this world; he could not live as we did. After the crops failed he—" I stopped again. The memory of those days was ever with me, yet the passing of time had made it quiescent; now my own words brought it savagely alive with a shrill, stabbing pain that swept the words away. I was quiet for a while, waiting for it to fade, to regain calmness. He did not look round, perhaps he sensed my struggle.

"Enough of me," I said at last. "What of you and yours?"

He turned on me roughly. "What concern is that of yours?"

"None; save that I wish them well."

"Save your wishes," he said unpleasantly. "My wife has left me. My sons have been taught to forget me."

I tried and failed to imagine her, this woman who could after so many years renounce altogether her husband, break the bond that must surely have existed despite his long absences. Perhaps it is just this that has driven her to it, I thought. He is not without blame.

"You think it is my fault," he said. "Do not deny it, your face speaks plainly enough for me."

"Women need men," I said, shrugging. "It is not right to deprive a woman."

"Tell me also," he said. "Do you not think a man must choose his work?"

"Such a man as you, yes," I replied.

"What then if his wife cannot accompany him?"

"Cannot?" I said. "She must. A woman's place is with her husband."

He sighed impatiently. "You simplify everything, being without understanding. Your views are so limited it is impossible to explain to you."

"Limited, yes," I agree. "Yet not wholly without understanding. Our ways are not your ways."

"You have sound instincts," he said.

For the first time since I had known him I saw a spark of admiration in his eyes.

"I am not a fool," I said, speaking in a low voice, pleased by the commendation in his eyes, a little hurt by it as well. "Have I not so much sense to see that you are not one of us? You live and work here, and there is in your heart solicitude for us and love for our children. But this is not your country and we are not your people. If you lived here your whole life it still would not be."

"My country," he said. "Sometimes I do not know which is my country. Until today I had thought perhaps it was this."

He sounded bitter and weary: his forlorn spirit touched mine, and a great emptiness seemed to unfold in me. I wished I could have my words back, locked away safely in myself, unsaid, powerless to wound.

"Save your regrets," he said. "You have told me nothing I did not know."

I rose to go. "My husband and children will be happy to see you. We shall be glad to welcome you in our house."

"You are not without riches, as I have said before," he said, speaking half to himself. "How is your daughter? She was a pretty young woman."

"Well; she is carrying."

"So her coming to me was not in vain."

"Had she been barren forever, it would have been better."

"Why? Was it not your wish—"

"Not this way," I said, "with the father any one of a dozen men."

"I suppose it was necessary," he said quietly. "I have seen it happen before."

"She would go," I replied. "She was devoted to the child; she would go. But of course she knew nothing, being inexperienced in such matters, and now she is with child. She conceived quickly."

"You will feel better when it is born," he said. "A baby is no worse for being conceived in an encounter."

"You may be right," I said bitterly, "but you do not realise the shame of it. People have not spared us."

He stared at me impatiently.

"That is all you can think of: what people will say! One goes from one end of the world to the other to hear the same story. Does it matter what people say?" His tone was contemptuous. Well, I thought. It is easy for you, but perhaps not quite so simple for us.

I walked home, musing over what he had said, and presently it seemed to me there was truth in his words, and I felt a little comforted. Nathan had said much the same thing: he and Kenny, so different in other ways, were yet united in their views about this.

Chapter 19

Kᴇɴɴʏ's ʀᴇᴛᴜʀɴ ᴡᴀs ᴛʜᴇ ʙᴇɢɪɴɴɪɴɢ of another change in our lives, and in Selvam's. Selvam, who for all that he had been reared on the land and had the earth in his blood, yet did not take to farming. Like his brothers, he was hard-working and conscientious, but he had no love for it and in return it did not yield to him. He had a knowledge of crops and seasons, born of experience; but where crops thrived under Nathan's hand, under his they wilted. Despite anxious care, the seed he planted did not sprout, the plants that sprouted did not bear.

One day he came straight from working in the fields, threw down the spade he was carrying and announced he was finished with the land.

"I am no farmer," he said. "The land has no liking for me, and I have no time for it."

"What then will you do, my son?" I said, worried. "How will you live when we are gone?"

He did not reply at once, but sat down cross-legged, looking out absently beyond the small courtyard to the cool green of the paddy fields. But he was not thinking of them.

"Kenny is building a hospital," he said. "When it is ready he will need an assistant, and he has offered me the job."

"But what can you know of such work?"

"Nothing. He is going to train me, starting as soon as possible. He says it will not be too difficult for me, for I am not without learning."

It was true. Selvam had been cast in the same mould as his brothers. He had quickly learned what I had to teach and had progressed from there by his own efforts and enthusiasm. Study came to him naturally; he wrote and read as I had once done, avidly, with pleasure. He will learn, I thought. This is the chance he has been waiting for.

Selvam began to fidget.

"I have told my father," he said hesitantly. "He is very willing."

I smiled at him. "So am I. I wish you well."

He relaxed. "I am glad. I thought you might be—were—displeased."

"Not displeased. Perhaps disappointed, since all our sons have forsaken the land. But it is the best way for you."

"It is the best way," he repeated after me. "It will be a great venture. We have many plans and much hope."

We both relapsed into silence. I watched him covertly, wondering whether I should say, "You must be prepared: this new association will not be taken at face value, there will be vilifiers who will say it was done not for you, but for your mother, who will seek to destroy your peace"; but then I thought resolutely, I will not take the fire from his resolve or sow suspicion between them, and so I held my peace. But his steady eyes were on me, calm and level.

"I am not unaware," he said quietly. "But is it not sufficient that you have the strength and I have trust?"

"It is indeed," I said with relief. "I wanted only that you should know."

We smiled at each other in perfect understanding.

I sought out Kenny again.

"We are once more in your debt. My son is overjoyed. This is something he has waited for without knowing it."

"I am indebted to him as well. I need an assistant; he promises to be a good one and will I hope be the first of many. I could not carry on alone. The town has grown and is still growing, as you know."

"It will be bigger than what went before?"

"It will be a hospital, not a dispensary," he said coldly. "Let me show you."

He pulled out several papers, drawings, and long sheets covered with calculations, which I could not understand even when he explained them, though this I did not confess. I gathered only that it would be a big affair.

"Where is the money to come from?" I said bewildered. "Such a construction will need I do not know how many hundreds of rupees."

"I have thousands," he replied.

"I did not realise. You have lived like us, the poor."

"The money is not mine. It has been given to me—I have collected it while I have been away."

"In your country?" I said. "From your people?"

"Yes," he said impatiently. "Part of it came from my country and my people, part of it from yours. Why do you look puzzled?"

"I have little understanding," I replied humbly. "I do not know why people who have not seen us and who know us not should do this for us."

"Because they have the means," he said, "and because they have learnt of your need. Do not the sick die in the streets because there is no hospital for them? Are not children born in the gutters? I have told you before," he said. "I will repeat it again: you must cry out if you want help. It is no use whatsoever to suffer in silence. Who will succour the drowning man if he does not clamour for his life?"

"It is said—" I began.

"Never mind what is said or what you have been told. There is no grandeur in want—or in endurance."

Privately I thought, Well, and what if we gave in to our troubles at every step! We would be pitiable creatures indeed to be so weak, for is not a man's spirit given to him to rise above his misfortunes? As for our wants, they are many and unfilled, for who is so rich or compassionate as to supply them? Want is our companion from birth to death, familiar as the seasons or the earth, varying only in degree. What profit to bewail that which has always been and cannot change?

His eyes narrowed: whether from our long association, or from many dealings with human beings, and whether one kept silent or spoke to cloak one's thoughts, he always knew the heart of the matter.

"Acquiescent imbeciles," he said scornfully, "do you think spiritual grace comes from being in want, or from suffering? What thoughts have you when your belly is empty or your body is sick? Tell me they are noble ones and I will call you a liar."

"Yet our priests fast, and inflict on themselves severe punishments, and we are taught to bear our sorrows in silence, and all this is so that the soul may be cleansed."

He struck his forehead. "My God!" he cried. "I do not understand you. I never will. Go, before I too am entangled in your philosophies."

Chapter 20

NOT IN THE TOWN, where all that was natural had long been sacrificed, but on its outskirts, one could still see the passing of the seasons. For in the town there were the crowds, and streets battened down upon the earth, and the filth that men had put upon it; and one walked with care for what might lie beneath one's feet or threaten from before or behind; and in this preoccupation forgot to look at the sun or the stars, or even to observe they had changed their setting in the sky: and knew nothing of the passage of time save in dry frenzy, by looking at a clock. But for us, who lived by the green, quiet fields, perilously close though these were to the town, nature still gave its muted message. Each passing day, each week, each month, left its sign, clear and unmistakable.

The tender budding of our new year, the periwinkles and the jasmine, the soft, scented champak blossom, had yielded place to the fierce flowering jacaranda and gold mohur, before Ira's time came for giving birth. When my daughter was in labour I erected the bamboo paling outside to warn my husband and son, as is the custom for those who have only one room and one dwelling; and when I had scoured the hut and poured wet dung on it I brought out the pallet of plaited straw I myself had used, for Ira to lie on; and went and gathered the petals the trees had shaken about them and took them in to her, a vivid basket of layer upon layer of gold and red and mauve and purple.

"A child of summer," I said, "should be sturdy."

She smiled and laid her hands on the petals.

"He is. I feel it."

While I waited I thought of the other births this very hut had seen. First Ira herself, then the long, long interval and after that almost every passing year I bore a son. There had been hope and expectation, perhaps some anxiety, before each birth; they were natural feelings. But now fears came swarming about my head like the black flying ants after a storm, and I cowered from the beat of their wings. A child conceived in an encounter fares no worse than a child born in wedlock . . . so Kenny had said; but could one be sure? A man takes his wife with passion, as is his nature, yet he is gentle with her: amid the fire of breast on breast and bared thigh on thigh he still can hold himself, and give as much as he takes, leaving the exultant flesh unbruised. The woman is his, his wife, not only now for this surging experience, but tomorrow and next year. She will carry his seed and he will see her fruitful, watch while day by day his child grows within her. And so he is tender and careful, and comes to her clean that their fulfilment may be rich and blessed.

But the man who finds a woman in the street, raises an eyebrow and snaps his fingers so that she follows him, throws her a few coins that he may possess her, holds her unresisting whatever he does to her, for this is what he has paid for—what cares such a man for the woman who is his for a brief moment? He has gained his relief, she her payment, he merges carelessly into the human throng, consigning her back into the shadows where she worked or to the gaudy streets where she loitered.

Of the thousands of men in the village, in the town, perhaps another village, another town, one man unknown is the father: of the vast range of manhood, who is to say he was not of the unsound, the unclean? What care or safeguard is there when the consequences of one's act are hidden from one's thankful eyes, and the woman is one of many, soft, desired, lost, forgotten!

If Ira had any tears she did not show them: perhaps she had fought her battles out alone when I was not there to see and when her face could not betray her; or perhaps her love for children swamped every other feeling. She was meant to have children: I had always known that. It was a cruel twist of Fate that gave them to her this way.

Then at last the birth began, and while I was ministering to her all these thoughts coiled back into my brain, leaving only the present and the imme-diate future which every passing second converted instantly into the past. Then there was no past or future, only now, the present, as I received the child and held him, while the fears that were nameless descended on me and shrieked their message and were no more nameless. I held him, this child begotten in the street of an unknown man in a moment of easy desire, while the brightness of the future broke and fell about me like so many pieces of coloured glass.

I did not want his mother to see: I washed him slowly, and massaged oil into his body, hoping to mitigate the whiteness of it, hoping to give colour to his skin, while he cried lustily, for he was a healthy child: and finally his mother called for him. I swaddled him carefully before I gave him to her hoping—still hoping—that she would not notice.

"Your son," I said, handing her the bundle, hovering near in my anxiety. She took it, smiling and relaxed.

"A lovely child," she said, gazing at the small face fondly. "Fair as a blossom."

Fair! He was too fair. Only his mother failed to see how unnatural his fairness was, or to notice that the hair which grew slow and unwilling from his pate was the colour of moonlight, or that his eyes were pink. Sometimes

I wondered whether her mind was gone, since she could not see what was so plain to others: or whether it was a ghastly pretence fashioned from her mother's pride and sustained through who knows what superhuman effort. However, if she dissembled she dissembled well; no sign of strain or fear crossed her face, she was as happy as a bird with her son, singing to him, playing with him, clucking and chuckling as if he were the most beautiful baby any woman could have. Perhaps he was to her. Such heaviness of spirit as there was, pressed not on her but on us, her parents, and of us Nathan was the most burdened.

"She has lost her reason," he said. "She does not see her child as he is, but as she would have him be. To her he is only fair, whereas it is clear he resembles nothing so much as a white mouse. She has done great wrong to herself and the child, and has given up her sanity rather than face the truth. My fault," he said, rocking slowly on his heels. "I might have prevented this."

"Hush," I said. "Do not torment yourself. You could not have stopped her, for she was determined."

"It is a cruel thing in the evening of our lives."

"Cruel, but not unbearable. The girl is happy and the child is doing well."

"I have seen him in the sun," Nathan said sadly. "He turns from the light, groping instead for the darkness which is kinder to him. Already he is beginning to be aware of his difference, baby though he is."

"Foolish talk," I said. "He turns from the light because his eyes are weak. Kenny has told me it is always so with such children."

"It may be the one or the other," he replied. "Who can be sure? But whatever the cause, the result is terrible. Sunshine is meant for men, darkness for bats and snakes and jackals and other such creatures."

In his pain he was exaggerating, for the child flinched only from direct sunlight; within the hut, or in the shade of a tree, he was perfectly content, and would lie on the ground or slung from a branch, sucking his toes and gurgling like any other baby. And I myself preferred not to see him in strong sunshine, for his pale, membranic skin was no barrier to the light, which pierced deep into the flesh and illumined it to a hideous translucency. Apart from this he burnt easily, even an hour or so in the sun would bring up red, scaly patches about the neck and forehead and make him fretful, whereas my children had grown up in the open and thrived on it.

The news travelled far and fast. People came to see the child, and I do not know what tales they told but more people came, their faces avid with curiosity to see him—a curiosity which was never sated although they stared and stared with bulging eyes; and they went away with appropriate comments on their lips and mouths bursting to describe the poor little albino mite they had seen. Some who came were kindly, most had a ready, sterile sympathy, and all went away with the unmaskable relief that men experience when they see others who have fared worse than themselves.

It was for us a prolonged ordeal. One day, after an especially long line of callers had come and gone, Nathan said bluntly that he was having no more of it.

"We will have a naming ceremony," he said. "Ask those we know and get it over. After that no one will have an excuse to call."

It is the custom to have a ceremony on the tenth day from birth: this is the custom, and I had followed it for all my children. But what was proper for this child, fatherless and marked from birth? However, Nathan made the decision and once it was made I felt better for it. Despite my wavering, I had not been altogether unaware that this was the right thing to do.

So they came: friends, neighbours, bringing sugar cane and frosted sugar and sticks of striped candy for the new baby. Ira accepted them in his name, smiling, graceful as ever, unperturbed. I think her bearing astounded and even awed them. Old Granny, bent low on her stick, came bringing a rupee which she gave me to keep for the child. I did not want to take it but she insisted: if I had known it was her last I would have resisted her blandishments. But I took it and thanked her.

"You are a good friend to us."

"In my intentions," she said, "little else. It was a poor marriage I arranged for your daughter. I have brought this on her."

She still refused to forget. I made some sort of soothing reply, but with the licence of age she did not listen, hobbling away mumbling that it was her fault. Not hers, not Nathan's, not mine or Ira's. "Not the man's," Kenny said. "A freak birth." Whose the blame then? I thought wearily. Blame the wind and the rain and the sun and the earth: they cannot refute it, they are the culprits.

Nathan's voice reached me from a distance:

"What is the matter with you? Are you not feeling well?"

"I am all right. I was thinking."

"Give it a rest," he said. "Give it a rest."

I was relieved that Kali, most garrulous of women, had not come, but it was a short-lived relief. She had been suffering from one of her periodic attacks of ague, and as soon as she had got rid of it she came, waddling, for she had put on a lot of fat when prosperity had returned to the land.

"I would have come before," she puffed, "but for the ague. The shivering was bad this year and the fever! I tell you, I hardly know how I survived." She lowered her voice confidentially. "You know how it is—not too easy at my age."

"I hope you are better," I said.

"Ah well, one must not expect too much. I am well enough. But I did not come to talk about myself."

I looked at her without favour: it was plain enough why she had come. She lowered her voice again.

"Is it true about the baby? People say he is milk-white!"

"He is fair," agreed Ira equably. "See for yourself," and she held out the sleeping child in her arms. Kali bent forward eagerly, quivering in her excitement, and at that moment as ill luck would have it the child woke, opened his weak, pinkish eyes, yawned and began to yell piercingly. Kali stepped back as if she had been deliberately affronted: and such pity as she might have had in her perished.

"He looks peculiar," she said frankly. "Not a bit normal. Who ever heard of pink eyes in a human child?"

I did not know what to say. Nathan was looking at her sourly: he had never liked her. Ira's face was strained and taut and queerly defensive, as if she had been hurt and was wondering where the next blow would fall. So she does know, I thought with something akin to relief, yet of course not wholly so. She hides her knowledge well. . . . The silence went on, everybody afraid to speak, thoughts crisscrossing in the over-full air, eyes averted, shifting, lowered at last to the ground. Then I heard Selvam clearing his throat to speak, and at once heads turned, surprised, lightened of suspense, very much alert.

"Just a matter of colouring," he said, "or lack of it. It is only a question of getting used to. Who is to say this colour is right and that is not?"

The words of a boy—Selvam was not sixteen—shaming us all.

"But pink—" Kali began.

"A pink-eyed child is no worse than a brown-eyed one," he said, looking at her with cold, rebuking eyes. "I should have thought your instincts as a woman if nothing else would have told you that."

He turned away from her contemptuously and began clicking his fingers to the child. Sacrabani, who had been screaming vigorously, began to quieten down: he gave one or two more tentative wails, then his mouth split in something like a smile and his fingers curled round Selvam's.

Selvam turned and smiled at us, raising eloquent eyebrows: Was not the child exactly the same as other babies? Had he not said so?

Triumphantly he turned to look for Kali but she—unnoticed—had gone.

Chapter 21

FROM THE DAY CONSTRUCTION BEGAN on the hospital, Selvam ceased to belong to us. During the preparations, while the site was bought and cleared, and a contractor engaged to find men and material, he spent his time with Kenny, and what they discussed I do not know, but sometimes he came home elated and sometimes he was morose and dejected; and it was clear enough that the many delays they encountered irked his spirit beyond the telling. Then when construction actually started, the bricks stacked high, the cement in heaps, whatever time he could spare he spent at the site watching while brick was laid on brick and mortar flowed between: and occasionally when the labourers let him (which was not often, for they were a jealous crew), he would take a hand in the building himself, for nothing gave him more pleasure than that. What he did not know was that seven more tedious years were to pass before the building was complete: both he and Kenny, possessed by their fierce enthusiasm, had, I think, reckoned on a much shorter time. Maybe it was as well they did not know: seven years is a long time to be patient.

If things had gone as they had hoped, the hospital would have been completed within a year, and Old Granny would not have had to die in the street as she did. There was nowhere else she could go: she had lived in the street and she died there. Day by day she sat beside her torn gunny sack selling handfuls of nuts and berries, growing progressively older, more ragged, less healthy. She had no relatives left—no person on whom she had any claim—certainly there was no one to enquire whether she made a living or how much longer she could continue to do so. Better to avoid such questions, better to pass quickly by with a cheerful word, than to stop and ask, for who would lightly take on the burden of feeding another mouth? And so one day she quietly disappeared. They found her body on the path that led to the well, an empty mud pot beside her and the gunny sacking tied around her waist. She had died of starvation.

Once a human being is dead there are people enough to provide the last decencies; perhaps it is so because only then can there be no question of further or recurring assistance being sought. Death after all is final. I could not avoid the thought, which came from my own uneasy conscience, harsh and bitter, as I watched them lift her up, light as dust, on to the bier; as mourners came with flowers, as oil and camphor were laid unstinted on the pyre, as rosewater and sandalwood paste were sprinkled on her corpse. So it had been with my sons, so it was now with Old Granny, one day it might be the same for me, for all of us. A man might drift to his death before his time unnoticed, but when he was dead and beyond any care then at last he was sure of attention. . . .

* * *

Old Granny's death bore especially hard on me: for apart from the fact that we had been friends since my marriage I could not forgive myself for having accepted the rupee which might have fed her for several days. I wanted to throw it away—give it to the next old crone I saw—anything to gain my relief; but the money belonged to Sacrabani, not to me.

"You are being very childish," Nathan said. "How long would a rupee have kept her?"

"A few days at least," I said.

"And what when those few days ran out?"

"I don't know . . . something may have turned up. It is a pity the hospital was not ready. She could have gone there."

"A hospital is not a soup kitchen," he said.

I did not know what he meant by a soup kitchen and I stared at him. He repeated the words, pleased that he knew and I did not.

"Where the poor are fed free of charge," he explained. "In other countries. Selvam tells me this is a fact."

"And how should he know? He has not been out of this town since his birth?"

"From books he has read perhaps—or Kenny may have told him. I do not know *how* he knows."

"Well, anyway," I said, going back to what we had been discussing, "soup kitchen or not, they would not have refused an old ailing woman."

"Why go on about it?" he said exasperated. "You are only distressing yourself and it might never have been. I tell you a hospital is only for the sick. There is nowhere for the old."

The hospital was no more than a few months old and a few feet high when people began attempting to stake their claims. They went to Kenny and they came to Selvam and they even approached me, his mother, and from the numbers who came I soon knew that not one-tenth could enter. And what I of little perception knew Kenny and Selvam knew twofold: but we none of us said anything, for we had woven about us a net of silence in whose meshes were precariously held our fears and our misgivings.

Meanwhile, work on the hospital did not progress smoothly; twice the contractor was changed, and each man in turn appointed new foremen, and these brought their own labourers. One year there were not enough men; the next, not enough material. During one very hot summer the workmen's huts caught fire and before it could be put out it had spread to the timber stacked nearby. The loss had to be made good, as had also the theft, despite the presence of a chowkidar, of a cartload of bricks and the cart itself. Several times work stopped altogether, for what reasons I do not know, while Kenny and Selvam strode about the deserted site in exasperation, dark as thunder, unapproachable. Kenny made frequent trips away from the town from which he came back tired and often dispirited; but always work was resumed on his return.

"Every pie has to be fought for," Selvam said. "It cannot be easy."

"He told me he had enough," I said. "He was away a long time collecting the money."

"There can never be enough," Selvam said, turning away.

I could not help wondering what bottomless pit they were trying to fill, or from what bottomless purse. It is not as simple as Kenny said, I remember thinking to myself. It is not enough to cry out, not sufficient to lay bare your woes and catalogue your needs; people have only to close their eyes and their ears, you cannot force them to see and to hear—or to answer your cries if they cannot and will not. Once I dared to say as much to Kenny and he looked at me a little sadly and said there were other ways which he could not explain to me. There was much talk between him and Selvam of various funds and grants and so on, but I do not know whether anything came of these. At any rate building went forward, slowly, painfully slowly, but at least it did go on.

Before long Selvam began his training. The small whitewashed cottage was once again in use, with my son now assisting Kenny. By the second year of his training he began treating minor cases by himself, and from then onwards Kenny paid him a small wage, not regularly but as and when funds came his way. Once in a moment of thoughtlessness I asked how he would contrive to pay all his staff when the hospital was finally established, for it was certain many people would be needed to run it. His face darkened: he would, he said, find ways and means. It had become his most frequent saying.

Chapter 22

Selvam and Ira had always been close, the years of separation when my daughter went to her husband having affected their relationship not at all; she treated him more as if he were her son than her brother, and he in turn accepted her love and returned it in his own deep, quiet way. He understood her well, better than I did who was her mother; in fact, I wonder whether parents ever know their children as they know one another. At any rate in our family my sons and daughter had always been as one in their thinking: such schism as there was opened between them and us, never between themselves. Kali said this was so because they were better read, more learned, than we were: but ever since the troubles at the tannery in which her sons had become involved, and for other reasons, she had been prejudiced against any kind of learning. In her view most of the troubles in the country sprang from the pages of books.

Selvam's easy attitude towards her son brought Ira even closer to him. From the beginning Selvam had accepted the child's albinism: accepted it and thought no more of it. From infancy he treated Sacrabani exactly as if he were a normal child. The pity of it was that it was a forlorn battle. No amount of such action on his part or ours could bring others to the same persuasion. Sacrabani was isolated from the start, a white crow in a flock of black, a grain of wheat among the rice. By the time he was four, Sacrabani was used to being a hanger-on—forever on the fringes of others' activities. Because of his difference, the other children never included him as a matter of course in their games: if they were short of a player, or for some other good reason, they sometimes invited him to join them, but on no account was he to do so of his own accord. In the hope of being thus asked he had to tag along, patient and submissive. His physical disabilities alone would have ensured his dependent role; for his skin was unable to stand the sun, and the light affected his eyes. The sight of him crouched in the shade with reddened face and streaming eyes evoked from his companions not pity but ribaldry. Poor child, he had even to suffer the behaviour of his elders, who stared—those who had not seen him before—and nudged each other and whispered and rustled, while those who *had* vied with each other to be the first to enlighten them. Then one day, sprung from who knows what taunts flung at him, his questionings, first of many, began.

"Mother, what is a bastard?"

What does one say to a child? What possible answer is there? I saw Ira eyeing the boy, startled, wary, trying to guess how much innocence and how much knowledge lay behind the question, wondering how little and how much she could tell him, questioning in her turn to gain time.

"Why do you ask?"

"I want to know."

"It is a child whose birth his mother did not wish for."

"Oh," he said, looking at her speculatively. "Did you wish me to be born?"

"Yes, of course, darling," Ira cried, and all the guilt of her efforts to have an abortion was in her voice. "I would not lose you for anything. Why do you have to ask?"

"I wanted to know," he repeated lightly, noncommittally, not knowing how cruelly he had hurt his mother.

Some days later he tackled her again.

"Mother, have I got a father?"

"Yes, dear, of course."

"Where is he?"

"Not here, my son; he is away."

"Why does he never come to see us?"

"He will when he can."

"But why not now?"

"Because he cannot. You will understand when you are older."

"How old?"

"I do not know myself. Now run away and play. You must not ask so many questions."

The first lie; many to follow. The distressing, inescapable need for lying.

"I would have told him his father was dead," I said, "as he certainly is to all intents and purposes. It would have been easier."

"Do not interfere," Nathan said. "It is for Ira to decide."

Ira looked heavy-eyed and hurt. "Yes; you are right," she said. "I should have told him that. I was not prepared for the question—he is such a baby still."

"He did not think of it himself," I said. "He is as yet too young. No doubt one of his companions."

"Leave it, leave it," said Nathan. "Do not upset the girl any more."

He put out his hand to Ira, but she shied away from him. I saw her leave the hut.

"It is no use going to her," Nathan said sadly. "Such comfort as there is to be had must come from her own spirit."

Nevertheless, after a little while he did go to her and his gentleness melted her last remnants of control, for she began to weep. I heard her crying for a long time.

Chapter 23

MY THIRD SON, MURUGAN, who was a servant, married a girl from the town in which he worked. We had not seen her, nor did we know her family, and the marriage, in the second year after Sacrabani's birth, was solemnised at her parents' house without either of us being present. Had it been at all possible we would have gone, but it proved beyond our power. The town was over a hundred miles away, and since the harvest had been a poor one and Selvam was earning very little we had not the money to go by rail. Durgan, it is true, had a bullock in addition to his milch cows, and a cart which he offered to lend us for a small sum, but Nathan was not fit enough to undertake the journey there and back. He was nearing fifty and no longer as healthy as he had been. He had begun to suffer from rheumatism, and apart from this had had several attacks of fever, from each of which he recovered more slowly and emerged weaker. Sometimes in the middle of sowing or reaping or tilling, or the innumerable tasks the land demanded, he would stop and straighten up, breathing hard and trembling. Often he was unable to continue work and was forced to lie down in the hut for a while. Ira and I did what we could; but the land is mistress to man, not to woman: the heavy work needed is beyond her strength. Several times Kenny came to see him bringing food and sometimes medicine; he told me bluntly that my husband was not getting enough to eat.

"We eat well enough when the harvest is good," I answered him, "but of course we have our lean times."

"Too many," he said. "Your husband needs milk and vegetables and butter, not plain rice day after day."

I looked at him incredulously. "Those can only come our way when the yield is rich," I said. "It cannot be always or indeed even frequent, for we are not rich, you understand."

"I was not thinking," he muttered. "Of course I know this too." Then one day he told me that my husband would not recover until he stopped worrying.

"He is very anxious about you," he said. "You must try and reassure him."

"I would do so if only it were in my hands. But what comfort can one offer a man who sees his family wholly dependent on him and no one else to see to them?"

When I had said the words, I thought, Perhaps he will despise me for my weakness; perhaps this will make him think I am a self-pitying good-for-nothing, anxious only for my own well-being, and I added quickly: "There are others to consider besides myself. . . . I do what I can but it is not much."

"I had not thought otherwise," he said gently. "Tell me, is there no one else apart from your husband?"

"No one. My sisters have children of their own—besides, they live very far away, we have not seen them for many years. My sons—well, they have made their lives elsewhere, as you know."

There was a silence, and I thought, Now I have wounded him. . . . I did not mean to. I made a move towards him, but he seemed to shrink back. Both hands came up to bury his face.

"I do not grudge—" I began timidly. He took his hands away, I saw the imprint of pain on his face.

"And I have taken the last of them," he said. "Why do you not say it? It is true. I have taken him and there is no recompense."

For a moment the words would not come; there was room in me only for feeling, very deep, very tender, for this man who felt for me.

"You have taken nothing that was or would have been ours," I said at last. "Selvam never belonged to the land; he would never have been a farmer like his father. Do not torment yourself that he has turned from it and found his peace with you. We would not have had it otherwise."

"Yet in your hearts you may have wished for something else."

"If so, we have long since forgotten it. We would not wish for our son other than what he would wish for himself. He has chosen well."

Another silence.

"Do you never," he said, "think of your future? While you still have your strength and can plan?"

"Naturally we think. But plan! How can we? It is not within our means."

"Is there nothing you can do?" he asked. "Nothing at all?"

"What can we do? There are many like ourselves who cannot provide for the future. You know it yourself."

"Yes; I know. . . . I do not know why I asked; it was needless. There is no provision at all," he said, speaking half to himself, "neither for old nor young nor sick. They accept it; they have no option."

He looked so stern that I grew alarmed.

"Do not concern yourself," I said diffidently. "We are in God's hands."

He looked up sharply, abruptly as if some chain of thought had been rudely broken: then he left me.

Nathan was lying within. "What happened?" he asked, turning to face me. "You were a long time."

"We were talking, that is all."

"What about?"

"You are as persistent as your grandson," I said, "but being older you should know better. We were talking about Selvam. Kenny thinks he will be good. He is shaping well."

"I am glad. Tell me, did he not say anything about me?"

"Only that you were not to worry and then you would soon be on your feet."

"Worry? What about? Did he say?"

"About anything. You are to rest."

"Well," he said. "I can see you are guarding your tongue. Never mind; I can guess. But I shall be well soon—you will see."

A few days later he was up and to my astonishment for the next year or so he had no further trouble. Then one day when I was congratulating my-self on his recovery the blow fell.

I was out gathering cow dung, I did not see Sivaji come, and he left quickly as soon as he had delivered his message. I came with my basket half-laden and saw my husband sitting on the floor staring out before him, a dazed expression on his face and his lips trembling loosely. Sacrabani was crouched in a corner, hugging his knees in his arms and his pink, fascinated eyes half-curious, half-terrified, fixed on his grandfather. I sent the child out and went to Nathan, thinking he had had another of his attacks, but he seemed to wake up when he heard my voice and waved me away.

"I am all right."

"Here—drink this. You will feel better." I tipped the mud pot and filling his bowl handed it to him. He drank obediently as if to please me, spilling a little in the process. He was still shaking. I sat beside him waiting.

"The land is to be sold," he said. "We are to move. Sivaji came this morning. He says there is nothing to be done."

I could not take it in. I gaped at him unbelieving. He nodded as if to emphasize that what he had said was so.

"The tannery owners are buying the land. They pay good prices."

The tannery! That word brought instant understanding. Realisation came like a rocket, swift and fiery.

"They can't," I remember saying helplessly. "It is our land; we have been here thirty years."

Nathan opened his hands, trembling, impotent.

"Sivaji tells me there is a profit to be made. The landlord has completed the deal, papers have been signed. We must leave."

Where can we go? I wanted to ask; but that was a question at present without an answer, and I refrained. Instead he put the question. "Where are we to go? What shall we do?"

"How much time have we got?" I asked, preparing for the worst.

"He does not expect us to leave at once. He has given us two weeks' time in which to go, which is lenient."

A dozen lines of thought began and continued in my brain without ending; crossing, tangling, like threads on some meaningless warp. My head was whirling. I must sit down and think, I said to myself, but not now, later. Follow each thought to its conclusion, decide what we are to do for ourselves, plan as Kenny said for ourselves and our children. This present chaos is madness.

"I do not know why they need this bit of land," I said, in the manner of people who must say something for the sake of the sanity which speech can bring.

"Certainly they cannot build on it; it is a swamp, meant only for rice-growing."

Nathan shrugged. "Who knows. Perhaps they can drain it, tighten the soil; they have resources beyond our imagining. Or perhaps they wish to grow rice for their own men."

He too was speaking like me, automatically, for the sake of speaking. I made another effort, a pitiful one, for the words I said were the last to bring comfort.

"At least we shall not have much to carry. The granary is almost empty."

He nodded in dull agreement. Then once again we relapsed into silence, sunk in our own thoughts.

Somehow I had always felt the tannery would eventually be our undoing. I had known it since the day the carts had come with their loads of bricks and noisy dusty men, staining the clear soft greens that had once coloured our village and cleaving its cool silences with clamour. Since then it had spread like weeds in an untended garden, strangling whatever life grew in its way. It had changed the face of our village beyond recognition and altered the lives of its inhabitants in a myriad ways. Some—a few—had been raised up; many others cast down, lost in its clutches. And because it grew and flourished it got the power that money brings, so that to attempt to withstand it was like trying to stop the onward rush of the great juggernaut. Well, I suppose there were some families who saw in it hope for their sons: indeed, many still depended on such earnings, and if my sons had still been there my thoughts might have been different; but for us as we were now, and others like us, there could be only resignation and resentment. There had been a time when we, too, had benefited—those days seemed very remote now, almost belonging to another life—but we had lost more than we had gained or could ever regain. Ira had ruined herself at the hands of the throngs that the tannery attracted. None but these would have laid hands on her, even at her bidding. My sons had left because it frowned on them; one of them had been destroyed by its ruthlessness. And there were others its touch had scathed. Janaki and her family, the hapless chakkli Kannan, Kunthi even. . . .

Yet I must be honest, as my husband and sons have always been: the tannery cannot be blamed for every misfortune we suffered. Tannery or not, the land might have been taken from us. It had never belonged to us, we had never prospered to the extent where we could buy, and Nathan, himself the son of a landless man, had inherited nothing. And whatever extraneous influence the tannery may have exercised, the calamities of the land belong to it alone, born of wind and rain and weather, immensities not to be tempered by man or his creations. To those who live by the land there must always come times of hardship, of fear and of hunger, even as there are years of plenty. This is one of the truths of our existence as those who live by the land know: that sometimes we eat and sometimes we starve. We live by our labours from one harvest to the next, there is no certain telling whether we shall be able to feed ourselves and our children, and if bad times are prolonged we know we must see the weak surrender their lives and this fact, too, is within our experience. In our lives there is no margin for misfortune.

Still, while there was land there was hope. Nothing now, nothing whatever. My being was full of the husks of despair, dry, lifeless. I went into the hut and looked about me. Brown mud walls that had crumbled many a time and been rebuilt many a time. Coconut thatching, some of it still part of the old palm lightning had destroyed, as I could tell from the colour. Bare, beaten floor of baked mud, hardened with dung-wash. This home my husband had built for me with his own hands in the time he was waiting for me; brought me to it with a pride which I, used to better living, had so very nearly crushed. In it we had lain together, and our children had been born. This hut with all its memories was to be taken from us, for it stood on land that belonged to another. And the land itself by which we lived. It is a cruel thing, I thought. They do not know what they do to us.

When Selvam came home that night from his studies my husband broke the news to him. I do not know what I expected—indignation, anger, perhaps sorrow: but he betrayed no emotion. He put the books he was carrying in the wooden crate he had made, then he sat down, still keeping his own counsel; the wavering light from the wick in its saucer of oil fell on his face, sombre and serious as it always was in repose. Well, I thought, this cannot affect the life he has chosen and so he is tranquil; and then I reminded myself that he was ever like this, that he seldom spoke until he had paused to reflect, and I felt ashamed.

In the brooding silence I heard Nathan shift his position again, and I thought, Naturally he is impatient; he has good cause.

"We have two weeks before we leave," I said. "They have agreed to let us stay till then."

"You think that is good of them?" Selvam said, his voice hard and sharp like crystals. He lifted his eyes to mine, I saw they were black and smouldering as if some deep flame of anger or hatred burned in him. Nathan made reply for me.

"It is better than being sent out at once, as others have been."

Selvam turned on his father.

"You have accepted it? You have made no protest?"

"What option have I, my son! Naturally, I protested, but it has availed me nothing."

"It is not just," Selvam said. "It is not right."

"Yet there is no law against it," said Nathan wearily. "We may grieve, but there is no redress."

"Where will you go?"

"We must go to Murugan. He has a good job—I am sure he will welcome his parents."

"It is a long way. With respect, you are not as young or as fit as you were."

"Yet the effort must be made," said Nathan, "for we cannot live except by the land, for I have no other knowledge or skill; and as you say I am getting on and for me it would be impossible to find another landlord. Who indeed would rent his land to such as I am, past hard labour and uncertain of paying what I owe?"

His words pierced me, hardened though I was, realist as I wished to be.

"Do not say these things," I said. "I cannot bear to hear them."

"They are true."

"Whether they are true or not," I cried, "I will not have you saying them."

"I would not distress you," Nathan said quietly, "yet must we not face the truth so that we can make our decisions? Have I told you anything you do not know yourself?"

No, I thought desolately, but I could not say it. Could not. I closed my eyes and felt his hands on my temples where the pulses beat, gently stroking, soothing me in the only way he could. He suffered for me, not so much for himself, and I likewise, so that although together there was more strength there was also more suffering, and if each had been alone the way might not have seemed so hard; yet I knew neither could have borne it alone. Thus confused, my mind turned this way and that, like a paper kite dipping to every current of air, unsure of its own meanings.

At length in the midst of the blackness I heard Selvam speaking and I opened my eyes. He seemed to be struggling with himself, for the words did not come easily and the fierce inner battle he waged had brought the sweat out on his forehead and left his lips dry. He was addressing his father alone— No doubt he dismisses me as an hysterical woman, I thought. He is not far wrong.

"I can always return to the land," he was saying. "I am young and able-bodied . . . together we can rent another piece of land . . . live as we did."

I saw my husband's eyes kindle, I saw in them, fearfully, the light of hope. You should not have said it, I cried silently to my son. It is too difficult for him, cruelly difficult. But already Nathan was shaking his head.

"No, my son. I would not have it so." He spoke resolutely. "There are some things that cannot be sacrificed . . . besides I would never be happy. Certainly your mother would not let me rest," he added, smiling a little.

"No; we must go. Ira and Sacrabani must come with us of course; there is nothing for them here."

"I will stay," said Ira, whom we had supposed asleep, and she rose and came and knelt beside her father. "I will not be a burden to you. I am happy enough here, people are used to me and to my son. I cannot start a new life now."

"If I can," said Nathan, "whose youth is only a memory now, why should not you, my child? You are very young; it will not be difficult for you."

"I must think of my son," she replied.

"How will you eat?" I said. "Where will you live?"

"If she decides to stay," said Selvam, "she will be with me. I will look after her. I swear it."

"And the child?"

"And the child, of course."

"Is it possible?" Nathan asked. "It is little enough you have for yourself."

"Do I not know it?" said Selvam bitterly. "It is perpetual shame to me that I have nothing to offer my parents. Yet I promise they shall not go in need."

If it had not been so late at night—if we had been less tired and dispirited—we might have argued with Ira, partly for her sake and partly for Selvam's. As it was we said no more—not that night at any rate, although subsequently we had more discussions than I can recount—accepting only that we were to go and that our children and grandchild were to stay.

Part Two

Chapter 24

I TOOK DOWN THE MATS on which we slept from the wall where they hung and rolled them up. Inside I placed the cloth bundle which contained two ollocks of rice, some chillies, tamarind and salt, and the two wooden bowls, Nathan's and mine, tying the ends of the rolled mats to make sure nothing fell out on the way. Most of the cooking vessels I had brought with me on my marriage had been sold to pay our debts, of the remainder I left two for Ira and the other two I put aside for ourselves. The grindstone, pestle and mortar were too heavy to take; in any case my daughter-in-law would be providing these. My cooking days are over, I thought a little sadly, and suddenly what I had formerly performed without thought, or even with impatience—the gathering of fuel, and the blowing of the fire, and the waxing of the flames under the steaming pot, with all the business of smoke down the lungs and in the eyes—acquired a sweet and piercing poignancy. There would be meals to cook on the journey, however, since we were travelling by bullock cart and expected to be on the road at least two days, and for these I took the hand-made bellows and six cakes of dung. Under the granary floor our money lay buried: three rupees of our own, three that Selvam had given us out of his earnings, and a ten-rupee note that Kenny had sent through Selvam. When everything was done I took out the money, counted it and tucked it in securely at my waist. Then we were ready.

The morning of our departure comes. It is a still morning, hazy, dewy, for it is yet early. The bullock cart lumbers up, the bells around the animals' necks jangling, they have tiny bells fixed to caps on the tips of their horns too, which tinkle as they move. The cart is piled high with bales of tightly packed skins, for we are passengers on a return journey, but there is room enough for two. We clamber on. Selvam hands us the two or three bundles we are taking with us which we hold on our laps until the carter tells us to stow them on top of the bales. We do so, carefully.

Then it is time to go. Selvam steps back. Ira comes forward from the courtyard where she has been standing, she is holding her son by the hand. The three of them stand in line waiting to see us on our way. The carter flicks both bullocks with his whip, the animals strain forward, the cart gives a lurch. Nathan holds out his hands, our children bow their heads. Then we begin to move and the three of them come after us a little of the way, walking in the dust the wheels grind out of the earth, until the bullocks begin to trot and they fall back. The bullocks have found their own rhythm now, moving so that their hoofs strike the earth together and the yoke is borne steadily on their shoulders: we are travelling fast. The hut—its inhabitants— recedes behind us and yet in front of us, for we are sitting with our backs to the bullocks. Our beloved green fields fall away to a blur, the hut becomes a smudge on the horizon. Still we strain our eyes to pierce the reddish dust the wheels throw up. We are farther away with every turn of the wheels. I stare at them fascinated until the spokes begin to revolve backwards while the rim is inexorably borne forward. I feel dizzy, my throat is dry. I lean against my husband, he is already leaning on me, together we achieve a kind of comfort.

The carter is asleep on his jointed perch: the bullocks know the route well, they keep on without guidance from him. At midday we halt near a small wayside well. The carter wakens, snorts, stretches himself before climbing down. We are to eat here, he says, and he unyokes the bullocks to water them. I see one of them has a large raw patch on its shoulder where the yoke has rubbed the skin off.

"The animal is not well," I say to the man.

He shrugs: "What can I do? I have no other. I must make these trips since they are my livelihood."

We wash, eat, wash again, then proceed.

Mile after mile of dusty road stretching out straight before us, lined here and there with cool shady banyans or tamarind trees. The bullock with the sore patch is slowing the other up; the carter turns, impatient and brings out his whip. It is no use, its pace does not alter. We pass other bullock carts, are passed by some, eat again, sleep again. At night we stop while the carter lights the lantern slung beneath the cart, then we move on in the darkness and the small yellow light-disc travels with us like a comforting beacon. On and on, and on and on, we journey.

The cart driver roused us when we reached the outskirts of the city where my son worked. It was mid-afternoon, the sun was streaming down hot and at its most powerful.

"Here you are. This is as far as I can take you." He nudged Nathan, who sat with his head lolling against the bales, fast asleep. I shook him, pushing his head erect.

"Wake up, we have arrived."

He opened his eyes, reddened and with drooping lids.

"I could easily sleep the whole day through," he said, yawning and stretching.

"We are late already," the carter was grumbling. "I should have got here by morning . . . if only this bullock had kept better pace—"

He leaped down and lifted the yoke preparatory to watering his animals.

The raw patch on the bullock I had noticed had begun to fester, more skin had been eaten away and trickles of blood were running down the edges.

"This animal will soon be fit for nothing," he muttered to himself. "Heaven knows when I shall be able to afford another."

As soon as the animals had drunk he put the yoke back. The bullock cringed, but accepted the torment and as soon as the whip fell it began to pull again.

The carter leaned from his perch to call to us, his face hot and perspiring. "Good luck friends, keep well!" His voice was friendly.

"Goodbye, good luck," we called back.

For a little while we stood by the roadside, our parcels about us. There were three turnings before us and there was no telling which way lay the house of our son. Then Nathan picked up the mats.

"Come along. We may meet somebody soon."

We chose a road at random; walked for some time without seeing anyone. We should have asked the carter, I thought. He would have known. But I did not say so. At length we saw two men approaching, jogging along towards us with bundles on their heads.

"Can you direct us to Koil Street, friend?"

"Koil Street? Let me see," he put up his hand to scratch his head, but, the burden being there, withdrew it.

"No, I can not. Brother, can you tell these people what they want to know?"

His companion thought: "I have heard of it. Yes, I remember now, it is in one of the suburbs of the town. Quite a way from here, but this is the right road."

"How far?"

"About fifteen miles . . . If you keep to the road you may get a lift," he added good-naturedly, seeing our crestfallen faces.

We plodded on. Several bullock carts passed us and one or two jutkas, but none stopped. Most of them were fully laden already. The bundle I carried, for all that it contained so little, grew heavier with each step; my neck was stiff with the effort of holding my head steady, for the bundle was poised on top. Under each arm was a cooking pot; whenever the sweat came trickling down—which happened frequently, it was a hot day—I had to stop and put them down before wiping my face. My husband, similarly burdened, and troubled more than I was by flies and insects, had also to stop frequently, so our going was slow.

As we progressed the road broadened; it split and forked, other roads curled away from it and more came to intersect it, so that it was difficult to know whether we were keeping to the right road or not. Many people were about, walking quickly and intent on their business: we did not find it easy to stop and ask them the way. Not only people but traffic—bullock carts, jutkas, cars and bicycles, more than we had ever seen, many times thicker than in the town around the tannery. The noise never let up: car horns, bicycle bells and the cracking of whips, combined to produce a deafening bewildering clamour, amid which it was impossible to heed every warning sound. Several times we were nearly knocked down by impatient cyclists whose bells we had not heard. Once a jutka almost ran us over . . . the driver just managed to pull up the horse and while we stood palpitating he leaned from his seat, irate and frightened, to shout at us. His voice was very loud, and he shook his fist as he drove off. Several people stopped to stare at us curiously as we hurried on.

We had reached the city's centre, Koil Street lay some six miles away, and we were still not sure of finding it. I could see Nathan was very tired: the heat and the noise, the bustle of the city, had taken their toll. He was walking sluggishly, now and again he stumbled, and at last I said, "Let us rest for a while, it will do us both good."

He agreed at once; we found a quieter side street, and thankfully putting our burdens beside us sank down. No one paid any attention to us. We were allowed to sit there in peace. We had bought on the way a hand of plantains, of which four remained, and as we had not eaten since morning I brought these out, giving two to my husband and eating two myself. It was nearly dusk: the activities of the city were beginning to die down, the noise was decreasing. Soon street lights were winking and in the shops gas lamps and hurricane lanterns were lighting up; but in the little side alley where we sat it was dark—darker than the air and the sky above us from the shadows cast by the buildings on either side.

It was such a relief to rest, and the thought of continuing the search was so unwelcome, that we sat on while the gloom thickened and night crept up on us. When at last we rose, stars were bright in the sky. We have stayed too long, I thought uneasily. We shall not reach our son tonight.

Nathan did not seem too happy either. As we stood there undecided, our bundles spread about us, wondering what next to do, an old man whom I had noticed asleep in a doorway came up to us.

"Where do you go, friends, at this late hour?"

"To Koil Street. Our son lives there, we are going to him."

"That is a long way yet. You look tired."

"We have rested too well. We should have been on our way long since."

"Well, if you do not arrive tonight there is a temple not far from here where you can eat and sleep." He pointed. In the distance we saw the outline of a temple, not too distant however, with a yellow oil flare burning from the top. We looked, and it seemed to beckon to us, promising food and shelter.

"We are grateful to you. Perhaps it would be best, we are tired as you say."

We picked up our possessions and walked on, more firmly now that we had somewhere definite to go, helped by the yellow flare that burned so steadily ahead of us.

As we neared the temple we noticed several people, mostly old and crippled, going the same way. Obviously many of them were known to one another, for as they hobbled along in ones and twos and sometimes small groups, they exchanged greetings and news. They knew us at once for strangers—perhaps by the bundles we carried—but were not disposed to be unfriendly for that, and they smiled to us and one or two called out cheerfully, "Are you bound for the temple too?"

"Yes, we hope to shelter there for the night."

"Are you going to settle in this city?"

"Yes, our son lives here. He is married and we are to stay with him. His name is Murugan," we said eagerly. "Maybe you have heard of him?"

"No, no," they shook their heads indulgently. "Ah well, it is a big city."

In the precincts of the temple, shops and stalls were open, brightly lit with gas lamps with their owners standing or sitting within and calling out their wares to passers-by; but most had no money to spend. At one shop pilaus were being sold, mounds of saffron rice on buttered plantain leaves, glistening with ghee and garnished with red chillies and curling strips of fried onion. The smell from it, rich and tempting, swirled up with the puffs of steam from the boiling rice. Impossible to shut it out, useless to try . . . the fragrant smell was everywhere. I felt a cramp beginning in my stomach, held it with an effort that turned me giddy; when it had passed, the familiar symptoms of nausea began. Nathan pressed my arm in sympathy; he too looked queasy.

Through the outer courtyards and along the corridors we went, going with the crowd to whom this was evidently a nightly routine, and into a large vaulted chamber with arched entrances opening on three sides. Here we stopped and sat down to wait with the rest on the stone floor. In the dark inner chamber the God and Goddess were seated on their thrones, freshly anointed and garlanded with flowers. At their feet were piled betel leaves, rice and a host of sweetmeats.

A woman sitting beside me nudged and pointed.

"The food is given to the poor—to us—when it has been blessed. There is a lot tonight," she added. "You are lucky!" I saw her sucking her lips in anticipation.

After a while two priests with half-shaven heads entered. One carried a beakerful of water, the other a tray of more votive offerings, which they placed at the feet of the God. Bells began to tinkle; at their sound the priests began intoning the prayers, one taking up where the other left off. Everyone was standing, most of them with hands folded and closed eyes. I closed my eyes, too, pressing my hands over them. The eyeballs felt hot under the lids. I could see beneath them a black-rimmed orange glow against which floated the images of the past—my sons, Ira, the hut where we lived and the fields we had worked. The more I banished them the faster they came. I saw Old Granny again, toothless and wrinkled; Kenny, his eyes sorrowful when I told him we were going; Sacrabani's face, white and scared as it often was. I tried and tried, concentrating on the prayers that were being said and at last the images faded; I saw in their place the countenance of the God and his Consort, and it seemed to me that they looked on me benignly and I was at length able to pray.

All about me was a deep intense silence, and in it I heard my prayer, voiceless, wordless, rising up and up endlessly like the incense which burnt perpetually upon the altar. And when at last I opened my eyes the silence which had enfolded me had given place to a pervasive murmur, the sound from the suppliant lips and beseeching throats of the multitude.

A drum struck savagely through the hush, sent it shivering, flying . . . people blinked and stared, called thus rudely to take up their ordinary existence. One of the priests began to sprinkle holy water, people manœuvring to get near the precious drops; the other was handing out the food to a third man, and as soon as this was done the gilded doors of the inner chamber were closed. Almost at once the people began moving to the courtyard which opened from the assembly hall.

"The food will be distributed there," a woman whispered to me. "There is not always enough to go round: it is best to be first."

A lot of people had had the same idea and were jockeying energetically for position. The murmuring silence gave, the crowd burst into loud chatter: it was as if the thought of food had loosened all tongues; and the pushing and thrusting became more violent. The friendliness that had existed before was gone; men and women struggled to be in the forefront, fighting their way with ferocity, thrusting forward with strident urgency. I found myself in the middle of the throng: Nathan had got separated and looking round I saw him on the outward fringe among the very old and crippled. He had never been one for pushing. Well, I thought. I can tell them my husband is here and take two portions. Then I saw two men enter bringing the food and all other thought ceased. Craning my neck and body, standing on tiptoe, I saw the cauldrons they carried, cauldrons of rice heaped high and showing white gleaming peaks from which wisps of steam issued, and pots filled with a mixture of dhal and vegetables which sent forth a most savoury smell.

From a pile beside him one of the men took out a plantain leaf—not a whole one, but cut into pieces twice the size of a man's hand, on this he ladled out two spoonfuls of rice; the other filled a small cup, made from dried leaves held together with thorns, with the dhal mixture.

From the crush one man at a time—as much by pressure as by his own efforts—was ejected, like the palm-leaf stopper of a foaming toddy pot: collected his portion, drank of the holy water and made his way out. My turn came; the level of the rice was already fallen so low that it was only by going close to the vessels that I could see any rice at all. One of the men rebuked me sharply.

"Keep your distance. Do you want to devour pot and all?"

I must ask for my husband, I thought, and found myself quaking. The plantain leaf was handed to me, the rice placed on top, then the cup of dhal. Now.

"If you would be so kind, sir," I said, "I will take my husband's portion as well on my leaf."

They gaped at me, surprised, affronted.

"The woman is mad," one called out. "Expects a double portion."

"Not satisfied with one," the other rejoined in an offended voice, "but must try and make capital out of charity."

"I do not," I said. "I have a husband and he is here, I ask only for his portion."

"If he is here let him come and we will serve him in his turn. We cannot hand out food to everyone merely because they ask for it. Do you take us for fools? Keep your tales for the unwary!" cried one, and the other called out impatiently,

"Hurry up, hurry up! Do you want to keep us standing here all night?"

I went, taking my food with me. Those who had been served were sitting in the open a little way off eating, and I joined them. Perhaps I looked dejected, for one of the women said consolingly, "They were sharp-tongued tonight, probably they were tired . . . you must not mind."

There was a murmur of assent, except from one man who said in a hostile voice: "Well, they are right. Everyone must come in his turn or who is to know the truth from a lie when people ask for more than one portion," and again from the easily swayed crowd came a murmur of agreement. I must justify myself in the eyes of these people, I thought forlornly, and I said, "I spoke the truth . . . my husband is here, see, he is coming to me," as I saw him approach. I saw also that his hands were empty. Still, it was good to share what there was and eat, good to have food in the belly, good to feel the dizziness replaced by well-being. When we had finished we threw the empty leaves to the goats that had gathered, expectant but patient for their meal, and that too was a satisfying thing, to see them eating leaves and cups, crunching them in their mouths with soft happy movements and looking at us with their mild benign eyes. Then we went and washed our hands under the running tap, rinsing mouth and face as well in the cool water, and came back ready for sleep. It was only then that we remembered, with trepidation, our bundles.

We had left them propped against one of the carved stone pillars in the long corridor leading to the assembly hall. We went to it, but the bundles had vanished. Perhaps our memory is at fault, maybe it is not this particular stone pillar but another, there are so many and one is like another, I thought. To the next and the next and the next, there were hundreds of pillars and columns and we went to them all with fast-dying hope.

Three or four had seen us searching, three or four more joined these, soon a small crowd of advisers and helpers followed at our heels.

"Are you sure it was this Hall of Pillars? There is another on the West side of the temple."

"Quite sure. We have not been on the other side."

"How could they?" said a scornful voice. "That side is locked at night."

"Who was looking after the bundles?"

"No one, no one . . . we left them untended."

"Untended! Looking for trouble that was! There are many thieves and strangers about these days."

"What, even in a temple! We did not think—"

"Yes, even in a temple, of course. Many kinds come here, there can be no guarantee of their honesty."

"It appears not," Nathan said heavily. "Our possessions have gone."

There was futility only in further searching, further weariness. We gave up and leant our backs against the painted wall which encircled the temple, the vermilion and white striped wall we had foolishlessly thought meant safety. The promise of shelter had been kept however: food, and somewhere to sleep.

"At least the loss is not irreparable," Nathan said. "We have our money still, the pots and matting can be replaced."

"Best not to speak of it," I said, feeling cautiously for the money in my waistband, the coins hard and comforting to my touch. "We must be careful."

He smiled wryly. "After the horse has bolted?"

But I could not smile, and the ease with which he accepted the misfortune irritated me. Now I shall be wholly indebted to my daughter-in-law, I thought. I go to her without even a cooking vessel, like any beggar off the streets; and straightaway I determined to spend one or two of the coins I felt digging into my flesh at the nearest bazaar, for I would not go to her destitute. Soothed a little by the thought I drifted into sleep, broken often by bells ringing and the low rat-tat of drums for the prayers which went on at intervals throughout the night. Once in my half-sleep it seemed to me someone was tugging at my arm, but when I woke it was only Nathan clutching at me in his sleep. I dozed off again, and after a while I felt a soft fumbling about my face, noiseless, like fingers on spindle cotton. I strove to wake, to brush aside those pathetic flutterings, but strive as I would I could not . . . at last I sat up, sleep and dream alike banished, wide awake now. And whether from the fact of sleeping in new surroundings, or from the loss we had sustained, I was unable to sleep again.

I leant against that same wall by which we had laid ourselves down, watching the wind play with the yellow flare on top of the temple, looking into the darkness which varied its pitch from point to point. Gradually I was able to make out the forms of the carven Gods and Goddesses on the sides of the temple, on the colonnades, and in the niches of the walls, and as I gazed they seemed almost to live, their stone breasts gently breathing, their limbs lightly moving. Nearly—nearly could I believe what I saw, sitting there in the darkness by the temple wall. Until dawn, when the stars went out one by one, and the grey light changed the sculptured figures back into immobility.

Chapter 25

As ALWAYS NATHAN STIRRED with the first light; when he saw I was awake he sat up quickly, rubbing the sleep from his eyes.

"You slept well," I said, a little envious because I had not, yet glad since he looked so much better for it.

"Yes, I was tired. But you look as if you had been up all night."

"Almost . . . I could not sleep."

"You were worried no doubt," he said gravely, and the concern in his voice made me slightly ashamed of myself. "Still, we shall soon be with our son and you will be able to rest. Come, we may as well start now—the sooner the better."

We went to wash at the tap, threading our way among the heap of rags under which men and women lay huddled in sleep, their crutches or staffs and begging bowls beside them, and when we had done we went out the way we had come in.

Early though it was, many of the shops were open. From the food stalls came the spluttering of ghee and oil as bread and pancakes were fried, ready for the early worshippers who would soon be coming. As we passed, Nathan hesitated and I saw him eyeing the crisp golden pancakes laid out upon a platter.

"Let us buy a few," he said cheerfully. "I am hungry enough and you must be too."

I for my part hesitated, although the food was tempting enough, for the silver coins we had were few and precious and there was no telling what our needs might be; still I could not very well deny him when I had already made up my mind to spend some of the money on cooking vessels, and so I put my hand in my waistband to take out the money I had tied there.

The coins were gone. I felt in my bodice and again in my waistband. I shook out the folds of my sari, but there was no doubt the money was gone.

"It may have slipped out in the night," Nathan said, and we went back, unhopeful, to where we had slept but the ground was bare and innocent. And those who saw us entering again laughed and said free meals were only given in the evening, not in the morning, their laughter changing to concern when we explained what had befallen us: but their concern was only perfunctory since they were after all lookers-on and not partakers, and I noticed one or two glances exchanged, pitying yet scornful, which said as plainly as words,

These are simple careless country folk. Lost and bewildered though I was I could contain myself no longer and I said sharply there was not too little care but too many thieves, and saw them nodding in facile agreement. Yes, thieves and pickpockets were very skilful; one needed to exercise the utmost care.

Well, we had not, and so we went our way with nothing to call our own save what we wore, past the food stall with set steadfast face, past the bazaar with never a glance, pressing on to reach the shelter of our son's house before worse should overtake us.

Through the streets of the terrifying city, amid the unaccustomed traffic and crowds, screwing up our courage each time we asked our way, we went slowly along. Some we questioned would not stop to answer, others did not know, many in trying to be helpful directed us wrongly. Without exception they were confusing—or we were dull. There were so many turnings we were to take, so many not to, that by the time we had followed the instruction to about the third turning, we were completely lost and had to stop and ask again. . . .

"I am a little slow," Nathan said humbly. "They speak so fast I can hardly follow, and I cannot remember all they say."

"If you are, so am I," I said stoutly, "for I also find it difficult."

It being near midday we sat down to rest by the roadside. A dozen or more children were playing there, dodging in and out of the traffic with a skill and indifference which I could not help admiring. For all their play they looked as if they had never eaten a full meal in their lives, with their ribs thrust out and bellies full-blown like drums with wind and emptiness; and they were also extremely dirty with the dust of the roadside and the filth deposited upon it; and the running sores many of them had upon their bodies were clogged with mud where blood or pus had exuded. But they themselves were forgetful of their pains—or patient with them as the bullock had been—and played naked and merry in the sun. Merry, that is, until a crust of bread fell on the road or a sweetmeat toppled from an over-ambitious pyramid when, all childishness lost, all play forgotten, they fought ferociously in the dust for the food . . . my children had fought thus too, I remembered, but time had mellowed the memory or dimmed it, for it did not seem to me that they had struggled like these: teeth bared, nails clawing, ready, predatory like animals. But when a man of wealth passed they were as tender and pitiful as fledglings, beseeching with soft open mouths and limpid eyes, their begging bowls meekly held before them and altogether changed with an artfulness which surely my children had not at their command. And however much they played and were children, still their faces were scored with the knowledge and cares that children should not have, their eyes were knowing and guileful beyond their years.

"We may yet be forced to that," said Nathan, pointing to their begging bowls, "if we do not find our son—"

"Never," I protested, a little frightened by his dejection. "Come, we must be on our way."

"Let us ask these children," he said. "They seem quick."

He clicked his fingers and called, and they came with bright curious eyes, twittering like sparrows.

"Tell me, my son, do you know where Koil Street is?"

"Koil Street? There are three or four. Which one do you seek?"

"Three or four!" exclaimed Nathan. "No wonder we have been chasing our tails!"

"If you tell me the name of the people," a boy said, "there are few I do not know."

"That I can well believe. We are looking for my son who is named Murugan, and he works with one Birla, who is a doctor."

"I do not know of Murugan," the boy said frankly, "but everyone knows Birla. For a small sum," he added, "I will take you there myself."

"I have less than you," Nathan sighed. "I can give you nothing."

"Oh," the boy said, disappointed, his voice falling away. Then an idea seemed to strike him and he said shrewdly: "Yet I will myself take you there, and if you prosper you can pay me."

"And how shall I know you?"

"I am called Puli after the king of animals, and I am leader of our pack. I am as well known as Birla."

"Then I shall know where to find you," Nathan said smiling, for there was an impudence in the boy which was somehow attractive, "Lead on, my young friend."

The boy turned and said something to his companions, and there was no doubt that he was their leader, for they dispersed at once; then he beckoned to us. "Follow closely," he said firmly—this child who might easily have been our grandson, "or you will be lost!" and he motioned us forward. And as he did so I saw that he had no fingers but only stumps. The disease which was rotting his body had eaten away nail and flesh to the first knuckle.

Prudently we took his advice to follow closely, although he went at a pace which we found difficult to match, and presently he brought us to a small whitewashed house set in a street on the corner of which stood a church.

"This is the street—this is the church—this is the house," he said rapidly pointing, and at once turned and made off, his head down and his shoulders moving as he ran.

We stood and looked at the house, arrived but uncertain how to proceed, and it looked back at us neither inviting nor forbidding. There was a wooden paling around it, broken by a small wooden gate, and at length—there being nobody in sight to ask—we walked through to the garden and so to the house. The doors and windows in it were wide open as if the occupants needed all the fresh air there was, and we could see right to the back of the house where two or three men were sitting wearing the white tunics of servants, and one of them at length saw us and came forward, saying mechanically as if he had used the same words many times before, "Beggars are not allowed here, only those who need—"

Then seeing we neither carried begging bowls nor held out our hands for alms he stopped short. "What have you come for?"

"Our son works here," Nathan said. "His name is Murugan."

"Murugan? No one of that name works here."

"Doesn't work here! Are you sure?"

"Of course I am sure. There are only three servants employed, and Murugan is not one of them."

"There must be some mistake," Nathan muttered. He pulled out the slip of paper on which the address was written and handed it to the man, looking anxiously at him as he read—or perhaps pretended to read, for he handed it back quickly saying:

"Yes, yes; no doubt it is written there—but you must take my word, he is not here now."

Why did we not write? I thought miserably. We should have written. But we had been so sure he would be here, we had relied on it, it had never struck us that he would leave without telling us.

Just then we heard a car driving up, and from it stepped a figure wearing shirt and trousers, carrying a small black bag.

"The doctor is here," the manservant said hurriedly. "You must go now."

But we had come too far, hoped too high, endured too much, to turn back now.

"I will stay and ask him," Nathan said stubbornly. "Maybe he will know," and he stood firmly.

The doctor meanwhile was approaching. Under the thin shirt I saw the figure of a woman and I whispered hastily to my husband: "Be careful—it is a woman." Nathan turned bewildered eyes on me. "The trousers—" he began, but there was no time to say more and he stopped short confused and stammering.

"Who are you? What do you want?" A woman's voice, unmistakably.

"Our son came here to work some years ago," I said. "We have come to seek shelter with him."

"His name?"

"Murugan."

"Oh yes, he came through Kennington, did he not?"

"Yes," I said eagerly. "Kenny gave him the recommendation. He has been very good to me and mine."

"How is he?" she asked, forgetting we thirsted for news. "I have not seen him for a very long time."

"Well," I said, "and happy, since he is building this new hospital. My son works for him."

She looked at me thoughtfully and I could see she wanted to know more about the hospital, but she only said: "Of course, you are anxious about your son. I am afraid I cannot help you, he left here nearly two years ago."

Left . . . two years ago. Where could he go? Why go with no word to us? We stood mute and miserable. At last I felt I must know. "Has anything happened—I mean had he done some wrong—?"

"No; nothing like that. He was a very good servant and he went after higher wages."

Well, I thought. This at least is better hearing, and I licked my dry lips and said, "If you would tell us where he went—we must go to him, there is no one else. . . ."

"I am not sure," she said with a hint of pity in her eyes, "but I have heard that he works for the Collector. He lives on Chamundi Hill," she added. "Anyone will show you the house: it is big enough."

We were at the gate when she came after us. "You look faint—have you not eaten?"

"We were fed at the temple," I said, not meeting those shrewd eyes.

"It is a long time since," she said. "You had better have a meal here before you go." She called to the servant and spoke to him rapidly, and he came, looking none too pleased, to lead us to where we had to go.

The servants' quarters lay behind the house and some distance away. They consisted of three godowns standing in a row, square rooms with brick walls and stone floors, each with a separate low doorway. At the first one the manservant, Das, stopped and beckoned us to enter. Inside it was half-dark, for there was only one window high up on the wall and a thick blue smoke was rising from a corner where a young woman was busy cooking.

"These people are to eat with us," Das said. "They are the parents of one Murugan who was before me."

The young woman rose and came to us cheerful and smiling, nursing a round, chubby baby. "You are more than welcome—you seem very tired. . . ."

Her friendliness, her smile, were warming like the sun on old limbs, gentle as the rain on parched earth. I felt the stiffness that had collected in me departing, felt a new upsurge of hope. Nathan was visibly relaxed. "The rice is nearly cooked," the young woman was saying. "Perhaps you would like to wash before we eat—the tap is outside, my husband will show you."

Das was on his feet. "Ah yes, I had forgotten. Certainly a wash will do you good." He sounded more friendly.

We followed him out to the tap, which was about a furlong away. A cement floor had been built around the base of the tap, but the water which dripped constantly from the pipe ran off the cement so that the ground for some distance around was wet and muddy with scores of footprints leading to and from it.

Beyond it was the latrine. I had not used one before, and I entered with misgiving. There was no door, merely four walls built of tin which did not meet at one corner, thus leaving enough space for one person at a time. No roof; along one side a shallow trench from which rose a most foul stench; no covers; no kindly earth to hide what lay there open to the blue offended skies; no water to wash it away. I went out and stepped through the mud to the clear running water and when I had washed I felt better.

"You will have to get used to these things," Nathan said. "This is how life is lived in the city."

When we went back the young woman, still with the child at her hip, was straining the rice. Besides the baby there were now three other children in the room.

"Oh yes," she said in reply to my question. "All mine, and you can always find my brats here at mealtimes! I don't see them the rest of the day."

The children giggled delightedly, wriggling with pleasure. Their mother was peering into one of the pots on the fire, stirring and tasting. "Ready now," she said with satisfaction, wiping her streaming eyes with a corner of her sari. The smoke must have entered the baby's eyes too, for he began screaming.

"Let me hold him," I said. "You will be able to work better."

"It's a girl. She very seldom cries," she said, handing the baby to me, and as if to earn the compliment it immediately quietened down.

The young woman had several pieces of plantain leaf cut and ready. She laid these out and began serving the rice and dhal, generous portions such as we ate at harvest times and ours larger than theirs.

"You are very kind to feed us so well," I said.

"We are fed free," she replied. "The doctor is very good to us and gives us rice and dhal. Today she sent extra for you."

So we ate with easy conscience, for I would not like to have taken from the store of a family who were for all their kindness only strangers to us, and who moreover had enough mouths of their own to feed.

As evening wore on the mother brought out a striped mat, for she had persuaded us to stay the night, on which to sleep. And sleep we did, the deep sleep of those who being tired have fed well and rested well.

The next morning early we departed, after thanking the doctor who was a woman, and Das and his wife who had cared so well for us, and she came to see us go with her curious-eyed children about her, sunny and smiling as when we had first seen her and to this day I see her as she was then, young and kind, with a warm smile ever ready on her lips.

Chapter 26

THE COLLECTOR'S HOUSE on Chamundi Hill was simple enough to find: the hill itself could be seen for miles around, and everyone had heard of the Collector and knew where he lived. It was as the doctor had said a very fine house, taller than the young casuarina trees that grew near it and so brilliantly white that it looked as if the painters had only just finished their work. Around the house and grounds, which stretched away on either side of the hill, ran a low compound wall. A number of peons were standing about, turbaned and belted, much more imposing than the tannery chowkidars had been.

When he saw us approaching, one of the peons came up to us.

"No beggars are allowed here."

"We are not beggars. We have come for our son Murugan, who works here."

The man's manner changed. He looked at us almost sympathetically and was about to say something but changed his mind, instead swinging the heavy gate open for us and indicating that we should follow him.

"I will take you to his wife. The servants' godowns are at the back of the house."

My son's wife, the girl we had never seen. My son, who had been gone so long. A queer excitement took hold of me, I felt myself trembling. Nathan beside me quickened his step: his excitement was part of me too.

"This is Ammu's godown," the man said, pointing. "Make yourselves known to her . . . I cannot wait. . . ."

He was gone. The godown he had pointed to was much the same as the one we had left, a small square room set in a row, only here the row was much longer, there were some ten or twelve godowns. The door stood open, from within came the sound of a baby's fretful crying.

"Come," Nathan said in a cracked voice. "Let us go in."

But we could not, although the door stood open, for sudden shyness had set a stranglehold upon us and the sense of intrusion was strong . . . and in the end we stood by the open doorway and called.

A thin girl with untidy hair came out: the baby we had heard crying at her hip, a small boy clinging to her sari; stood staring at us with a slight frown.

"Who is it? What do you want?"

No smile, no welcome. Perhaps she thinks we are beggars, I thought. No wonder since we look it, and once more the humiliation of having nothing, not even a cooking pot, smote at me.

"We are Murugan's parents," Nathan said gently. "You must be his wife."

The girl nodded, then recollecting herself she drew aside so that we could enter, came after us and stood biting her lip as if uncertain what to say.

"These must be our grandchildren," I said, trying not to notice her attitude. "I have long wanted to see them."

"No doubt . . ." the girl said, her lips twisting a little. "No doubt you want to see your son, too. He is not here."

"Not here," Nathan repeated. "I was told he was here! When is he coming back?"

"I wish I knew," she replied. "I do not think he will ever come back."

"What do you mean? Are you not his wife? What makes you say he will never return?"

"He left me," she replied bitterly. "He has been gone nearly two years."

We had come a long way to meet bad news and now it seemed there was neither going back nor going forward. What we had saved had been taken from us, there was nothing more . . . nothing left to sell; neither youth nor strength left to barter.

I looked about the room in which my son's wife lived, and I knew that at any rate we could not stay here. Such resources as she had were not enough even for herself, they would certainly not stretch to cover our needs. Except for a small bowlful of rice there seemed to be no other food in the place. The little boy was thin and hollow-cheeked, his mother looked worn and haggard and was obviously hardly able to feed the baby who kept whimpering fitfully: the cry of hunger which is different from the other cries of infants.

"Is there no way of finding out where he has gone?" Nathan said at last. "Perhaps if we tried . . ."

"I have tried," Ammu said brusquely. "Do you think I haven't? He has left the city: nobody knows where he has gone."

There was about her a faint air of hostility, as if in some way she held us responsible for his defection. As indeed we are, I thought sadly. We gave him life, we should have taught him better. Yet looking back it was difficult to see how or where the mistake had been made.

We had been there about an hour, perhaps less, when Ammu rose. "I must go to my work . . . it is late already. I shall be back at midday to feed the children, stay till then."

"Do you go far?"

"No . . . only to the house. I sweep and clean."

"It must be hard work," I said. "You do not look very strong and the house is a large one."

She shrugged. "I am not the only one . . . besides one must live. It is not everywhere one can earn fifteen rupees a month and have a godown to live in free."

The baby was still astride her hip, now she arranged a few rags in a corner of the room and laid him down. Instantly he began to wail. "Let me take him," I said. "He may quieten down."

"As you wish," she said indifferently, picking him up and handing him to me. "Of course you realise he has nothing to do with you. . . . I mean he is not your grandchild."

"Of course."

"One must live," she repeated, defiant, challenging, sensing reproach where none could be; for it is very true, one must live.

At midday, as she had said, she came back. She had told us to wait, yet now her attitude said very clearly: You should not have taken me at my word, what I said was said in duty and for no other reason. In a sullen silence she began preparing the meal, lighting the fire, fetching the water, boiling the rice, the baby astride her hip as before and whimpering unheeded. She did not speak until we had eaten. Then she looked up.

"Where will you go? Can you return to your village?" And when? said her hostile questioning eyes. I cannot keep you here indefinitely, the sooner you go the better.

"We must return to our village," Nathan agreed. "There is nothing for us here. We came only because of our son, you understand."

She nodded. "Yes; he has let us all down."

"Maybe there were reasons," I said. Whatever claim this woman had on him, still he was my son; I could not let her heap all the blame on him. Her face darkened, anger bloated her lips and lit fires behind her black brooding eyes.

"They were the usual ones: women and gambling," she said harshly.

We looked at each other, trembling on the brink of a quarrel, bitterness parting the threads of forbearance one by one, but while a few still held, suddenly, the outward semblance fell away. I saw only that she was a very young girl, frail beyond most, deserted by her husband and doing her best to feed herself and her children.

"I am sorry," I said jerkily. "I must have been out of my senses."

She nodded very slightly, accepting my explanation, the blaze dying out behind her face.

"It is better that we should go now," said Nathan, rising, "while it is still light. We are not yet used to this city . . . darkness does not help."

"Where will you go?" Ammu repeated her question. Her voice had taken on anxiety; behind the relief which she could not hide, I sensed her troubled uneasy mind moving from doubt to doubt. No words, the meaning clearer than if there had been. These people are old . . . they are mine through my husband . . . I have a duty to them, but what of myself and my children? Are we not poor enough, ragged enough, without two more coming to share our resources? Yet what of them, they have nothing. The shadows of her thought, dull and heavy, moved across her pale thin face.

"We will return to our son and daughter," Nathan said, not replying directly. "But what of you, my child? It is we rather than you who should ask. We have had our day, you are still young . . . the mother of children who cannot help you for many years yet."

She stared at him as if unused to consideration, hardly credulous, almost suspicious. "I can look after myself and my children," she said, slightly emphasising the "myself" and "my children" so that we might understand, "but not my in-laws as well." "I have managed for a long time now."

There is no touching this girl, I thought. Misfortune has hardened her, which is just as well, she will take many a knock yet. There seemed nothing more to say, nothing left to keep us. Ammu had begun to fidget, moving restlessly where she sat, pulling nervously at her fingers until the joints cracked. I nudged Nathan, who was sunk in thought.

"We must go."

"Yes, yes," he said, starting. "It is getting late."

We looked again at our grandchild who was part of ourselves, and at the poor little waif who lay quietly now on the rag-heap, and we said farewell. Ammu came to the doorway with us. Now that we were actually leaving, her manner became more cordial, the stiff unfriendliness she has displayed had gone with the fear that we might have come to stay.

"Take care of yourselves," she called. "Godspeed and may you get home safely." Her lips were smiling, she brought the boy to the door to wave to us.

Though we had known them so short a while there was melancholy in the parting. Maybe we shall never see them again, I thought sadly, and I heard Nathan beside me heave a sigh. Both of us absorbed in our thoughts, we did not understand the shouting we vaguely heard until one of the peons came running after us puffing and angry.

"Are you deaf?" he bawled. "I have told you three times that servants are not allowed to use this gate, yet you continue as if you had not heard!"

"We are not servants."

"Servants or not, it is all one! You must use the back gate. Come on, if you are seen here I will lose my job."

We followed him. Some distance from the main gate was a smaller one, and to this he pointed. "There! And remember to use it next time as well."

"There will not be a next time," said Nathan gently, "but we shall remember."

Chapter 27

ONE OR TWO OF THE REGULARS in the temple recognised us.

"What, you back again? Trouble with your daughter-in-law no doubt?"

"No, no trouble. All is well."

Some sniggered knowingly, others were sympathetic. "Ah well, things often turn out unexpectedly. Perhaps your luck will change soon."

A few were antagonistic and openly so; like Ammu they saw their share of the food shrinking with each additional mouth.

"Outsiders should not be allowed," they grumbled. "Are there not enough destitute in this city without the whole of India flocking in?"

We looked at them resentfully: were we not as hungry as they? Soon we were looking at newcomers with a fearful eye, wondering with each fresh arrival how much less there would be.

Each night was a struggle, more fierce now that we were daily engaged in it. I saw, night after night, what I had not observed before: the lame with their crutches knocked away from them so that they fell and were unable to rise; the feeble separated from their supporters so that their numbers were halved. Many a time my husband stood aside unable to face the fray: if I had not reproached him his distaste of the whole procedure would have led him to starvation. As it was, more often than not one meal sufficed for two.

And when the crowd had dispersed, to sleep, to beg, to scavenge, in the cool of the night and early dawn we sat in the quiet courtyards, or leaned our backs against the pillars in the paved corridors, making our plans and thinking, always thinking. With each passing day the longing for the land grew; our plans were forged against a background of brown earth and green fields and the ripe rustling paddy, not, curiously, as they were, but as we had first known them . . . fresh, open and unspoilt, with their delicate scents and sounds untainted, with the skies clear above them and the birds finding sanctuary amid the grasses. And at the same time, keeping pace with these longings, our distaste for the city grew and grew and became a sweeping, pervading hatred.

"Better to starve where we were bred than live here," Nathan said passionately. "Whatever happens, whatever awaits us, we must return."

But how? We have no money. My husband can till and sow and reap with skill, but here there is no land. I can weave and spin, or plait matting, but there is no money for spindle, cotton or fibre. For where shall a man turn who has no money? Where can he go? Wide, wide world, but as narrow as the coins in your hand. Like a tethered goat, so far and no farther. Only money can make the rope stretch, only money.

Then one day I thought I would set myself up as a reader of letters such as there are in most villages, and surely also in cities?

"Whoever heard of a woman reader?" said Nathan. "No one will come to you."

"If I ask little, and less than the others, custom there will surely be," said I. "In any case one must try. Even a few annas would help."

"Do you think you could?" Nathan was half-despondent, half-eager, and somehow the eagerness alone communicated itself to me.

"Yes, I am sure. If I write letters as well as read them, I shall earn even more."

"How can you write without paper or ink?"

"Who asks must provide," I said confidently. "Leave it to me."

We looked at each other and hope stirred, albeit cautiously, making us cheerful.

"We shall need about ten rupees," Nathan said. "For our food on the way, and to pay the carter . . . say two rupees more in case we are three days travelling."

"Eight letters a day at an anna each," I said. "Say half that for rice each day . . ."

We made our calculations, crushing optimism whenever it arose so that we might be certain, absolutely certain. And at last we said to each other . . . "Soon we shall be back."

All that day and many following, I sat by the side of the road leading to the bazaar calling to those who passed, adding to the general clamour. Men hurrying by stopped to stare inquisitively before moving on, idlers stood or sat around lazily indulging their curiosity. Youths sauntered by insolent of eye and manner, speaking loudly and with exaggerated clearness to each other that I might hear.

"Says she can read! These village folk are certainly getting above themselves!"

"She is a *writer* as well! What do you suppose she writes with?"

"Probably uses her . . .!" Whispers, laughs.

"Oh, come away! she is past all that. . . ."

"She must be mad to imagine . . ."

Grimly I took no notice and went on with my cries.

By the end of the day my voice was hoarse: my mouth tasted of the dust that each passing pair of feet raised, my hair was full of it. I had earned two annas, and I spent it on a rice cake for us to eat in the morning.

One year ended, a new one began. Worshippers at the temple brought garlands of jasmine instead of chrysanthemums, and roses had disappeared from the feet of the Gods. Still we stayed on in the city. And whether from its fumes or from the blighting of our hopes, my husband began to suffer again from rheumatism, and at the same time the old bouts of fever began. Over and over again I told myself, we must go from here; especially at night, when my husband lay beside me twisting and straining in his sleep, it seemed to be the one hope for him, and I would look at the yellow flare burning from the top of the temple and at the carven Gods vigilant about us, and only one prayer did I utter.

I was returning to the temple one evening, hurrying so that I should be in good time for the meal, when I heard someone running after me, shouting something I could not understand. I stopped at last and looked round, peering at the boy who had come up panting, but it was dusk and I did not recognise him.

"Do not pretend you do not know me," he said accusingly. "I am Puli; I have come for my payment."

"Payment? What payment? I owe no one anything."

I walked on quickly, and the lad came after me.

"I took you to the doctor's house . . . not so long ago either . . . and you promised to pay."

I remembered now. It was the boy with the impudent face who had guided us.

"If you do not," he continued threateningly, "it will be the worse for you. I am not used to being bilked."

I could not help smiling, this child spoke like a man using the words of a ruffian.

"I would pay you if I could," I said placatingly, "but I have nothing. Come and see for yourself if you do not believe me."

"I do not," he said frankly. "I will see for myself."

I hurried on and he came after, dogging my footsteps in a suspicious silence. Nathan came running to meet me.

"Where on earth have you been? The food has all gone. Luckily today I was able to get near, otherwise we should have starved."

"Blame this lad," I said. "He would stop and argue."

Nathan peered at Puli. "Who is he? What does he want of you?"

Before I could reply the boy advanced. "I want payment; that's what I want," he said truculently. "I shall see that I get it."

"Payment? What for?" asked Nathan, bewildered. He too had forgotten.

"He guided us to the doctor's house," I explained, "when we first came."

There was a pause. Nathan began sharing out the rice and dhal, carefully tearing the plantain leaf he carried into three pieces on which to put each portion. I had with the day's earnings bought as usual one rice cake which I now broke to hand around. The boy stared at it: "You must have money! Otherwise how could you buy rice cakes?"

I sighed. "I earn two annas a day by writing letters—sometimes a little more, sometimes a little less. I buy food with it."

"Which is not unreasonable," Nathan said impatiently, "seeing how one portion has sometimes to be stretched to three!"

At last Puli seemed satisfied. He began to eat, and once more I saw that he had no fingers, only stumps. He himself did not appear to find any difficulty in managing without, except that once or twice he had to use both hands, and there was a certain awkwardness in his handling of the food. Despite myself I could not keep my eyes off his hands; the harder I tried to keep my gaze fixed elsewhere, the more it fastened itself to those stumps. Puli, seemingly unaware, continued eating stolidly. He is used to it, I thought. He knows and accepts the shameful probing curiosities of human beings.

When we had eaten, and fed the leaves to the goats, and washed, Puli to my surprise lay down beside us.

"You had better go home," I said, nudging him. "What will your poor mother think if you stay here all night?"

"I have no mother, poor or otherwise," he said. "There is no one to worry about me and none to worry me either, which is a good thing," and turning on his side he fell instantly asleep.

I might have felt apprehensive for him, but that I knew him to be eminently capable of looking after himself; or sorry, save that he so patently did not desire it; but I could not help feeling a vague responsibility which certainly I knew I was in no position to fulfill.

"He is probably better fitted to fend for himself than we are—" Nathan began, but although he was echoing my thoughts I found myself turning on him indignantly: "How can you say such a thing! He is only a child . . . no more than nine or ten! And he is not whole either, as we are."

But that he was right Puli demonstrated the next morning. When we woke we found him sitting cross-legged beside us, frowning thoughtfully.

"You earn two annas," he asked, "after working all day?" I nodded: "Sometimes three or four."

"Between two and four then," he amended impatiently. "Have you no wish to earn more?"

I stared at him.

"If only I could," I said, half breathless. "Is there some way?"

"There is a stone quarry," he said, "not far from here. Stone-breakers earn good wages."

"And who will employ us," said Nathan sadly, "at our age! Such heavy work would in any event be beyond us."

"Age doesn't matter," the boy said impatiently. "As for who will employ you, there is no such thing. Anyone can go and work and be paid by the results—so much for each sackful."

"Are we not beyond such labour?"

"Indeed no! All kinds work in the quarry, men, women and children. I would work too," he added, "but I cannot hold a hammer or stone firmly enough. One can earn a lot if one works quickly."

"Lead on," Nathan said. "We are in your hands."

We heard the noise of the stone-breakers long before we reached the quarry; a clink-clank of stone on stone with intermittent dull explosions. As we drew near, the din grew louder; we had to shout to make ourselves heard.

The quarry was on a hillside, not the calm and pleasant Chamundi Hill, but another, lesser hill, bare and rocky, with here and there a few clumps of prickly pear. On one side of the hill the land fell away sharply, almost vertically, and here was revealed the actual quarry, an enormous irregular crater strewn with boulders and lined with jagged rocks, its sides pitted with holes of varying size. People were everywhere; some working in the quarry itself, others scattered about the hillside; the heftier among the men splitting boulders, the women and children chipping fragments off the larger stones. Movement everywhere: a myriad arms, rising and falling, hands flailing, backs bending and straightening in a relentless rhythm. At intervals I observed a red flag being hoisted which seemed to be some sort of a danger signal, for those working in the vicinity immediately dispersed to wait at a safe distance; a shrill whistle also blew as a warning to those who had not seen, or who had disregarded, the red flag; and within a few seconds followed the explosions we had heard when approaching the quarry.

"The sheet rock is blasted by gunpowder," Puli explained. "The municipality sends special men to do that, but the other work can be done by anyone."

So it seemed: there were all ages and sizes here; but we were at a loss where to begin. "Begin here," Puli said. "It is some way from the quarry, where most of the blasting is done, and you won't have to run so often." He sat himself down, keeping a watchful eye on us.

"I have never done this kind of work before," I said uncertainly. "I hardly know—"

"Oh, it is quite simple. You merely hammer the stones until they break. The only thing is you must get them the right size. See that pile there?" he pointed to a heap of stones, most of which were about the size of a child's fist. "Try and get them like that."

And that was precisely the difficulty: to break the stones to the required size. Sometimes they were too big, sometimes too small. We struck lightly and only chips glanced off the stone: we struck hard and it fell to fragments.

The air was full of flying dust and stone particles, part of the trouble lay in keeping one's eyes open while striking.

"It is not a simple way of earning," I said, "and it is more difficult than it looks." And Nathan grumbled, "If we had a hammer, at least we should not have so much waste." Yet there were many like us without hammers and using only stones, who were making very good progress. Once or twice I stopped to watch, admiring and envious, while the stones broke obediently to the right size under their skilful blows and the knobbly heaps before them grew. Only once were we disturbed by blasting near us. Engrossed in our work, neither of us had observed the red flag, nor with the hammering constantly beating upon our eardrums, did we hear the whistle go; but Puli, more alert than either of us, hustled us to safety, and as we ran we felt the ground shake beneath us.

"You must learn to be careful," Puli said severely, while stones and earth still rained down on us like hailstones. "Did you not hear the whistle, or the people who shouted to you? This blasting is a nuisance," he went on. "You will find your stones are scattered; but you will get used to it."

The stones were indeed scattered, and mixed inextricably with those of other workers: but when we had collected what we reckoned to be our pile no one raised any objections. "Sometimes one loses, sometimes one gains," a man said philosophically. "It evens itself out."

I was thankful there was this spirit of amity: we were neither of us anxious to engage in futile disputes.

The sun was setting before we finished. The heap of stones before us was not very large; nor, to our proud eyes, very small. All about us people were stopping work. As the light faded so the clink-clank died; in the gathering darkness only a few faint sounds of hammering told of a solitary stone-breaker continuing his labours.

I turned to the boy beside us. "Well, what now? Who pays us?"

"We must get a sack first," he replied. "Your husband had better wait here while we are gone. Come, I will show you the overseer's hut."

I followed him. The hillside was full of moving people, some carrying laden sacks, others with wicker baskets on their shoulders which creaked with the weight of the stones, some of which tumbled from holes in the loosely woven wicker.

The overseer's hut was built some distance away from the quarry—a small affair with thatched roof and pressed-fibre walls. The two doors, one at either end, were both open. A long line of people was moving in slowly at one; from the other, people were coming away, not with sacks but with money. I joined the line, empty-handed. Puli was standing some distance away; from somewhere he had produced a begging bowl which he held in the crook of his elbow, while he displayed his mutilated hands to the passers-by. He had altered his voice, I noticed, making it weak and quavery while he uttered his sing-song plea: "Take pity on an orphan child, take pity . . ."

Wrong place, I thought. Only the poor come here. But to my astonishment I saw one or two had dropped pies into his bowl. Soon he was able to rattle it, thus attracting even more attention.

The line was moving slowly forward: I shuffled along with it. The man behind me was laden with two baskets; he kept prodding me with them until at last I turned round in irritation. Then I saw he was a very old man, the load he carried kept slipping over his lean shanks and every time he hitched the baskets up they bumped against me. My irritation vanished.

"You have been busy today, I see," I said.

"No more than usual. . . . I generally manage two baskets."

"We were two," I confessed, "but I doubt whether we have filled even one!"

"You will work faster when you are used to it. . . . You are new, are you not?"

"Yes; first time we have been."

"I thought so," he nodded. "You ought to collect your sack as soon as you get here, otherwise there is this long wait and then you have to come back and wait again."

I thanked him, feeling surprised that Puli had not known, he who was so competent in his way. Then I reminded myself that despite his airs he was only a child.

My turn. I entered. A man was sitting on the floor writing on a small raised wooden board resting on bricks before him.

"How many?" He did not raise his eyes.

"One only."

He entered something in a book and reached for some coins, then he looked up. "Where is your sack?"

"I have not got one . . . I have just come for it," I stammered.

"Why did you not ask for it in the first place?" he said crossly. "Are you trying to get money for nothing?"

He put the coins back on the pile, took a basket from those stacked behind him.

"Here you are . . . no sacks left. And hurry up, else you won't be paid tonight."

I took it and ran back to Nathan. Breathless with haste we filled the basket and I was back while the line of waiters still stretched before the hut.

"Two sacks, one rupee . . . three sacks, one-eight . . ." the overseer's voice kept calling, monotonous, slightly weary. Stooping I placed my basket in front of him.

"One sack, eight annas," he called; then impatiently, altering his rhythm, "Not there! Behind, with the others!"

I put the basket alongside the others. Now at last I was to be paid. He took out the money, two coins, each a four-anna piece, dropped them in my palm.

Nathan was waiting, eager and impatient. "How much?"

"Eight annas!"

We looked at each other, smiling, jubilant. "We shall soon be home," Nathan said softly. "Think of it!"

It seemed natural that we should wait for Puli, and sure enough he joined us a few minutes later. The boy had attached himself to us of his own accord and now both of us took it for granted he would remain.

"Well," I said as he came up. "How did you fare? I saw you were busy."

"Not well at all," he replied dolefully, holding out one anna. "That is all I got for my pains."

I myself had heard the rattling of many more coins, and apparently so had Nathan. "You must be very clever," he said drily, "to make so much clatter with only one coin!"

There was a silence, then Puli recovered himself.

"Ah that! True, there were other coins, but they were pies. I have exchanged them for this one anna."

He was an artful child in many ways, and more than a match for us.

Each day Puli accompanied us to the quarry, usually remaining with us while we worked and always returning with us to the temple. Whatever we earned we entrusted to him; the theft of the money from my sari while I slept had undermined not only my confidence but Nathan's: besides, Puli was manifestly more capable of caring for it than we were.

We calculated that if we earned eight annas each day and contrived to live on four, we could save the money we needed to return in forty days. "At any rate within two months," said Nathan, "allowing for everything." He turned to Puli, who had bought some marbles which he was tossing up and down in his begging bowl, being unable to use them in any other way.

"What of you? Will you come with us?"

The boy stared: the thought of leaving the city seemed to shock him. He shook his head. "No! I do not want to go to your village."

"It is much nicer than here," said Nathan enticingly. "More peaceful, with green fields and open air . . . and when the paddy is ripe—ah, such a sight as you have never seen."

"And what would I do there," said Puli contemptuously, "in these green fields of yours I know nothing about! What is more, they are not even yours, do you want me to starve with you?"

"You are right," Nathan said softly. "We have nothing to offer you."

"I do not know why you want to return," Puli continued. "You have told me yourself you have no land. What will you live on?"

We ourselves did not know. We had left because we had nothing to live on, and if we went back it was only because there was nothing here either. We ate once a day and that was all: when the day came for buying cloth to cover ourselves with, or a mat to lie on, or medicines for Nathan while he fevered, there would be nothing.

"You are too young to understand," said Nathan. "This is not my home, I can never live here."

"Yet you came?"

"I came because I was forced, and believing my son lived here. Now he has gone none knows where. I must return to my youngest son, he will somehow support us."

"Are you sure?" said the ruthless child. "You are too old to keep travelling up and down."

"At least," said Nathan, "I shall be where I was born and bred. This city is no place for me, I am lost in it. And I am too old to learn to like it." He changed the subject: "How will you fare when we go?"

"As I did before you came," said Puli indifferently. "We beg and work sometimes and filch from stalls when we can . . . I and the other boys. . . . I know every street and alley," he added proudly. "I have been chased often, but have never been caught. Now if I came to your village I would know neither where to hide nor where to seek. No, no! I will not leave."

We did not try to dissuade him, although the thought of going without him was saddening. In the short time he had spent with us we had become to be curiously dependent on the boy, respecting his independent spirit as much as his considerable knowledge of the city and its many kinds of people. Yet I thought, what I did not wish to think, of the time when the disease that had claimed his fingers would creep up, eating away his limbs—or attach some other part, his feet or his eyes. What then of this bright fearless child who boasted that he stood alone? There is a limit to the achievements of human courage.

Chapter 28

FROM COUNTING ANNAS, as the days went by, we began to count rupees. Four rupees, five, six. Even Puli began to show excitement. There was the time when we worked so well—or the stones were so kind—that we earned a rupee in a single day. I handed the coins as usual to Puli, who thrust it into the ragged pouch which covered his manhood. Where he transferred the money we gave him from there I do not know. It was his own business and he never told: certainly not one pie was ever lost. We walked back jubilant that day in the coppery twilight already edged with black, like ashes around dying embers. A thin drizzle was falling, so fine it might have been dew, the ground beneath my feet felt like the earth in the early morning and no longer a street. In fancy I was already home.

The single, twisting road that led from the quarry soon split into several streets, the main one leading to the bazaar, and it was this that I took.

"I will go on to the temple," said Nathan. "I am a little tired . . . besides it does not take two to buy rice cakes."

"Maybe a little more than rice cakes this time," I said cheerfully, winking at the boy. "You go on; we will give you a surprise."

I went to the small shop as I did each morning, Puli in eager step beside me, and the vendor hailed me as an old customer. He was a good man, for all that I bought so little from him: he sought out the largest rice cakes for the same money, and sometimes a lump of ghee to go with it as well.

"Wait a bit," I said, as he began to wrap the rice cake in a plantain leaf. "There may be a little more today."

"Come into money, have you?" he cried, chuckling and slapping his thigh with a loud report. "Well, you have come to the right man. I have a selection such as few have and, mark you, cheaper than anybody else! What will you have? Potato fritters, crisped in butter and melting inside, or these fried pancakes I have myself stuffed with onions? . . . Something sweet for the boy? . . . Sugar-whirls, or these exquisite curly-curlies?"

What shall it be, what shall it be? I inspected all the delicacies, which I had never dared to do before, and I found it next to impossible to decide between them. Puli, hopping up and down beside me, was likewise veering from one dainty to another. "The pilau there, such a lovely smell, and it has roasted nuts in it—or no, I think the fritters will last longer. . . ."

In the end we bought the fried pancakes, one each, paying six annas for the three, and four annas for two rice cakes.

"Well, if we are extravagant it is only once," I said, seeking to console my uneasy mind. "Ten annas is only a little over what we usually spend. The change will do us good."

But the recklessness did not end there. As we walked on we passed a hawker, and he had a sensitive nose and sniffed that we had a little money and little control to go with it and he came after us pulling out and ex- hibiting his wares, and at last he took out a small wooden cart on wheels to which he attached a string and pulled it along behind him as he came following us.

"A dum-dum cart," cried Puli, and he echoed after the man, "We need not buy, let us only stop and watch," and he tugged at my sari. So we stopped to look at the toy and indeed it was a pretty thing, lovingly made and exactly like a real cart, the wood skilfully carved, with painted spokes to the wheels and a yoke which moved on the necks of the painted oxen.

"Pull it and hear the drum beat," said the wily man, holding out the string to Puli, and how could he resist it, who was only a child, when I myself was enchanted! So he jerked the string and as the cart came towards him the legs of the oxen moved and the carter's hands rose and fell and the drum- sticks he held in them came down upon the tiny drum in front of him—a real drum, cunningly made with cords up the sides and skin stretched tightly over the top. Dum-dum-dum-dum went the drum, the quicker you pulled the faster it beat.

"Two annas only—you will never be able to buy cheaper. It cost me all of that to make. . . . There is no profit to me in it, I only sell because I must. I have not sold one toy all day."

I sneaked a glance at Puli and he was looking at me with eyes like lamps. He still held the string between the stumps of his fingers, and kept yanking at it as if the drumming was sweet to his ears.

"Why do you not pay for it with your own money if you want it?" I said uneasily. "I see you begging every day. . . . You know I have spent more than I ought already."

"Two annas more won't matter," he wheedled. "I promise I will never ask you for anything. . . ."

"But you have money of your own," I repeated. "I have seen it myself."

"I have spent it all," he said pitifully. "People gave at first but now they are used to me. . . . It is a hard world."

Again I thought, He is a child after all, still tender, still eager. Whatever he may say or do he has lived only a short time, not easily. And even as I nodded he began fumbling at his pouch, unable in his haste to undo it, until at last I had to do it for him, taking from it the coins I needed, still warm from his body, and handing them to the hawker.

Then extravagance grew frenzied, encouraged by this lapse, and I could not stop myself from taking out two more annas to buy another cart. For my little grandson, I thought, who has had so much to bear from his birth, and I pictured his white transparent cheeks flushing with excitement while Ira hovered nearby with her face like a flower and the rare smile that graced it.

The hawker took the money from me and made off quickly—no doubt fearing that I would come to my senses. We continued on our way, Puli dragging one cart behind him, I carrying the other together with the rice cakes, the pancakes and the two-anna piece which was all that was left of the day's earnings; while I thought again and again of what I would say to my husband.

Now we were within the precincts of the temple and I caught sight of Nathan and ran towards him, bidding the boy pick up the cart with its infernal drum: but no, he was bewitched, the cart must come dum-dumming behind him.

"I don't know what came over me," I blurted, penitent. "I shall work very hard tomorrow to make up. You will see."

Nathan looked at me, his eyes were dull. He is exasperated, I thought. No wonder!

"We have a surprise for you," I said with false cheerfulness. "Look, pancakes!"

Nathan gave them a glance, then rose hurriedly to his feet. I saw him stagger to one side, away from the stone corridors. When the spasm of sickness was over, he came back to lean against a pillar. He was shivering.

"It was the food," he gasped. "It turned my stomach."

"You have worked too hard," I said. "It does not do to strain oneself."

"The fever has been coming all day," he said. "Since this morning."

I felt his body and it was burning hot, the skin dry and stretched. He had obviously been ill for several hours. Why did you have to do it? I wanted to say. Why? But I only said, "Lie and rest. You will feel better." And I took his head in my lap and set my hands to massaging the pain from his limbs.

The rain which had been a fine drizzle had become by morning a heavy downpour. The air, as always at the beginning of the monsoon, lay like a blanket upon the earth, damp and suffocating, but when it blew the wind came through the rain wet and chill. Nathan was still shivering, but no longer violently. I broke up the two rice cakes and we ate in silence, depressed by the ceaseless rain. Nathan has eaten his share, I thought. He must be better; it is the cold which makes him shiver. Nevertheless I said to him anxiously: "Stay behind and rest—it is not good for you to go out in this rain. Tomorrow will be enough."

"Tomorrow and tomorrow it will rain," he replied. "It is the monsoon. I cannot sit here idling while the days slip past and we are still far from home."

We went, the three of us, to the quarry, joining the bedraggled groups of workers toiling along the winding, muddy road. Those who were richer bought and donned palm-leaf hooded cloaks which fell stiffly from head to thigh, making them look like walking beetles; but these protectors were expensive, twelve annas apiece; most of the workers did without.

Rain had softened the road, liquid mud came squelching up between my toes as I walked. Ahead and behind me were scores of footprints, many of them like small pools where water had seeped in. The cart-tracks were full of water too, long lines crisscrossing with mud flung up on either side of the trenches. Three or four empty bullock carts passed us on the way to collect the broken stones, the bullocks drawing them struggling to get through the morass, their hides slippery with rain. The cart wheels sank deep in the mud as they turned, mud spattered continuously from the creaking wheels.

"The worst season of the year," a voice was grumbling. "Next year whatever happens I shall not work."

"Pah, you say that every year."

"No, really, this time I mean it . . . even if it means not eating."

Plans, everyone had plans. They were all built on money. Save enough to keep dry, save enough to cast one's chains, save enough to go away.

The clink of stones came to us sodden with the rain, indistinct, unmistakable. A few brave souls had risen with the dawn. Up the hillside to join them, scrambling over the sharp slopes. Once I caught at a bush to help me up . . . it was a prickly pear, and I had to spend precious minutes pulling out the thorns. Nathan behind me was panting, the breath came and went so quickly that his chest resembled a bellows.

"I will rest when we are home," he said to me impatiently. "There will be plenty of time then."

And I listened to him. All day we sat there in the rain breaking stones, and for the whole of that week, and Nathan grew neither better nor worse. On the seventh day the ague came upon him again, but he did not stop work. A kind of frenzy drove him on.

Rain. Not heavy now but monotonous, dripping on to us, splashing on the stones. No shelter on that bare hillside. The wind came whistling round it and struck at the crouched wet bodies. Hammer on stone. Stone on stone. clink-clank-drip. The rain had even defeated Puli the lion-hearted; he would not accompany us to the quarry.

Dusk was approaching, early because of the sullen lowering clouds; when I took up the sack, not full today, the stones rattled loosely inside.

"Don't wait for me," I said to my husband. "I will be with you soon."

"Don't be long," he said.

I went quickly from him with the sack on my back; running to get to the head of the waiting queue. Six annas, less than we have earned before; but we have nearly enough now, I thought, coming through the gloom. I must see about a carter. Maybe it will not be as much as we have reckoned, then we can leave at once. My mind wandered to my home; would it still be there? I saw before me my daughter and the shy white-faced Sacrabani. And Puli . . . if only he would come, how happy we would be, my husband and I! Not Puli, though; he would certainly refuse. I shall miss him, I thought sadly. But he—he won't even notice our going.

Disjointed thoughts kept clattering through my brain—or was the clatter only the rain? I stumbled down the hill-slopes, treacherous with mud and stones, sighing with relief as I reached the road.

Half way along it, I saw a small knot of people gathered. Nothing can make me stop, I thought, hurrying along. Then one of the group called: "Ai! See to your man. He has fallen."

I stopped and my senses poised themselves on the brink of insensibility, ready to swoop away at the merest nod from me. I shook off the blackness and went to him through the gathered people, who parted to let me through, then closed their ranks as I knelt beside him.

He was lying by the side of the road where someone had carried him— not in the gutter but away from the road, to avoid the mud-churning cart wheels. His body had made a trough of the wet mud, in it he lay jerking and twitching. Next to him the swollen gutter ran like a stream, noisily; above it I could hear his hoarse breathing. I touched him and his body was as chill as the wind. The pitiless rain came splashing down uncaring. I had no shield for him. At last I unwound part of my sari, meaning to tear it, but the mate- rial would not tear: where my hands were it gave, limp and perished. In despair I wound the rags about me again. Nobody gave anything, nobody had anything to give; the men in loincloths, the women in saris tattered and sodden like mine. It makes no difference, I thought to myself, and found the words being murmured by another.

One man took him by the armpits, another his feet. I came walking behind; with me other women, whispering words of comfort that the rain washed away as soon as they were uttered. Sometimes there was a silence while they waited for my answer, waited while I groped for their words.

"Has he been ill long?"

"Yes; some time."

"Have you no sons to help?"

"Yes—no—not here."

I licked my wet lips. There was a taste on them of salt and of the fresh sweetness of rainwater. I did not know I had been crying.

Chapter 29

THE MEMORIES OF THAT NIGHT are hard and bright within me like a diamond, and the fires that flash from it have strange powers. Some are blue and wrap me gently in their glow; or green and soothing like oxen eyes in the night; but there are others, yellow and red, that sear me with their intensity. When this happens I call to the mists and they come, like clouds that cover the sun. But the fires themselves are always there, they will never be extinguished until my life itself is done.

What do I remember? Every word, every detail. I remember walking along the wet deserted street by the wall of the temple; I remember looking up for the flare that had ever burnt on the top of the temple, and it was quenched; and the black demons of fear came shrieking at my ear and would not be silenced, for all that I repeated like a madwoman, "Fire cannot burn in water." I saw the faces of men who were not there and of children from whom the life had been filched, and yet it was black night, blacker than black since the stars were hidden.

They laid my husband on the paved floor and I sank down beside him. Somebody brought a light, a hurricane lantern that burned steady in the stormy wind; somebody else, water. His body was caked in mud, wet and dirty. I wiped him clean, took his head in my lap. The knot of people who had come so far with me melted away into the darkness, in ones and twos, when they saw how it was.

Nathan's head kept twitching from side to side, he called to our sons and muttered words that I did not understand. The rays from the lantern fell on his wasted face, on the tight yellowed skin, on the lips split with fever, on his limbs which were like a child's. Sometimes his breath came between his chattering teeth in gusts, rising above the rain and the winds that swished down the corridors; at other times I had to bend to listen.

Hour after hour his body suffered; his mind had fled from the tormented flesh. Midnight approached. The time of in-between when it is neither day nor night, when nature seems to pause, to sigh and turn and prepare for another day.

Midnight, and, as always before, his paroxysms eased. The fits of shivering stopped, the stiff limbs fell limp and relaxed. In the calm stillness I saw him open his eyes, his hand came to my face, tender and searching, wiping away the unruly tears.

"You must not cry, dearest. What has to be, has to be."

"Hush," I said. "Rest and grow better."

"I have only to stretch out my hand," he said, "to feel the coldness of death. Would you hold me when my time is come? I am at peace. Do not grieve."

"If I grieve," I said, "it is not for you, but for myself, beloved, for how shall I endure to live without you, who are my love and my life?"

"You are not alone," he said. "I live in my children," and was silent, and then I heard him murmur my name and bent down.

"Have we not been happy together?"

"Always, my dearest, always."

"It is slipping away fast," he said. "Rest with me a little."

And so I laid my face on his and for a while his breath fell soft and light as a rose petal on my cheek, then he sighed as if in weariness and turned his face to me, and so his gentle spirit withdrew and the light went out in his eyes.

Chapter 30

THE DAYS WENT BY, Nathan no longer beside me; no more. Ashes and dust, scattered to the winds, moistened by the rain, unrecognisable. I picked up the fragments of my life and put them together, all but the missing piece; and out of my affliction I called to Puli. I do not know what words I used, when I think of what I may have said I shiver. Rich promise to lure a child, before I knew it could be kept. Priceless treasure of health, not mine to give. And he, compassionate creature, who drew from me the arrows of sorrow one by one, listened, and when I came home I was not alone.

So good to be home at last, at last. The cart jolted to a standstill. I looked about me at the land and it was life to my starving spirit. I felt the earth beneath my feet and wept for happiness. The time of in-between, already a memory, coiled away like a snake within its hole.

From the unfinished, scaffolded building a figure emerged, came running. Selvam, my son.

"Thank God," he said. "Are you all right?" and he held me. My daughter joined us, her haste making her breathless. Puli alone not of the family, standing a little apart awkwardly, clutching in his arms the dum-dum cart. I called to him.

"My son," I said. "We adopted him, your father and I."

"You look tired and hungry," Ira said, taking his arm. "Come with me and rest, I will prepare the rice."

They walked on ahead.

"Do not worry," Selvam said. "We shall manage."

There was a silence, I struggled to say what had to be said.

"Do not talk about it," he said tenderly, "unless you must."

"It was a gentle passing," I said. "I will tell you later."

Some Indian Words

Beedi	. .	cheroot
Bulbul tara	. .	stringed musical instrument
Chakkli	. .	cobbler
Chowkidar	. .	watchman
Dhal	. .	lentils
Dhoti	. .	garment worn by men
Ghee	. .	clarified butter
Godown	. .	servants' quarters
Golsu	. .	circlet, usually of silver, worn round ankles
Jaggery	. .	a kind of coarse sugar
Jutka	. .	light horse-carriage
Kohl or *Khol*	. .	eye black, similar to mascara
Kum-kum	. .	red powder, used for caste marks, etc.
Maidan	. .	open field
Namaskar	. .	greeting, salutation
Ollock	. .	about one pound in weight
Pandal	. .	marquee
Patt-has	. .	fireworks [onomatopœic]
Peons	. .	porters, messengers
Zemindar	. .	landowner

Words whose meaning is readily apparent have not been included.

Twelve pies are equal to one anna; sixteen annas, to one rupee. A pice is three pies.

Related Readings

Pictures of
Marriage

Ved Mehta

*In his memoirs of his childhood in India, Ved Mehta re-
creates the wedding festivities as well as the family debates
surrounding the arranged marriage of his eldest sister.
Growing up in the late 1940s, his sisters are adopting
Western ways and beginning to question the traditional
role of women in a Hindu household.*

MY SISTERS WERE GROWING BIG, and even though they protested,
and said they would never get married, there was constant talk of finding
husbands for them. . . .

I remember that when I had just gone blind Daddyji[1] put me in his
motorcar and we went for a long ride. Then we were in a completely new
place. There some cousin-brothers dressed me in a long, heavy coat and
tight shoes with curled-up toes. The coat and shoes had thin wire woven in
all over and felt shiny. I picked at a bit of the wire on the sleeve. "Don't,"
they said. "It's real gold." They put a silk turban on my head, and I pulled at
the free end, which hung way down my back, like a veil. "Don't," they said.
"The turban will come off."

They carried me into a strange room filled with familiar voices, and
everyone clapped. "A perfect child bridegroom!" they cried. "You would
think he was getting married instead of Cousin Dharam Bir."

"What's a child bridegroom?" I asked.

Everyone laughed.

We went outside. I was lifted onto a horse jingling with all sorts of
things and was made to sit on something still and slippery in front of Cousin
Dharam Bir. The horse snorted and shook as if it were getting ready to run.

"Get me down!" I cried.

Many hands reached up and patted me. Cousin Dharam Bir slipped my
hand under a little hollow in front of me and told me to hold tight. He put
his arms around me. Horns sounded, drums rolled, firecrackers went off, and
the horse started walking slowly.

---

1. -ji suffix denoting affection

"Where are we going?" I asked.

"To the wedding, child bridegroom," the horsewallah[2] said. "To get a new lady relative for you. There will be a Brahman, a fire, incense, and ghi."[3] He clicked his tongue and urged the horse forward.

"Will the new lady relative have a horse, too?" I asked, pulling at the coat of the horse with my free hand—the hair was matted but bouncy.

"Oh, no," the horsewallah said. "Only the bridegroom and the child bridegroom ride on the horse. She sits and weeps."

Cousin Dharam Bir said something over my head. The band got really loud. Then I was lifted off the horse, passed from hand to hand, and carried into another strange room. I felt restless and fidgety. A strange lady embraced me and said, "You think you're going to get married. Marriage is not for you." I slept.

When I awoke, my turban had fallen off, and unfamiliar hands were taking off my coat and shoes. Once more, I was in the motorcar. There were the familiar voices of Daddyji beside me in the driver's seat and Cousin Dharam Bir in the back. The voices were droning over the murmur of the motor. Someone rustled in the back seat. "Who's that?" I asked.

"She's your cousin-brother's wife, Satya," Daddyji said.

She leaned forward and put her arms around me. "Come to me," she said, her voice jingling like the things on the wedding horse. I climbed over the back of the front seat and sat with her and Cousin Dharam Bir.

When I was about eight, a cousin-sister from Mehta Gulli came to stay with us in Rawalpindi. She brought us the news that Daulat Ram Chachaji—one of my father's brothers—had broken off Cousin Sheila's engagement. "You all heard that Sheila was marrying a very rich boy," she said. "On the day of the engagement, he arrived with some coolies[4] carrying his engagement present. And what a present it was! A teakwood dressing table complete with a stool, a mirror, a cosmetic box, and hairbrushes. The hairbrushes had silver backs with Sheila's initials on them. Daulat Ram Chachaji liked the dressing table, but later he began worrying about the young man's big girth. He said, 'A rich son-in-law is all well and good, but from the health point of view his being fat is a distinct handicap, especially since he could not be a hair taller than five feet four.' Subhadran Chachiji"—Cousin Sheila's mother—"who has recently become very plump herself, tried to minimize the issue. She said that to her the fellow looked just healthy. The two argued for some days. Then Daulat Ram Chachaji had a brilliant idea. He knew that every morning the young man walked past

---

2. **-wallah** suffix meaning the person or thing concerned with a job or an object
3. **ghi** clarified semiliquid butter in India; also spelled *ghee*
4. **coolies** offensive term for unskilled Asian laborers

the door of the chemist's on the Mall Road. He posted himself there. When he caught sight of the young man coming along, he stepped on the weighing machine that, you remember, stands just outside the chemist's, and quickly inserted an anna.[5] He was studying the card giving his weight and fortune when the young man came abreast. Before the fellow knew what was happening, Daulat Ram Chachaji had maneuvered him onto the weighing machine. And practically before the card dropped out of the slot Daulat Ram Chachaji had read the weight—fourteen stone.[6] They looked at each other, and both knew that the engagement was off. The dressing table, hairbrushes and all, had to be returned. Sheila has now been engaged to a boy from a professional family, and that means no showy, extravagant presents but probably a healthy, long-lived husband."

A year or so later, we went to Kashmir and stayed with some relatives in Srinagar for a couple of days. For long stretches, Daddyji would disappear into the house across the road. "We don't see any more of you here than we did in Rawalpindi!" we children complained. "What's the point of being on a holiday in Kashmir?"

Daddyji wouldn't explain.

"It must be either a card game or a girl for Cousin Prakash," Sister Umi said. Prakash Anand was Dharam Bir's younger brother, and Daddyji's nephew. Since Daddyji was the most successful member of the family and was considered to have the best eye for feminine beauty, Prakash looked to Daddyji to help him find a wife.

Daddyji laughed, and admitted that he was indeed looking over a girl for Cousin Prakash. "She has large eyes and long, thick hair. Her height is good, and she has a very fair complexion. Her father assures me that she doesn't wear lipstick or fingernail polish. Her family is here from Lahore on holiday. She is affectionately called Rani."

Then, a few months later, when we were visiting Lahore, Cousin Prakash came to Daddyji while I was playing within earshot.

"She wears slacks!" he said.

"Who does?"

"Rani!"

"So? When? Where—on the Mall Road?"

"No, no, in her father's house. Sister Vidya went to visit, and Rani was sitting in the garden in slacks. That's worse than wearing rouge. She's too fashionable, too Westernized, to fit into our family pattern."

There was silence, and then Daddyji asked, "What would you like me to do?"

---

5. **anna** former coin of India equal to one-sixteenth of a rupee

6. **stone** unit of weight equal to fourteen pounds

"Tell them that the engagement is off."

"It will be done."

For a long time, I thought about Rani's slacks and about Cousin Vidya, who was the elder sister of Cousin Prakash. Daddyji used to say that he really admired Cousin Vidya for wearing homespun clothes and living simply on her small salary, and for being one of the first women in the Punjab to do an M.A. in economics and to make a career of teaching in a college—for living by her principles and being self-reliant. Yet it was clear to us children that while people respected her and made a fuss over her they also pitied her, because she had missed out on love and marriage.

"Why is Cousin Vidya a spinster?" I asked Mamaji one day.

"Why? No one would marry a girl with misshapen hands. Poor Vidya— her marriage train pulled out of the station before she was twelve, when she got the sickness in her wrists. After that, she never had a chance to wear good clothes, to have a man and a house, to bear children. Marriage was not in her karma.[7] Her dharma[8] was to live alone, wear spectacles, and strain her eyes at the books."

Cousin Vidya, when she spoke, had a way of pausing and breathing out hesitantly through her nose, doing a sort of reverse sniff. It made her sound very wise and thoughtful. Whenever she came to see us, I would try to copy the way she talked, with pauses and sniffs, and long after she had left, people would say to me, "Stop talking like Vidya." Without my knowing exactly why, people used to think there was a bond between her and me. I now asked Mamaji, "Will I end up a spinster?"

"Not a spinster—a bachelor," she said, without a moment's hesitation.

I remember that Sister Pom had a friend in Rawalpindi named Chinta. She was a year older than Sister Pom and, we thought, the loveliest of all her friends. Once, when I was about ten, Cousin Vidya came to stay with us. She saw Chinta, and the moment Chinta left she quizzed Sister Pom about her.

"She has been studying at Kinnaird College, in Lahore, and is the daugher of Uncle Tandon," Sister Pom said, and she explained that R. R. M. Tandon, divisional engineer of the railway, belonged to the small family of government officials in Rawalpindi.

Cousin Vidya suggested Chinta to Daddyji for her youngest brother, Dev. We children couldn't imagine how Cousin Dev could possibly do for Chinta. He was famous with us for lecturing, for scrimping,[9] for joking. Bhua Parmeshwari Devi—his mother, and our paternal aunt—used to say

---

7. **karma** fate; destiny

8. **dharma** duty

9. **scrimping** being very cautious with money

that when he was eight years old he had climbed up onto a mantelpiece and started lecturing, and that he had never stopped. Whenever we met him, he sang the same film song, "I'm Off to Meet My Beloved." But none of us had the pluck to say anything against the match in front of Cousin Vidya.

"Whatever you say goes with me, Vidya," Daddyji said.

"Chinta's very fair, but she looks to me to be a little bit on the short side," Cousin Vidya said.

"I think she's my height," Sister Pom said.

Everybody in the room started debating about Chinta's height.

"If you can't tell, what difference does it make?" I asked.

"It makes a lot of difference. Be quiet," Mamaji said.

"Why don't we just ring her up and ask her how tall she is?" I asked.

"That would be very rude," Cousin Vidya said.

It was decided that Cousin Vidya must settle the question for herself, and Sister Pom was deputed to invite Chinta to the Rawal Club, next door, for tea. As had been arranged, Sister Pom, who was the tallest of my big sisters, took Chinta for a turn around the club gardens, and the rest of us sat with Cousin Vidya on the club veranda as she compared the heights of the two girls. Cousin Vidya was satisfied that Chinta was only two or three inches shorter than Sister Pom. In subsequent days, Cousin Vidya closely observed Chinta talking, eating, sewing, knitting, and studying, and satisfied herself that she had good eyes, that she did not secretly wear spectacles, and that she was not a "modern butterfly type" who would polish her nails, use rouge, or wear slacks. Finally, she told Daddyji to make the proposal, and she left, confident that Chinta's parents would say yes, even though they had not yet met Cousin Dev.

"We don't know the young man," Daddyji reported Uncle Tandon as saying. "We've never seen him. But if he's your nephew he must be a chip off the old block—isn't he?"

"How unfair!" Sister Umi said. "Because of you, Daddyji, Chinta's parents have said yes without even seeing Cousin Dev. But Chinta will not be marrying you—she'll be marrying Cousin Dev."

"Umi, your tongue will get us all into trouble," Mamaji said.

"You don't only marry a man, you marry into a family," Daddyji said. "In the West, things are done differently—there women work and earn and are independent. But we live in India."

I remember that Cousin Dev came to see Chinta, and that Chinta's family and our family met at the Rawal Club for tiffin.[10] As we were all sitting around, Chinta's younger sister Sheila said to me in a loud aside, "Why are our parents torturing poor, fair Chinta into marrying Blackie-Black? He's

---

10. **tiffin** lunch

the color of an eggplant!" Cousin Dev was known to have a dark complexion. "Haven't there been enough unhappy marriages between Beauty and the Beast in the world already?" People often addressed me as if I were a lamppost, and told me things intended for someone else.

Auntie Tandon stirred her tea very loudly, but everybody had heard Sheila's remark.

Cousing Dev said good-humoredly, "Bridegrooms can be dark—Lord Krishna was dark. Only brides have to be fair and beautiful. Besides, what is there in color when I can recite Urdu[11] verses and set water on fire with them?"

One evening, in Lahore, as we were finishing our sweet at the dinner table, Mamaji said, "Thank God, Prakash is reëngaged and everything is settled between Dev and Chinta. Now let them get married, and be happy or sad in their own houses and not trouble your daddy." She was outspoken because Daddyji was away at a club.

"What would happen if Chinta was miserable with Cousin Dev?" Sister Umi asked rhetorically. "He's completely unsuitable for Chinta. Cousin Vidya has already let it be known that once Chinta gets married even her name will be changed—she'll be called Nishchint." Cousin Vidya objected to the name Chinta because it meant "worry;" Nishchint meant "without worry." "It's no wonder that when a daughter is born in our country the whole house becomes as silent as a mausoleum.[12] How different it would be if we girls could work and be independent, find our own husbands without any dowry and without relatives getting into it. I think I'll go and live in the West."

"What nonsense you talk," Mamaji said.

"Umi, you'll have to live here, like the rest of us," Sister Pom said. "Wait till your turn comes. Then you'll sing a different raga."[13]

"If I must live here, I'm never going to get married," Sister Umi said. "I'll have a boyfriend. I certainly won't come home crying for a dowry. If I ever did decide to get married, I'd just get married in the salwar and kemise[14] I had on. If he didn't like that—didn't take me as I was—I would show him the door and say, 'Ta-ta, goodbye, nice to have known you.'"

"I'll never forget the four girls I saw starving at the annual fair in Rawalpindi Division while their brother gorged himself," Sister Nimi said. "I almost cry whenever I think of them. If parents didn't have to worry

---

11. **Urdu** official language of Pakistan widely used in India
12. **mausoleum** building housing tombs
13. **raga** melodic scale pattern
14. **salwar and kemise** trousers and shirt

about dowries, maybe those girls would have been eating with their brother."

"I think the dowry system is detestable, just as you do, Nimi," Sister Pom said. "But some would starve anyway. You can't blame all that just on the dowry system and arranged marriages, because there still wouldn't be enough food to go around, and there would be just as many children dying from poverty."

"Yes, some must suffer and sacrifice," Mamaji said. "And it has to be women. It's in their nature. Otherwise, there's no happiness for anyone."

"But the suffering here is carried to such an extreme," Sister Nimi said. "It's all very well for us to talk like this, but we sisters haven't had to go hungry. Mamaji has never been beaten by Daddyji. If we were poor women, we would know what suffering and sacrifice really are—how deplorable the poverty is that forces mothers to take food out of their own daughters' mouths and give it to their sons, how deplorable the poverty is that drives husbands to beat their wives."

"But, Nimi, that's just the way of life in our crowded, poor country," Sister Pom said.

"I would like the man to suffer and sacrifice for me," Sister Umi said. "What happiness is there in suffering and sacrifice anyway?"

"The happiness in suffering and sacrifice is the same as the pleasure we get from giving without expecting anything in return," Sister Pom said. "We women may do all the suffering and sacrificing, but because of that we can also endure more."

"If that's marriage, Pom, I would rather go without, thank you very much," Sister Umi said.

"I think Umi is right," Sister Nimi said. "We shouldn't make our parents responsible for our marriage. That's where the trouble starts. The man says, 'If you don't give me a big dowry, I won't take your girl.' Then, when he gets her, he says, 'If she doesn't serve me hand and foot, I won't keep her.' The result: the parents suffer and sacrifice, the girl suffers and sacrifices, and what does the man do? Sits back and enjoys it all. This is fair? This is equality? This is freedom?"

"We don't have freedom and equality," Mamaji said. "We have only responsibility. I was the oldest in my family, and I took care of my brothers and sisters, just as Pom takes care of you when I'm away. Responsibility was all I ever knew."

"For myself, I think that if girls found their own husbands, boyfriends, or whatever, it would be better all around," Sister Umi said.

"You should do what Mamaji and Daddyji tell you to do, or you'll be very unhappy," I said.

"Who asked you for your opinion, Mister?" Sister Umi said.

"Umi, I don't see how you could make a better choice than Mamaji and Daddyji can," Sister Pom said. "Their experience is so much greater than yours. I wouldn't even know where to begin."

Sister Umi persisted. "If the customs were changed, we would know where to begin," she said. She continued, half laughing, "Pom, you have to admit that this is a man's world, especially in our country. I don't know why that should be. I'm just as good as Om, Yog, or any of them."

"Are you prepared to go and work like a man?" Sister Pom asked. "Bob your hair, give up your sari, and start wearing those horrible practical clothes—horrible slacks—that you have to wear to work in factories in the West?"

"If all of us, men and women, worked, perhaps there wouldn't be so much poverty in our country," Sister Umi said, undaunted. "I am prepared to bob my hair, wear slacks, and work like any mister."

"But can you imagine what our society would really be like if all the women started leading independent lives?" Sister Pom asked. "Who would have children? Who would look after them?"

"I believe in Russia they manage," Sister Nimi said. "Children are just brought up on a collective."

"That will suit me fine," Sister Umi said, "Society is bound to change after our country becomes independent. Whether we like it or not, women will become less subservient to men, and more independent. There will be less useless misery in Indian homes. Whatever Pom's theories, people will change, and change of their own accord. I can hardly wait for that day to come."

"If I'd acted the way Umi talks, I would have said 'Ta-ta, goodbye' in the first few weeks of our marriage," Mamaji said. "Then none of you would have been here. I know of only two ways of pleasing a man: quiet suffering and sacrifice, and saying yes to his every yes, and no to his every no. If your daddy pulled me up, even if I was completely in the right I bit my tongue and said 'Just as you say.' If the sun was shining and your daddy said that it was a beautiful moonlit night, I said it was a beautiful moonlit night."

"It might have been just as well if you had walked out," Sister Umi said. "You might have been happier."

"The kind of happiness you talk about is not for us Indian women," Mamaji said. "I was brought up in the Indian way, and it is that upbringing that has kept me going all these years. However our customs may be at fault, you girls will have to admit that ultimately our marriages work out very well."

Before we moved to Lahore, Daddyji had gone to Mussoorie, a hill station in the United Provinces, without telling us why he was going out of the

Punjab. Now, several months after he made that trip, he gathered us around him in the drawing room at 11 Temple Road while Mamaji mysteriously hurried Sister Pom upstairs. He started talking as if we were all very small and he were conducting one of our "dinner-table-school" discussions. He said that by right and tradition the oldest daughter had to be given in marriage first, and that the ripe age for marriage was nineteen. He said that when a girl approached that age her parents, who had to take the initiative, made many inquiries and followed many leads. They investigated each young man and his family background, his relatives, his friends, his classmates, because it was important to know what kind of family the girl would be marrying into, what kind of company she would be expected to keep. If the girl's parents decided that a particular young man was suitable, then his people also had to make their investigations, but, however favorable their findings, their decision was unpredictable, because good, well-settled boys were in great demand and could afford to be choosy. All this took a lot of time. "That's why I said nothing to you children about why I went to Mussoorie," he concluded. "I went to see a young man for Pom. She's already nineteen."

We were stunned. We have never really faced the idea that Sister Pom might get married and suddenly leave, I thought.

"We won't lose Pom, we'll get a new family member," Daddyji said, as if reading my thoughts.

Then all of us started talking at once. We wanted to know if Sister Pom had been told; if she'd agreed; whom she'd be marrying.

"Your mother has just taken Pom up to tell her," Daddyji said. "But she's a good girl. She will agree." He added, "The young man in question is twenty-eight years old. He's a dentist, and so has a profession."

"Did you get a dentist because Sister Pom has bad teeth?" Usha asked. Sister Pom had always been held up to us as an example of someone who, as a child, had spurned greens and had therefore grown up with a mouthful of poor teeth.

Daddyji laughed. "I confess I didn't think of anyone's teeth when I chose the young man in question."

"What is he like?" I asked. "What are we to call him?"

"He's a little bit on the short side, but he has a happy-go-lucky nature, like Nimi's. He doesn't drink, but, unfortunately, he does smoke. His father died at an early age of a heart attack, but he has a nice mother, who will not give Pom any trouble. It seems that everyone calls him Kakaji."

We all laughed. Kakaji, or "youngster," was what very small boys were called.

"That's what he must have been called when he was small, and the name stuck," Daddyji said.

In spite of myself, I pictured a boy smaller than I was and imagined him taking Sister Pom away, and then I imagined her having to keep his pocket money, to arrange his clothes in the cupboards, to comb his hair. My mouth felt dry.

"What will Kakaji call Sister Pom?" I asked.

"Pom, silly—what else?" Sister Umi said.

Mamaji and Sister Pom walked into the room. Daddyji made a place for Sister Pom next to him, and said, "Now, now, w, no reason to cry. Is it to be yes?"

"Whatever you say," Sister Pom said in a small voice, between sobs.

"Pom, how can you say that? You've never seen him," Sister Umi said.

"Kakaji's uncle, Dr. Prakash Mehrotra, himself a dentist, has known our family from his student days in Lahore," Daddyji said. "As a student dentist, he used to be welcomed in Babuji's Shahalmi Gate house. He would come and go as he pleased. He has known for a long time what kind of people we are. He remembered seeing you, Pom, when we went to Mussoorie on holiday. He said yes immediately, and his approval seemed to be enough for Kakaji."

"You promised me you wouldn't cry again," Mamaji said to Sister Pom, patting her on the back, and then, to Daddyji, "She's agreed."

Daddyji said much else, sometimes talking just for the sake of talking, sometimes laughing at us because we were sniffling, and all the time trying to make us believe that this was a happy occasion. First, Sister Umi took issue with him: parents had no business arranging marriages; if she were Pom she would run away. Then Sister Nimi: all her life she had heard him say to us children, "Think for yourself—be independent," and here he was not allowing Pom to think for herself. Brother Om took Daddyji's part: girls who didn't get married became a burden on their parents, and Daddyji had four daughters to marry off, and would be retiring in a few years. Sisters Nimi and Umi retorted: they hadn't gone to college to get married off, to have some young man following them around like a leech. Daddyji just laughed. I thought he was so wise, and right.

"Go and bless your big sister," Mamaji said, pushing me in the direction of Sister Pom.

"I don't want to," I said. "I don't know him."

"What'll happen to Sister Pom's room?" Usha asked. She and Ashok didn't have rooms of their own. They slept in Mamaji's room.

"Pom's room will remain empty, so that any time she likes she can come and stay in her room with Kakaji," Daddyji said.

The thought that a man I had never met would sleep in Pom's room with Sister Pom there made my heart race. A sob shook me. I ran outside.

The whole house seemed to be in an uproar. Mamaji was shouting at Gian Chand, Gian Chand was shouting at the bearer, the bearer was shouting at the sweeper. There were the sounds of the kitchen fire being stoked, of the drain being washed out, of water running in bathrooms. From behind whichever door I passed came the rustle of saris, salwars, and kemises. The house smelled of fresh flowers, but it had a ghostly chill. I would climb to the landing of Sister Pom's room and thump down the stairs two at a time. Brother Om would shout up at me, "Stop it!" Sister Umi would shout down at me, "Don't you have anything better to do?" Sister Nimi would call to me from somewhere, "You're giving Pom a headache." I wouldn't heed any of them. As soon as I had thumped down, I would clatter to the top and thump my way down again.

Daddyji went past on the back veranda. "Who's coming with Kakaji?" I asked. Kakaji was in Lahore to buy some dental equipment, and in a few minutes he was expected for tea, to meet Sister Pom and the family.

"He's coming alone," Daddyji said, over his shoulder. "He's come from very far away." I had somehow imagined that Kakaji would come with at least as many people as we had in our family, because I had started thinking of the tea as a kind of cricket match—the elevens facing off.

I followed Daddyji into the drawing room. "Will he come alone for his wedding, too?"

"No. Then he'll come with the bridegroom's party."

We were joined by everyone except Mamaji and Sister Pom, who from the moment we got the news of Sister Pom's marriage had become inseparable.

Gian Chand came in, the tea things rattling on his tray.

Later, I couldn't remember exactly how Kakaji had arrived, but I remembered noticing that his footfall was heavy, that his greeting was affectionate, and that his voice seemed to float up with laughter. I don't know what I'd expected, but I imagined that if I had been in his place I would have skulked in the *gulli*, and perhaps changed my mind and not entered at all.

"Better to have ventured and lost than never to have ventured at all," Daddyji was saying to Kakaji about life's battles.

"Yes, Daddyji, just so," he said, with a little laugh. I had never heard anybody outside our family call my father Daddyji. It sounded odd.

Sister Pom was sent for, and she came in with Mamaji. Her footsteps were shy, and the rustle of her sari around her feet was slow, as if she felt too conscious of the noise she was making just in walking. Daddyji made some complimentary remark about the silver border on her sari, and told her to sit next to Kakaji. Kakaji and Sister Pom exchanged a few words about a family group photograph on the mantelpiece, and about her studies. There was the clink of china as Sister Pom served Kakaji tea.

"Won't you have some tea yourself?" Kakaji asked Sister Pom.

Sister Pom's sari rustled over her shoulder as she turned to Daddyji.

"Kakaji, none of my children have ever tasted tea or coffee," Daddyji said. "We consider both to be bad habits. My children have been brought up on hot milk, and lately Pom has been taking a little ghi in her milk at bedtime, for health reasons."

We all protested at Daddyji's broadcasting family matters.

Kakaji tactfully turned the conversation to a visit to Mussoorie that our family was planning.

Mamaji offered him onion, potato, and cauliflower pakoras. He accepted, remarking how hot and crisp they were.

"Where will Sister Pom live?" Usha asked.

"In the summer, my practice is in Mussoorie," Kakaji said, "but in the winter it's in Dehra Dun."

It struck me for the first time that after Sister Pom got married people we didn't know, people she didn't know, would become more important to her than we were.

Kakaji had left without formally committing himself. Then, four days later, when we were all sitting in the drawing room, a servant brought a letter to Mamaji. She told us that it was from Kakaji's mother, and that it asked if Sister Pom might be engaged to Kakaji. "She even wants to know if Pom can be married in April or May," Mamaji said excitedly. "How propitious! That'll be the fifth wedding in the family in those two months." Cousins Prakash and Dev, Cousin Pushpa (Bhaji Ganga Ram's adopted daughter), and Auntie Vimla were all due to be married in Lahore then.

"You still have time to change your mind," Daddyji said to Sister Pom. "What do you really think of him?"

Sister Pom wouldn't say anything.

"How do you expect her to know what her mind is when all that the two talked about was a picture and her bachelor's exam in May?" Umi demanded. "Could she have fallen in love already?"

"Love, Umi, means something very different from 'falling in love,'" Daddyji said. "It's not an act but a lifelong process. The best we can do as Pom's parents is to give her love every opportunity to grow."

"But doesn't your 'every opportunity' include knowing the person better than over a cup of tea, or whatever?" Sister Umi persisted.

"Yes, of course it does. But what we are discussing here is a simple matter of choice—not love," Daddyji said. "To know a person, to love a person, takes years of living together."

"Do you mean, then, that knowing a person and loving a person are the same thing?" Sister Umi asked.

"Not quite, but understanding and respect are essential to love, and that cannot come from talking together, even over a period of days or months. That can come only in good time, through years of experience. It is only when Pom and Kakaji learn to consider each other's problems as one and the same that they will find love."

"But, Daddyji, look at the risk you're taking, the risk you're making Pom take," Sister Nimi said.

"We are trying to minimize the risk as much as we can by finding Pom a family that is like ours," Daddyji said. "Kakaji is a dentist, I am a doctor. His life and way of thinking will be similar to mine. We are from the same caste, and Kakaji's family originally came from the Punjab. They eat meat and eggs, and they take religion in their stride, and don't pray every day and go to temples, like Brahmans. Kakaji knows how I walk into a club and how I am greeted there. The atmosphere in Pom's new home will be very much the same as the atmosphere here. Now, if I were to give Pom in marriage to a Brahman he'd expect Pom to live as he did. That would really be gambling."

"Then what you're doing is perpetuating the caste system," Sister Nimi said. She was the political rebel in the family. "You seem to presuppose that a Kshatriya should marry only a Kshatriya, that a Brahman should marry only a Brahman. I would just as soon marry a shopkeeper from the Bania caste or an Untouchable, and help to break down caste barriers."

"That day might come," Daddyji said. "But you will admit, Nimi, that by doing that you'd be increasing the odds."

"But for a cause I believe in," Sister Nimi said.

"Yes, but that's a whole other issue," Daddyji said.

"Daddyji, you say that understanding and respect are necessary for love," Sister Umi said. "I don't see why you would respect a person more because you lived with him and shared his problems."

"In our society, we think of understanding and respect as coming only through sacrifice," Daddyji said.

"Then you're advocating the subservience of women," Sister Nimi said, "because it's not Kakaji who will be expected to sacrifice—it's Pom. That's not fair."

"And why do you think that Pom will learn to respect Kakaji because she sacrifices for him?" Umi said, pressing her point.

"No, Umi, it is the other way around," Daddyji said. "It is Kakaji who will respect Pom because she sacrifices for him."

"But that doesn't mean that Pom will respect Kakaji," Umi persisted.

"But if Kakaji is moved by Pom's sacrifices he will show more considera-tion for her. He will grow to love her. I know in my own case I was moved to the depths to see Shanti suffer so because she was so ill-prepared to be my wife. It took me long enough—too long, I believe—to reach that understanding, perhaps because I had broken away from the old traditions and had given in to Western influences."

"So you admit that Pom will have to suffer for years," Umi said.

"Perhaps," Daddyji said. "But all that time she will be striving for ultimate happiness and love. Those are precious gifts that can only be cultivated in time."

"You haven't told us what this ultimate happiness is," Sister Umi said. "I don't really understand it."

"It is a uniting of ideals and purposes, and a merging of them. This is the tradition of our society, and it is the means we have adopted to make our marriages successful and beautiful. It works because we believe in the goodness of the individuals going into the marriage and rely on the strength of the sacred bond."

"But my ideal is to be independent," Sister Nimi said. "As you say, 'Think for yourself.'"

"But often you have to choose among ideals," Daddyji said. "You may have to choose between being independent and being married."

"But aren't you struck by the fact that all the suffering is going to be on Pom's part? Shouldn't Kakaji be required to sacrifice for their happiness, too?" Sister Nimi said, reverting to the old theme.

"There has to be a start," Daddyji said. "Remember, in our tradition it's her life that is joined with his; it is she who will forsake her past to build a new future with him. If both Pom and Kakaji were to be obstinate, were to compete with each other about who would sacrifice first, who would sacrifice more, what hope would there be of their ever getting on together, of their ever finding love?"

"Daddyji, you're evading the issue," Sister Nimi said. "Why shouldn't he take the initiative in this business of sacrifice?"

"He would perhaps be expected to if Pom were working, too, as in the West, and, though married, leading a whole different life from his. I suppose more than this I really can't say, and there may be some injustice in our system, at that. In the West, they go in for romantic love, which is unknown among us. I'm not sure that that method works any better than our method does."

Then Daddyji said to Sister Pom, "I have done my best. Even after you marry Kakaji, my responsibility for you will not be over. I will always be there in the background if you should need me."

"I respect your judgment, Daddyji," Sister Pom said obediently. "I'll do what you say."

Mamaji consulted Shambu Pandit. He compared the horoscopes of Sister Pom and Kakaji and set the date of the marriage for the eleventh of May—

the year was 1946—between the wedding of Cousin Pushpa and the wedding of Auntie Vimla. "That's just three days after she finishes her B.A. finals!" we cried. "When will she study? You are sacrificing her education to some silly superstition."

But Shambu Pandit would not be budged from the date. "I am only going by the horoscopes of the couple," he said. "You might as well protest to the stars."

We appealed to Daddyji, but he said that he didn't want to interfere, because such matters were up to Mamaji. That was as much as to say that Shambu Pandit's date was a settled thing.

I recall that at about that time there was an engagement ceremony. We all—Daddyji, Mamaji, Sister Pom, many of our Mehta and Mehra relatives—sat cross-legged on the floor of the front veranda around Shambu Pandit. He recited the Gayatri Mantra, the simple prayer he used to tell us to say before we went to sleep, and made a thank offering of incense and ghi to a fire in a brazier, much as Mamaji did—behind Daddyji's back—when one of us was going on a trip or had recovered from a bout of illness. Servants passed around a platter heaped up with crumbly sweet balls. I heard Kakaji's sister, Billo, saying something to Sister Pom; she had just come from Dehra Dun bearing a sari, a veil, and the engagement ring for Sister Pom, after Romesh Chachaji, one of Daddyji's brothers, had gone to Dehra Dun bearing some money, a silver platter and silver bowls, and sweet meats for Kakaji. It was the first time that I was able to think of Kakaji both as a remote and frightening dentist who was going to take Sister Pom away and as someone ordinary like us, who had his own family. At some point, Mamaji prodded me, and I scooted forward, crab fashion, to embrace Sister Pom. I felt her hand on my neck. It had something cold and metallic on it, which sent a shiver through me. I realized that she was wearing her engagement ring, and that until then Mamaji was the only one in our family who had worn a ring.

In the evening, the women relatives closeted themselves in the drawing room with Sister Pom for the engagement singsong. I crouched outside with my ear to the door. The door pulsated with the beat of a barrel drum. The pulse in my forehead throbbed in sympathy with the beat as I caught snatches of songs about bedsheets and henna, along with explosions of laughter, the songs themselves rising and falling like the cooing of the doves that nested under the eaves of the veranda. I thought that a couple of years earlier I would have been playing somewhere outside on such an occasion, without knowing what I was missing, or been in the drawing room clapping and singing, but now I was crouching by the door like a thief, and was feeling ashamed even as I was captivated.

The whole house, it seemed, was turned into women's quarters, dividing the family right down the middle, like a parting in one's hair. The sisters preferred to keep their own company or to be with Mamaji. They spoke in whispers and gestures, or in what seemed like riddles. The dowry had to contain twenty-one saris and twenty-one blouses, because twenty-one was a lucky number; at the same time, it had to contain twelve gold bangles, twelve bedsheets, and twelve tablecloths, because the quantity "a dozen" sounded more impressive than the number "twenty-one." The dowry had to be lavish—in fact, had to include everything to start a home with except a house and a motorcar—because it might determine the kind of offers the other sisters received; at the same time, it had to be modest, because the dowries of the other sisters would be expected to match it. Since nothing ready-made was available, two tailors were engaged. They sat on the front veranda from morning to night cutting and stitching. Friends and relatives came at all hours with something they had knitted, sewn, or embroidered. Jewellers, cloth merchants, or quilt-makers called daily with samples or for fittings. Once, I found Mamaji bargaining with the family jeweller for some gold bangles and gold chains. "Why haggle, Mistress?" the jeweller asked sombrely. "They're your daughter's inheritance, her *istri dhan*. As our great lawgiver Manu has said, 'Ornaments which may have been worn by women during their husbands' lifetime, their heirs shall not divide; those who divide them become outcasts.'"

For weeks, it seemed, the wedding preparations blew through the house like a storm, displacing the furniture and familiar objects. I could scarcely move about the house without falling over trunks, crates, bedrolls, bundles, packages, baskets, sacks piled up everywhere helter-skelter. I sometimes felt that I was not in my own house but in a crowded, chaotic train compartment. ("Her marriage train pulled out of the station.") When I hurt myself, tradesmen and deliverymen would click their tongues with pity, ask questions about my eyes, and then bless themselves for having been spared my misfortune.

No one in the family seemed to have much time for me, so I spent most of my days and evenings standing around in the kitchen talking to the servants. They were a constant source of news and opinion: Kakaji was coming in a train with fifty male relatives and friends. He could have brought four times as many, but since the Second World War and the Great Bengal Famine the government had restricted the bridegroom's party to a mere fifty. The Big Sahib could easily circumvent the restriction, but he was a government servant, correct to a fault. Just as well, because this way the Big Sahib would be able to save money. The bridegroom's relatives and friends would pay their train fare, of course, but their maintenance and feasting during the wedding would be on the shoulders of the bride's father, and weddings, even in these hard times, lasted at least three days. And to feed fifty healthy men was no joke. Only healthy men came, because the bride had to be protected and guarded—the world was full of bride thieves. Besides, the train journey back to Dehra Dun was more than two hundred miles long, and the route was infested with dacoits—tribes of gypsy thieves who roamed the country-side and who were known to jump on trains in the middle of nowhere and abscond with the dowry and God knew what else. Police? They were good in their way, but they couldn't take the place of blood relatives.

In Mehta Gulli, people were arranging to double up to make room for Kakaji and his force. They were engaging barbers to come and shave the men and cut their hair, washermen to wash and starch their clothes, boy ser-vants to keep their boots polished, cooks to produce Dehra Dun-type fare at a moment's notice, a twenty-piece band to accompany them for the wed-ding. Tradesmen had already delivered countless tins of ghi and bags of flour. It had definitely been decided to have five weddings, one after an-other: first cousin Prakash was going to get married, and then Cousin Dev (although their weddings were to take place in the brides' houses, there were to be many related festivities in Mehta Gulli); then Cousin Pushpa; then Sister Pom; then Auntie Vimla. For days, there would be only wedding preparations at 11 Temple Road, in Mehta Gulli, and at 16 Mozang Road. The whole city was in turmoil.

It was the morning of Sister Pom's wedding. Nearly two hundred of our own relatives and friends who lived at a distance had already arrived, and practi-cally every spare inch of floor in Mehta Gulli and at 16 Mozang Road and in our house was taken up with cots and bedding. The train with Kakaji and the bridegroom's party was due in a few minutes, and many of our male rela-tives had driven off to the station to receive them. Daddyji and Brother Om and I could not go; we had to wait and meet them in the evening at the *milni,* the formal meeting ceremony. All day, servants ran in from Mehta Gulli with snatches of news: Kakaji and the bridegroom's party had arrived at dawn. They looked bright but tired. Three of them were having a haircut. Kakaji had finished his breakfast, and two barbers were vying for the honor of shaving him. Some of the party had gone out for sightseeing. They had finished their lunch, and the cooks were gratified because they had eaten heartily. Kakaji was having his tiffin and had eaten three pastries.

I ran around the house like a top, touching everything, greeting every-one, trying to find out what was happening. In the back part of the inner courtyard, where the confectioners were stoking makeshift fires, patting dough for *puris,*[15] stirring something in vats, I breathed lungfuls to savor the

---

15. **puris** wheat cakes

cooking. They must be getting ready to make a *puri* a second, I thought, and I remembered the Great Bengal Famine. In the center of the inner courtyard, I paced around the *vedi*—four banana trunks firmly set in the ground under a canopy, and forming a biggish square. I helped hang branches and twigs with lots of leaves between them, to form arches, and, on the arches, fruits, flowers, balloons, and strings of lights. I barged into Mamaji's bedroom, and was chased out, because Sister Pom was being dressed there. I wandered into the drawing room, where women were looking over the articles of the dowry, counting them, exclaiming at them. They, too, shooed me away. I went upstairs and downstairs, into the garden and out to the gate, feeling the strings of lights on walls and bushes, eaves and pillars, to see if the bulbs were warm, only to have other people shout at me that I would electrocute myself, that I was spoiling the decorations, that I should get out of the way, that I should go and sit down quietly somewhere. But there was no place to sit. The whole house was restless and hot. Everywhere were rotating table fans and whirring ceiling fans, and smells of frying, incense, marigolds, powder, kohl,[16] pulling me this way and that way.

A band of trumpets, clarinets, drums, and cymbals struck up from the direction of Mehta Gulli, with a Noor Jehan song from "Zeenat"—"Dance, O Stars, Dance!" "Kakaji is about to get on his mare and ride over here!" Cousin Yog shouted, rushing in. "All his party is gathering behind his mare. They will be here for the *milni* any moment." Suddenly, the steps of our front veranda were thronged with our close male relatives. Sister Umi shouted from somewhere for the servants to bring out the buckets of flower petals and to put more bottles of lemonade on ice.

I slipped into my long coat woven all over with gold wire and ran into Daddyji's room with my turban, gathered, pleated, and starched like a long rope. Daddyji was busy tying his own turban, and I danced around him, impatient for him to tie mine, the long coat rustling behind me like a sari.

"I don't think I've ever worn a long coat before," I said.

"You did, too, at Dharam Bir's marriage," Daddyji said from over my head as he wound my turban.

I followed Daddyji, touching his coat, out to the veranda. The band music became a little distant, as if the band had turned back.

"What's happening? What's happening?" I asked.

"They have probably taken a detour to show off Kakaji," Brother Om said, coming up behind me.

Daddyji and Shambu Pandit arranged and rearranged us, sometimes by age, it seemed, and other times by our relationship to Sister Pom and gave each of us a garland and an odd number of rupees for the *milni*. The band

---

16. **kohl** cosmetic preparations used to darken the skin around the eyes

moved closer and closer, each medley sounding a little louder than the last, as if Kakaji and his people were now coming very slowly along our *gulli*.

I collared my younger cousin Ravi. "What's happening?"

"It's a young mare he's riding," he whispered, tittering. "But he has a sword at his side. I think he uses the sword to get Cousin Pom to say yes."

We both laughed, and felt very smug and knowing.

Kakaji's mare halted right in front of the gate, between us and the wedding guests. The band stopped playing, and the absence of its sound made the place seem quieter than it really was. Shambu Pandit recited Vedic hymns in a soft, melancholy voice. Then he called Daddyji to step forward for his *milni* and embrace Kakaji's uncle, Dr. Prakash Mehrotra. I wondered what it was like to be fatherless, like Kakaji, and to have an uncle stand in the father's place. Then Shambu Pandit called Brother Om and me to meet our counterparts. Brother Om met one of Kakaji's relatives, but Kakaji had no younger brother or stand-in for my *milni*, so I thrust the money back into my pocket and let the garland drop from my hand.

Brother Om and I helped Kakaji to alight from the mare, and we were surrounded by girls, who teased Kakaji and threw buckets of flower petals at him.

We all escorted Kakaji to the steps of the veranda, where my big sisters and Mamaji were now gathered. Servants ran around spraying everybody with scented water. Shambu Pandit announced, "Time for *jaimala, jaimala*."

Sister Pom, who was dressed in a filmy dark-red wedding sari with a rich gold border and gold decorations wonderful to touch, shyly garlanded Kakaji. (Shambu Pandit later insisted that, technically, until the *jaimala*— or victory garland—Sister Pom had the choice of refusing Kakaji.)

The band struck up again, and Brother Om and I led Kakaji to Daddyji's room. He joked with us about the elaborate arrangements and about his warm woollen coat with its closed collar. Sisters Nimi and Umi came in and took him upstairs to the terraced roof for his dinner. Servants ran to and fro serving the band in the *gulli*. Our *chachas* (paternal uncles) led the bridegroom's party upstairs for its dinner.

As I moved about, everyone commented on my glittering coat, and I felt at once like a wedding ornament with legs on and like a walking coat watched by all eyes. Wedding guests were milling about as they waited for the bridegroom's party and the band to finish eating, so that they could eat. At one point, I carried some bottles of lemonade to the band. The drummer proudly showed me the heavy ornamental buckle on his uniform belt, while clucking to his neighbors, "What a pity the little fellow cannot see all these beautiful clothes and lights."

"I've been looking for you," Brother Om shouted over the din, coming up to me. "Daddyji wants you upstairs for a photograph."

The feasting was over by midnight. The band and most of the wedding guests had eaten and left. Only close relatives and a few of the bridegroom's party remained. I remember that there was much confusion as people went around the house calling, *"Vedi! Vedi!* . . . Time for the ancient vows from the Vedas. . . . Come to the *vedi."* Ravi thought that it was a perfect wedding joke—my nickname was Vedi, and I had been named after the Vedas. I wasn't so sure: the journey to the *vedi* seemed long and treacherous—a mere pair of slacks or a deficiency of an inch or two in height could end it. I thought that I'd never felt so blind.

We sat on the ground around the *vedi,* I next to Sister Nimi. Now and then, she whispered to me. "Kakaji and Pom are sitting on low stools next to Mamaji and Daddyji. . . . Shambu Pandit is sitting under the *vedi.* . . . Shambu Pandit is lighting the sacred fire."

There was the sizzle and aroma of ghi and sandalwood chips in the fire. A huge platter of perfumed salts was passed around, and I took a fistful.

"A pinch will do," Sister Nimi whispered.

I aimed my fistful at the fire. It crackled, and wafted scented smoke.

Shambu Pandit chanted the Vedic hymns over the fire, and then he asked Kakaji and Sister Pom to repeat the marriage vows after him, and paused now and then to translate the Sanskrit into Punjabi, so that they would know what they were promising: to live according to the Hindu creed, to be true to each other, to share each other's burdens, to propagate the race, to beget sons, to remain rock firm and faithful. Kakaji and Sister Pom sounded odd as a duet—like a parrot and a sparrow chirping alternately in the distance, he sharp, she barely audible in the still night.

"Now they are putting their feet side by side on a stone. . . . Now they are circling the *vedi.* . . . That's one time around. . . . That's two. . . . That's . . ."

"Become thou my partner," Shambu Pandit sang out.

"Become thou my partner," Kakaji repeated after him.

"As thou hast paced all the seven steps with me."

"As thou hast paced all the seven steps with me."

"Apart from thee I cannot live."

"Apart from thee I cannot live."

"Apart from me do thou not live."

"Apart from me do thou not live."

"We shall share alike all goods and power combined."

"We shall share alike all goods and power combined."

"Over my house you shall bear full sway."

"Over my house you shall bear full sway."

Shambu Pandit said the benediction. Then all around there were the sounds of people standing up and stretching. Before I knew what was happening, Kakaji and Sister Pom had left the courtyard.

"Why is he taking her away?" I asked. "Where are they going?"

"He's telling her that he's the master and that she now belongs to him," Mamaji said, through tears.

"He's just taking her to Mehta Gulli for a few minutes," Daddyji said, "to show her off to the members of his party who were not invited to the *vedi*. She'll be back. There are still two more days of feasting."

All of Sister Pom's dowry and belongings were packed up and sent ahead to the station. With many of our close relatives, we silently escorted Sister Pom and Kakaji out of the house, out of the gate, to a borrowed motorcar waiting in the *gulli*, our footfalls like little firecrackers going off haphazardly one after another. Still silent, we showered Kakaji and Sister Pom with handfuls of flower petals, and the motorcar pulled away. Kakaji's party quickly got into other borrowed motorcars, which then formed a line behind Kakaji's. Daddyji, Mamaji, and we children followed in our motorcar. It was almost the first time since the start of the wedding that our family had been alone, and our motorcar seemed suddenly very roomy. There was no need to lean forward or to sit with our shoulders firmly against the back of the seat. Yet the motorcar felt extremely hot, as if the *vedi* fire itself were burning at our feet. I wiped streams of sweat off my face and struck out at a fly buzzing around my ear.

"All our loving relatives must be discussing the dowry and its worth in real gold," Sister Umi said, breaking the silence. "After a wedding like that for your first daughter, Daddyji, you'll never have to worry about proposals for any of us."

"What'll happen to Sister Pom now?" I asked.

"She'll go to her new home in Dehra Dun, to more receptions and feasts," Daddyji said.

"I'm giving everyone fair warning that I'm going to get married in a chapel, as Westerners do, with no crowds of loving relatives around," Sister Umi said.

I waited for Mamaji to contradict or to argue, but she said nothing.

The station was noisy and hot. Daddyji hailed a coolie, took down his badge number, and told him to take the luggage to the coupé near the end of the train. I didn't know what a coupé was, and I remember that Daddyji later took me inside and showed it to me: a small, two-berth compartment with a little fan in the ceiling and blocks of ice placed in the corners to keep it cool. The berths were covered with grainy leather and smelled of saddle soap and polish. The coolie brought in Kakaji's luggage and wanted to undo the bedrolls. There wasn't room enough, and Daddyji and I got out onto the platform. Abruptly, Daddyji's hand wasn't there to guide me. I couldn't take a step forward, for fear of the gap between the track and the train, or take a step back, for fear of the handcarts that were clattering past at great speed. Though I stood on a crowded platform, I felt alone. I remembered the frightening train that had taken me far, far away and deposited me in a strange city, in a strange school, among terrifying strangers, and remembered how, no matter how much I cried and begged, there had been no way to get back home.

The guard trilled his whistle very near my ear. Train-compartment doors slammed shut. The engine let out a deafening burst of steam. The train screeched, jolted, and began pulling out, shaking the platform with a roar.

"Goodbye! Ta-ta!" I cried, with the full force of my lungs, but I didn't hear my voice.

As if in a dream, I heard Daddyji's voice, through the clatter and thunder, the sounds of finality itself: "Kakaji, take the journey gently. . . . She's very innocent."

"Yes, Dad—" The rest of the word was lost in the forlorn, retreating clackety-clack.

Letter to Lord Irwin

Mahatma Gandhi was a leading figure in India's struggle for independence from Great Britain. In these two writings, he explains his creed of nonviolence and civil disobedience. Since independence, India has been engaged in a long and difficult period of modernization as typified by the experiences of the narrator of the poem "Rice." The narrator's family is exchanging centuries of tradition for new values and beliefs.

Satyagraha Ashram, Sabarmati
March 2, 1930

DEAR FRIEND,

Before embarking on civil disobedience and taking the risk I have dreaded to take all these years, I would fain[1] approach you and find a way out.

My personal faith is absolutely clear. I cannot intentionally hurt anything that lives, much less fellow human beings, even though they may do the greatest wrong to me and mine. Whilst, therefore, I hold the British rule to be a curse, I do not intend harm to a single Englishman or to any legitimate interest he may have in India.

I must not be misunderstood. Though I hold the British rule in India to be a curse, I do not, therefore, consider Englishmen in general to be worse than any other people on earth. I have the privilege of claiming many Englishmen as dearest friends. Indeed much that I have learnt of the evil of British rule is due to the writings of frank and courageous Englishmen who have not hesitated to tell the unpalatable[2] truth about that rule.

---

1. **fain** gladly
2. **unpalatable** unpleasant; disagreeable

And why do I regard the British rule as a curse?

It has impoverished the dumb millions by a system of progressive exploitation and by a ruinously expensive military and civil administration which the country can never afford.

It has reduced us politically to serfdom.[3] It has sapped the foundations of our culture. And, by the policy of cruel disarmament, it has degraded us spiritually. Lacking the inward strength, we have been reduced, by all but universal disarmament, to a state bordering on cowardly helplessness. . . .

Unless those who work in the name of the nation understand and keep before all concerned the motive that lies behind the craving for independence, there is every danger of independence coming to us so changed as to be of no value to those toiling voiceless millions for whom it is sought and for whom it is worth taking. It is for that reason that I have been recently telling the public what independence should really mean.

Let me put before you some of the salient points.

The terrific pressure of land revenue,[4] which furnishes a large part of the total, must undergo considerable modification in an independent India. Even the much vaunted permanent settlement benefits the few rich zamindars,[5] not the ryots.[6] The ryot has remained as helpless as ever. He is a mere tenant at will. Not only, then, has the land revenue to be considerably reduced, but the whole revenue system has to be so revised as to make the ryot's good its primary concern. But the British system seems to be designed to crush the very life out of him. Even the salt he must use to live is so taxed as to make the burden fall heaviest on him, if only because of the heartless impartiality of its incidence. The tax shows itself still more burdensome on the poor man when it is remembered that salt is the one thing he must eat more than the rich man both individually and collectively. The drink and drug revenue, too, is derived from the poor. It saps the foundations both of their health and morals. It is defended under the false plea of individual freedom, but, in reality, is maintained for its own sake. . . . If the weight of taxation has crushed the poor from above, the destruction of the central supplementary industry, i.e., handspinning, has undermined their capacity for producing wealth. The tale of India's ruination is not complete without reference to the liabilities incurred in her name. Sufficient has been recently said about these in the public Press. It must be the duty of a free India to subject all the liabilities to the strictest investigation, and repudiate those that may be adjudged by an impartial tribunal to be unjust and unfair.

---

3. **serfdom** the condition of being servants legally bound to landowners
4. **revenue** amount of income produced by a source
5. **zamindars** landowners
6. **ryots** peasants

The iniquities sampled above are maintained in order to carry on a foreign administration, demonstrably the most expensive in the world. Take your own salary. It is over Rs. 21,000 per month, besides many other indirect additions. The British Prime Minister gets £5,000 per year, i.e., over Rs. 5,400 per month at the present rate of exchange. You are getting over Rs. 700 per day against India's average income of less than annas 2 per day. The Prime Minister gets Rs. 180 per day against Great Britain's average income of nearly Rs. 2 per day. Thus you are getting much over five thousand times India's average income. The British Prime Minister is getting only ninety times Britain's average income. On bended knees I ask you to ponder over this phenomenon. I have taken a personal illustration to drive home a painful truth. I have too great a regard for you as a man to wish to hurt your feelings. I know that you do not need the salary you get. Probably the whole of your salary goes for charity. But a system that provides for such an arrangement deserves to be summarily scrapped. What is true of the Viceregal salary is true generally of the whole administration.

A radical cutting down of the revenue, therefore, depends upon an equally radical reduction in the expenses of the administration. This means a transformation of the scheme of government. This transformation is impossible without independence. Hence, in my opinion, the spontaneous demonstration of 26th January, in which hundreds of thousands of villagers instinctively participated. To them independence means deliverance from the killing weight.

Not one of the great British political parties, it seems to me, is prepared to give up the Indian spoils to which Great Britain helps herself from day to day, often, in spite of the unanimous opposition of Indian opinion.

Nevertheless, if India is to live as a nation, if the slow death by starvation of her people is to stop, some remedy must be found for immediate relief. The proposed Conference is certainly not the remedy. It is not a matter of carrying conviction by argument. The matter resolves itself into one of matching forces. Conviction or no conviction, Great Britain would defend her Indian commerce and interests by all the forces at her command. India must consequently evolve force enough to free herself from that embrace of death.

It is common cause that, however disorganized and, for the time being, insignificant it may be, the party of violence is gaining ground and making itself felt. Its end is the same as mine. But I am convinced that it cannot bring the desired relief to the dumb millions. And the conviction is growing deeper and deeper in me that nothing but unadulterated non-violence can check the organized violence of the British Government. Many think that non-violence is not an active force. My experience, limited though it undoubtedly is, shows that non-violence can be an intensely active force. It is my purpose to set in motion that force as well against the organized violent force of the British rule as [against] the unorganized violent force of the growing party of violence. To sit still would be to give rein to both the forces above mentioned. Having an unquestioning and immovable faith in the efficacy of non-violence as I know it, it would be sinful on my part to wait any longer.

This non-violence will be expressed through civil disobedience, for the moment confined to the inmates of the Satyagraha Ashram,[7] but ultimately designed to cover all those who choose to join the movement with its obvious limitations.

I know that in embarking on non-violence I shall be running what might fairly be termed a mad risk. But the victories of truth have never been won without risks, often of the gravest character. Conversion of a nation that has consciously or unconsciously preyed upon another, far more numerous, far more ancient and no less cultured than itself, is worth any amount of risk.

I have deliberately used the word "conversion." For my ambition is no less than to convert the British people through non-violence, and thus make them see the wrong they have done to India. I do not seek to harm your people. I want to serve them even as I want to serve my own. I believe that I have always served them. I served them up to 1919 blindly. But when my eyes were opened and I conceived non-cooperation, the object still was to serve them. I employed the same weapon that I have in all humility successfully used against the dearest members of my family. If I have equal love for your people with mine it will not long remain hidden. It will be acknowledged by them even as the members of my family acknowledged it after they had tried me for several years. If the people join me as I expect they will, the sufferings they will undergo, unless the British nation sooner retraces its steps, will be enough to melt the stoniest hearts.

The plan through civil disobedience will be to combat such evils as I have sampled out. If we want to sever the British connection it is because of such evils. When they are removed the path becomes easy. Then the way to friendly negotiation will be open. If the British commerce with India is purified of greed, you will have no difficulty in recognizing our independence. I respectfully invite you then to pave the way for immediate removal of those evils, and thus open a way for a real conference between equals, interested only in promoting the common good of mankind through voluntary fellowship and in arranging terms of mutual help and commerce equally suited to both. You have unnecessarily laid stress upon the communal problems that unhappily affect this land. Important though they undoubtedly are for the

---

7. **Satyagraha Ashram** one of several communities where followers practiced Gandhi's teachings

consideration of any scheme of government, they have little bearing on the greater problems which are above communities and which affect them all equally. But if you cannot see your way to deal with these evils and my letter makes no appeal to your heart, on the 11th day of this month, I shall proceed with such co-workers of the Ashram as I can take, to disregard the provisions of the salt laws. I regard this tax to be the most iniquitous[8] of all from the poor man's standpoint. As the independence movement is essentially for the poorest in the land the beginning will be made with this evil. The wonder is that we have submitted to the cruel monopoly for so long. It is, I know, open to you to frustrate my design by arresting me. I hope that there will be tens of thousands ready, in a disciplined manner, to take up the work after me, and, in the act of disobeying the Salt Act to lay themselves open to the penalties of a law that should never have disfigured the Statute-book.

I have no desire to cause you unnecessary embarrassment, or any at all, so far as I can help. If you think that there is any substance in my letter, and if you will care to discuss matters with me, and if to that end you would like me to postpone publication of this letter, I shall gladly refrain on receipt of a telegram to that effect soon after this reaches you. You will, however, do me the favour not to deflect me from my course unless you can see your way to conform to the substance of this letter.

This letter is not in any way intended as a threat but is a simple and sacred duty peremptory[9] on a civil resister. Therefore I am having it specially delivered by a young English friend who believes in the Indian cause and is a full believer in non-violence and whom Providence[10] seems to have sent to me, as it were, for the very purpose.

I remain,
Your sincere friend,
M. K. Gandhi

H. E. Lord Irwin
Viceroy's House
New Delhi-3

---

8. **iniquitous** unjust; wicked
9. **peremptory** allowing no denial or refusal
10. **Providence** God

<table>
<tr><td>Mahatma
Gandhi</td><td></td></tr>
</table>

Mahatma Gandhi | # About That Letter

MY LETTER TO THE VICEROY went on the 2nd instant as anticipated by the newspapers. Forecasts have been published of its contents which are largely untrue. I wish these correspondents and the news agencies will, instead of making the publication of news a matter merely of making money, think of the public good. If there had been anything to give to the public, surely Pandit Jawaharlal Nehru would have given it. But it was thought advisable to wait for an acknowledgment from Delhi before publishing the letter. I am not intent on a fight. I am leaving no stone unturned to avoid it. But I am ready for it the moment I find that there is no honourable way out of it. Premature publication of news indirectly obtained by means not always straight ought not to be the function of journalists. I know that the newspaper said to be the greatest in the world makes it a boast to obtain by secret methods news which no other agency can. It makes it a boast to publish news which the keepers are most anxious often in the public interest to withhold for the time being. But the English public submits to the treatment, because moneyed and influential men conduct *The Times*. We have blindly copied the rulers' code of manners without discrimination in the matter of publication of news as in many others of still greater importance. I know that mine is a voice in the wilderness, though I speak with the authority of an unbroken experience of practical journalism for over twenty years, if successful conducting of four weeklies[a] can be regarded as such. Be that as it may, the imminent fight includes among the points of attack this slavish habit of copying everything English. No one will accuse me of any anti-English tendency. Indeed I pride myself on my discrimination. I have thankfully copied many things from them. Punctuality, reticence,[1] public hygiene, independent thinking and exercise of judgment and several other things I owe to my association with them. But never having had the slightest touch of slave mentality in me and never having even a thought of materially benefiting myself through contact, official or otherwise, with them, I have had the rare good fortune of studying them with complete detachment. On the

1. **reticence** restraint; reserve

eve of battle therefore I would warn fellow journalists against copying the English method of obtaining and publishing news. Let them study my original method which was introduced long before I became a Mahatma and before I had acquired any status of importance in the public life of India. It was a hard struggle, but I found in the field of journalism as in many others that the strictest honesty and fair dealing was undoubtedly the best policy. Any shorter cut is longer at least by double the length sought to be saved. For there must be a retracing. I say all this not for the sake of reading a lesson to fellow-journalists but for the sake of the struggle in which I would value the co-operation of journalists whether they approve of or oppose my methods of political warfare. Let them not add to the risks I am already taking. The rule I would like them to observe is never to publish any news without having it checked by someone connected with me and having authority.

With this long preface I may inform the reader that the letter was sent through a special messenger to be personally delivered to the Private Secretary to His Excellency the Viceroy. The messenger selected was a young English friend Reginald Reynolds who came to India some months ago and who has identified himself completely with the Indian cause. For me the sending of the letter was a religious act as the whole struggle is. And I selected an English friend as my messenger, because I wanted to forge a further check upon myself against any intentional act that would hurt a single Englishman. If I have any sense of honour in me, this choice should prove an automatic restraint even upon unconscious error. It pleases me also to have the unselfish and unsolicited association of a cultured, well-read, devout Englishman in an act which may, in spite of all my effort to the contrary, involve loss of English life.

As for the letter itself, when the reader has the text before him he will see that it is not an ultimatum, but it is a friendly, if also a frank, communication from one who considers himself to be a friend of Englishmen. But the reader must hold himself in patience for a while.

---

a. *Indian Opinion, Young India, Navajivan* and *Hindi Navajivan*

Chemmanam Chacko | # Rice

I

I come home at the end of four years of research
in North India, having earned a doctoral degree
and generous praise for my work on making toys with husk;
bored with eating chapaties[1] day after day,
5   I'm eager to eat a meal of *athikira* rice.

It will be the planting season when I get there,
and my father—his handloom dhoti[2] stained with yellow mud,
excited about the waters of the Varanganal canal—
will greet me from the fields below our house,
10   amidst the shouts of ploughing[3] with several oxen.

The oxen will stop when they see me
walking with my suitcase, and my father,
without smiling the smile slowly forming on his lips,
will call from the field: "And when did you start from there?"

15   My little brother, carrying the tender saplings
to be planted in the field where the ploughing is done,
will run when he sees me, and call out loud
within earshot of the house: "Mother, brother's arrived!"

Walking cautiously along the dyke[4]
20   so as not to upset the baskets full of seed,
I'll reach home in good time, at last,
just as my mother drains the well-cooked rice.
O train, will you run a little faster—
let me get home quickly and eat my fill.

---

1. **chapaties** a round, flat bread
2. **dhoti** loincloth
3. **ploughing** plowing
4. **dyke** British variant of *dike*; bank of earth constructed to confine water

II

25 The bus stops on the road across from the house.
When I left this place, palm-thatched houses could be seen
in the distance on the right—but now there's nothing,
except for trees. How the place has changed!

Rubber plants, twice my height,
30 now stand in rows around me on the ridge
where *modan* and *vellaran* used to be sown,
and confuse my path as I walk home.

There's no bustle of men below,
no shouts of ploughing; and when I look,
35 the whole field is planted over with arecanut palms,
and in the corner, along the canal, stand the dealwood trees.

I enter the house. Beyond the southern wing,
my father's watching them fix up the machine
for making rubber sheets—how happy
40 and contented the look on his face!

My father says, with obvious pride:
"Son, we've stopped working on all the rice.
It was quite inconvenient. The farmer gained nothing—
only fools turn to rice-farming for gain.
45 This is better money—what good times!
The government gives rice to those who don't have paddy fields."

My little brother runs in to meet me—
I, eager to have a full meal of *athikira* rice.
He's carrying the rations for the whole household—
50 he trips over something and scatters the wheat all over the yard.

Above us, a "ship of the sky" roars northwards,
drowning my brother's loud cries—
the Chief Minister's off like an arrow to the Centre
to clamour for more grains, now flying high
55 above the cash crops, now growing tall like the trees,
since no one here promotes the farming of rice.

Can we get some husk from the Centre, too,
to make toys with it? I don't know.

Translated from Malayalam[5] by K. Ayyappa Paniker

---

5. **Malayalam** a language spoken in southwest India

**Translated by
Dwijendra Nath
Neog**

Snatched from Death

Marriage customs and the family unit occupy an important place in the Hindu religion. The princess of this story, a mortal being, dares to outwit the gods to bring her husband back to life. Hindu women worship her in a ceremony that they believe ensures they will not lose their husbands.

KING ASVAPATHI OF UJJAYINEE belonged to the Solar race of monarchs. His vast dominions, which comprised seas and islands, had no joy for him, for though he had been married for more than twenty years he and his queen had not been blessed with any children. He performed the great *Putreshti* sacrifice to the gods in hope of being blessed with a child and impatiently awaited the result. The gods seemed to listen to his prayers, for the queen conceived and in due time gave birth to a charming daughter. The King named her Savitri. As Savitri grew up, the delight of her parents, she received such education as was appropriate to her sex and rank. Soon the time came when her royal father thought of marriage for her, but he could not find an eligible youth. At last he gave her liberty to choose her own husband, and as a result she visited cities and hermitages, attended only by her maids.

On one of these trips she met a handsome youth, the son, presumably, of a hermit, and was struck with love at first sight. This was Satyaban, who in his turn was also stung by passion. But they both chose to keep their feelings to themselves. A few months later King Asvapathi, under the impression that his daughter had not yet met with anyone whom she could love, called a council of the elders of his court for consultation as to the desirability of holding a regular *svayaṁvara*, or ceremony of self-choice, to which young princes from all the states of Bharatabarsha should be invited. He felt that Savitri could not fail to find a husband worthy of her love among so many guests. These grave councillors had not been long in the council-hall before Savitri, who had guessed their purpose, came like the prudent girl she was to set them right.

"Father," said she, addressing the King, "you need not think of a *svayaṁvara*, for I am already more a married woman than a maid. Please don't be startled, my Lord. You have heard of and seen Satyaban, the son of the hermit. It is he who is the chosen companion of my life here and here-after. It is he, father, who occupies my heart fully—there is no room for another!"

Now the King and his grave councillors were in a quandary.[1] How could a princess be married to the son of a hermit? Bred in the lap of every con-ceivable luxury, she could not endure the life of an ascetic.[2] Besides, would the hermit allow his son to marry beneath his caste?

But to help them out of this difficulty, who should knock at the door just at that moment but Nārada himself, the celestial hermit, son of Brahmā, the grandsire of all the universe.

After he had been received with the customary *padya* and *arghya* (water to wash the feet and a present of honey, ghee, curd, milk, etc.) and had been conducted to a seat of deerskin with the deepest reverence such as was due to him, the question was referred to him for solution. Nārada, to whom nothing was unknown, said:

"O King, when you have heard my story you will agree that Savitri had better live single than unite herself to Satyaban. For this Satyaban is no son of a hermit: the old, blind man, his father, who wears an ascetic's garb, is none other than King Dyumatsena himself, reduced to this condition by the enemies of his house. He was met in the field, conquered, and driven from his throne and palace. Here you see him now. But what concerns you most," continued the celestial sage, "is that there is a terrible curse upon Satyaban, and he is fated to die within a year of his marriage."

Savitri shuddered involuntarily at this, but quickly regained her self-possession.

"Reverend Father," she said, addressing Nārada, "if it is to be as you say, let it be. As for me, I am at this moment a widow if you resolve I am not to marry him. I cannot marry another, for that would be a sin. One can elect a husband only once, not twice. In my heart I have given myself to him. Let me also tell you that I can bear widowhood for eternity after having Satyaban as my husband for a day."

Upon this, and after some further deliberation, it was determined that Savitri should wed the beloved of her heart.

The scene now shifts to the forest—to the hermitage of Dyumatsena, where Savitri and Satyaban, who were now wedded, lived. Savitri made an

---

1. **quandary** a state of uncertainty
2. **ascetic** one who leads an austere life, especially for religious reasons

exemplary[3] wife and an affectionate daughter-in-law, in spite of having discarded every luxury and comfort to which she had been accustomed. She was the stay of her father-in-law and mother-in-law in their old age, and made Satyaban so happy that he did not feel the loss of a prospective throne. He, it may be mentioned, did not know that a heavy curse was hanging over him, and Savitri did not wish to make her husband unhappy with the foretaste of death.

Month after month passed quickly away; and at last the time came when it lacked only a day to the date on which his doom had been foretold.

Savitri had passed the whole day in worshipping the gods as, indeed, she had done all through the year, praying to them to avert the terrible decree. When she retired to bed at night, she begged Satyaban to take her with him on the following morning on his daily excursion into the woods for fruits, roots, and sacred fuel. He wondered at her unusual request, but consented to comply with her wish.

On the following morning, the loving couple went together into the depths of the forest. Savitri followed her husband like a shadow, and when he climbed up a tree to pluck fruits, she stood beneath with her eyes fixed on him, for there was no way of knowing at what particular moment the curse, like the sword of Damocles, might fall on her dear husband's head.

Satyaban was not many minutes aloft, when he felt a severe headache. Coming hastily down and unable to support himself, he fell prone on the ground at his wife's feet. Although the shock to Savitri was a great one, it was not one for which she was altogether unprepared. "Savitri, my darling," Satyaban gasped, "I am dying. O what a pain there is in my head! Let it rest on your knees—Savitri, my darling!" The next minute all was over.

Savitri wept not. With the remains of her lord in her arms she sat there, a statue of grief, watching what might follow. It was in a happy age when wonderful things were wont[4] to happen. No sooner had Satyaban breathed his last than the messengers of Yama, the King of the dead, came down to take their victim to his place in the other world. But the chastity that hedged in the person of Savitri was like a burning flame, and those grim messengers did not dare approach her for fear of being consumed by it. They returned to their master saying, "Lord, we cannot." Yama was astonished, but he resolved to see for himself what it all meant. So, armed with his club, robed in scarlet, and mounted on his favorite buffalo, the dread deity set off to where Savitri held her dead husband in her embrace. Yama himself felt her influence and he, too, was struck with awe. He did not, however, shrink

---

3. **exemplary** worthy of imitation
4. **wont** likely

from his duty, but gently approaching the damsel, "Daughter Savitri," said he in his softest voice, "I am here to take your husband away: he is mine now. You, I suppose, know who I am."

"I know you by your words," she replied gently but firmly, "you are Yama. My husband may now be your property, and so will I be too: you can take him, but not without me."

"How can that be?" cried the dread visitor. "Such is not my mission. You must part with your husband, girl. The living cannot accompany the dead."

"You cannot persuade me of that," returned Savitri, holding the corpse tighter in her embrace.

Yama was struck by the devotion of the young wife, and anxious to do what he could for her, said, "Savitri, you may keep your husband's body, and as I am exceedingly pleased with you, I wish to give you anything you may wish for except one thing, that is the life of your husband."

"If you are pleased, great Lord of the Dead, and will grant me a boon,[5] kindly let my father who has no son have one who will live to hand down his name to posterity."

"It shall be so," said the other, "but go home now, for it is not well to stay here alone."

So saying, he turned his back upon her and, taking with him the soul of Satyaban, proceeded on his journey. A few minutes after, he looked back, thinking of the poor faithful wife. Lo! she was at his heels. "Where are you going?" cried he in surprise. "What good is there in following me, child? Go home!"

"Go home?" replied Savitri quietly. "Whither[6] my lord goes I go. I have no home but where he is. O King of the Dead, you know a true wife follows her husband through life and death. A god though you are, you cannot stop me."

And Yama, who was greatly affected, said, "Savitri, ask for still another boon excepting, of course, the life of your husband, and you shall have it."

Savitri replied, "If you are pleased, dread god, let my father-in-law, King Dyumatsena, recover his lost kingdom and his sight."

"He shall," answered Yama, "and now go your way home, and let me go mine."

He held on and lessened not his pace, until out of curiosity, he turned his head once again to see if Savitri was out of sight.

Savitri was still close behind him!

"Savitri, why are you following me?" exclaimed Yama, unable to suppress his surprise.

---

5. **boon** something beneficial; a blessing
6. **whither** to what place

"I cannot choose but do so," was her calm reply. "You have in your possession all that I hold dear in heaven and on earth: and besides, you are so good and kind. Why should I stay behind?"

"My girl," said Yama, his heart melting with pity, "I would give you your husband back, if I could: but ask for a third boon, and if it is not the life of Satyaban, it shall be given to you."

Whereupon said Savitri with folded hands, "Great God, as you have so far granted every request of your poor supplicant, grant that I may have a hundred sons by Satyaban, each born after an interval of a hundred years!"

"It shall be so," said Yama thoughtlessly, bent only upon pleasing his fair petitioner and inducing her to leave him alone.

Then Savitri stood right across Yama's path and smilingly said, "Let me have my husband!"

"How now?" cried Yama. "You are unreasonable, child!"

"Unreasonable? Indeed I am not," answered Savitri gaily. "Consider the boon you have just granted me and say if it can be accomplished without your returning me my Satyaban."

Yama perceived the truth of what she said, and was conquered, as he had never been before; and that too by a girl! But she was strong by virtue of her undying love, her pious and self-sacrificing devotion. Yama yielded his charge not unwillingly, in that it gave the world an example to follow. Savitri returned home with her husband, rejoicing.

Her father-in-law was now no longer a hermit and her husband a hermit's son. The old man regained his sight and with it his kingdom. But the cares of a kingdom are a sore weight to one in the shady vale of life and who has, moreover, tasted the calm of a hermit's life. It was not long before he resigned his crown in favor of his son Satyaban, who mounted the throne of his fathers with Savitri, a queen who was to be forever glorious because of her undying love and chastity.

So, all you that have listened to this sacred *kathā*, cry, "Victory to Savitri," and may you all be even as she was!

Sheila Tefft

In India, Marriages Made by Computer

For some modern-day Hindu families, the network of relatives, friends, and matchmakers who helped find suitable spouses for their children has been replaced by classified advertisements and computer services, according to this newspaper article.

IN A CENTRAL DELHI OFFICE BUILDING, a stream of names and code numbers blip across the computer screen. Suddenly, blue lights flash and a loud *Beeeeeep!* breaks the machine's steady hum. Life Partners Computer, one of India's new high-tech marriage brokers, has found another match.

For generations, Indians have married under the watchful eyes of their parents and families. Marriages often are arranged through a network of relatives, friends, and acquaintances. In towns and villages, the go-between may be the local busybody or the barber.

However, in major cities, newspaper ads and, most recently, computer services have become key cogs[1] in the matchmaking process. Every Sunday, newspapers run pages of ads searching for the perfect bride or groom. At publications like the Hindustan Times—one of the largest English-language newspapers—families placing a matrimonial ad may try computerized matchmaking for no extra charge.

"The traditional ways of finding a match are becoming increasingly difficult because the joint family is breaking up," says O. P. Sharma, advertising

---

1. **cogs** subordinate, but vital, parts

manager of the Hindustan Times, which operates the Life Partners Computer service. "The traditional is giving way to the scientific."

Computerized matchmaking is the rage among India's emerging, status-conscious middle class. The Hindustan Times—which pioneered the concept of matrimony-through-advertising 60 years ago—runs up to 1,200 of the ads every Sunday.

Many would-be partners also opt for the free computer service which the newspaper launched as a promotion four years ago. Fifty to sixty computer forms are submitted daily. Almost 100 tidbits about the person and his or her preferences are punched into a computer. Although caste and religion remain key factors in marriage for many Indians, job and living standards are of increasing importance.

Each prospect gets a printout of possible matches to pursue. Flexible Indians get as many as 40 candidates. The too-picky may get none.

"There are not many cases where marriage by newspaper or computer has failed," the ad executive insists, although he has no survey to support the claim.

Playing matchmaker can be dangerous, however. When the Life Partners Computer matched up a brother and sister, Mr. Sharma had the angry and offended father raging in his office. Woman's rights activists have also protested some ads, saying that they are degrading.

Sharma says he is careful that the computer not be used for dating, which is considered risqué[2] by Indian standards. "We are very vigilant. This is not a dating service," he says.

---

2. **risqué** almost improper

Samuel Taylor
Coleridge

Work Without Hope

Lines composed 21st February 1825

The title Nectar in a Sieve *is an allusion to the final lines of
this poem by Samuel Taylor Coleridge. Although Coleridge
was one of the most influential poets and literary critics of
his day, he was highly critical of his own work and often
suffered from bouts of depression.*

All Nature seems at work. Slugs leave their lair—
The bees are stirring—birds are on the wing—
And Winter slumbering in the open air,
Wears on his smiling face a dream of Spring!
5   And I the while, the sole unbusy thing,
Nor honey make, nor pair, nor build, nor sing.

Yet well I ken¹ the banks where amaranths² blow,
Have traced the fount whence streams of nectar³ flow.
Bloom, O ye amaranths! bloom for whom ye may,
10   For me ye bloom not! Glide, rich streams, away!
With lips unbrightened, wreathless brow, I stroll:
And would you learn the spells that drowse my soul?
Work without Hope draws nectar in a sieve,
And Hope without an object cannot live.

1. **ken** know about; see
2. **amaranths** flowers that never fade
3. **nectar** drink of the gods that made immortal all who drank it

Santha Rama Rau

from
A Passage to India

Since its publication in 1924, E. M. Forster's novel,
A Passage to India, *has become synonymous with the*
cultural and social divide between colonial officials and
native peoples. The first act of this play, based on the novel,
shows the tensions and misunderstandings between East
and West as the characters try not to offend members of the
other race but, at the same time, are quick to take offense.

CHARACTERS
in order of appearance

DR. AZIZ, Assistant Civil Surgeon in the Government Hospital at Chandrapore

MR. FIELDING, Principal of the Government College at Chandrapore

MRS. MOORE, an elderly lady visiting her son in Chandrapore

MISS ADELA QUESTED, informally engaged to Mrs. Moore's son and travelling with her

PROFESSOR GODBOLE, Mr. Fielding's assistant at the Government College

RONNY HEASLOP, District Magistrate of Chandrapore, son of Mrs. Moore

The action of the play takes place in the small provincial town of Chandrapore, in Eastern India, near Bengal. The time is April of a year in the early [1920s. The play opens in the living room of] Mr. Fielding's house in the grounds of the Government College at Chandrapore, early in April at about 4 o'clock in the afternoon.

AZIZ (*shouting cheerfully from the entrance*): Mr Fielding! Mr. Fielding! Mr. Fielding? (*sees his shadow on the glass door*) I have simply walked in unannounced. Will you forgive this informality?

FIELDING (*from the bedroom*): Of course, of course! Please make yourself at home.

AZIZ (*takes this literally*): May I really, Mr. Fielding? It's very good of you; I like unconventional behaviour so extremely.

FIELDING: I'm delighted.

AZIZ: The fact is I have been wanting to meet you for a long time. But where is one to meet in a wretched hole like Chandrapore. (*with a touch of irony*) Where will the poor Indian doctor run across the Exalted European Principal of the Government College?

FIELDING: My dear fellow.

AZIZ (*walks to the bedroom door*): When you first came here—I'll tell you what I used to wish. I used to wish that you would fall ill so that we could meet that way.

[FIELDING *laughs.* AZIZ *joins in the laughter. He begins to improvise.*]

I said to myself, "How does Mr. Fielding look this morning? Perhaps pale? And the Civil Surgeon is pale too. Malaria, without a doubt. He will not be able to attend on Mr. Fielding when the shivering commences. They will have to send for me instead."

FIELDING: You know me by sight then?

AZIZ: Of course, of course. Not only that, but I have heard your lectures. You're a celebrated student of Persian poetry. You know me?

FIELDING: I know you very well by name.

AZIZ: I say, Mr. Fielding.

FIELDING: Yes?

AZIZ: Guess what I look like before you come out. That will be a kind of game.

FIELDING: You're five feet nine inches tall—

AZIZ: Jolly good!

FIELDING: Well, it should be. I can see that much through the door.

AZIZ: Well, what else? Have I not a venerable white beard?

FIELDING: Oh blast!

AZIZ: Anything is wrong?

FIELDING: I've just trodden on my last back collar stud.

AZIZ: Take mine, take mine.

FIELDING: Have you a spare one?

AZIZ: Yes, yes, one minute.

FIELDING: Not if you're wearing it yourself.

AZIZ: No, no, one in my pocket.

[*He steps away from the door so that* FIELDING *cannot see his outline, wrenches off his collar and pulls out the back stud, a gold one.*]

Here it is!

FIELDING (*after a pause*): But nobody carries a spare collar stud in his pocket.

AZIZ: I, always! In case of emergency.

FIELDING: Nonsense.

[AZIZ *stares at the stud in his hand, dismayed. He puts it in his pocket, touchily.*]

AZIZ: Indians are famous for talking nonsense, doubtless you know that.

FIELDING: All I meant is that I don't want to deprive you . . .

AZIZ (*sarcastically*): No depriving, rest assured. It should be the highest of honours for me.

FIELDING (*matching his sarcasm, clearly irritated*): Look, Dr. Aziz, keep your stud. I can easily send for a new one.

AZIZ: By all means! Yes, yes, by all means! Send your servant to the bazaar—get your new collar stud—an unsoiled collar stud—that is what Indians are for, isn't it?

FIELDING: What are you talking about?

AZIZ (*even more excited*): Only an Englishman is friend enough to do a favour. I am wrong to offer. I see that.

FIELDING (*after a long pause*): Dr. Aziz, please forgive me. Just a moment. It seems absurd to quarrel with a man one hasn't even seen. I am delighted and grateful to wear your collar stud.

AZIZ (*responding at once*): Of course, of course! No trouble!

[FIELDING *is seen tying the sash of a dressing-gown. He is wearing the trousers of his suit under the dressing-gown, socks and slippers. He is a large, shaggy man, untidy, greying, loose and easy in his movements. He smiles, shakes hands with AZIZ, takes the stud.*]

> FIELDING: Many thanks. I'm ashamed of my boorishness.
>
> AZIZ (*graciously*): Such a small thing . . .
>
> FIELDING: The fact is that my nerves are frayed. I've had a beastly day with Government inspection committees. (*he shakes his head*) Oh, God! Do sit down while I finish dressing—if you will forgive the unconventionality.

[*He continues his dressing slowly through the next few minutes.*]

> AZIZ (*looking around the bedroom inquisitively*): Very gladly. It makes me feel that we have been friends for a long time.
>
> FIELDING: Well, that may be. I've been hauled over the coals all day about it. I'm not very popular with the higher-ups just now. They do not like unconventionality. "The British and the Indians must each keep their place," they tell me—like teams in some tiresome sort of game.
>
> AZIZ: Don't Englishmen like sports?
>
> FIELDING (*laughing*): I can't be bothered with that sort when I'm trying to get my work done. However, I'm sure you didn't come here to listen to my troubles. Do sit down.
>
> AZIZ (*enthralled with the room*): But I always thought Englishmen kept their rooms so tidy. It seems this is not so. I need not be so ashamed.

[*He sits down gaily on the sofa, and forgetting himself entirely, draws his legs up under him.*]

> Everything ranged coldly on shelves was what I thought. Shall I tell you something, Mr. Fielding? This is the first time I have ever been invited to an Englishman's house. Sometimes I have been summoned in case of sickness when my superior Major Callendar is away. But for a jolly social occasion like this—informal, as equals—never. No, no, never, never.
>
> FIELDING (*looking at him intensely*): Really? How—how astonishing.

AZIZ: Yes, really. But not astonishing. For I am not a bootlicker. I am not one of those.

FIELDING: I don't mean that. I mean that there seem to be no bounds to our stupidity in India. Why must we add social insult to political injury, I wonder?

AZIZ: Very good! Very good, Mr. Fielding. Social insult to political injury. I shall remember that to tell my friends.

FIELDING: It can't be a new idea to them, surely.

AZIZ: The idea, no. But to hear it from an Englishman, yes. Let me assure you, oh yes. We talk such things among ourselves, my friends, and I—

FIELDING: However, if it's all the same to you, I'd appreciate it if you didn't mention that remark to them. It was just—just a casual observation.

AZIZ: And a true one. If you so wish, I shall not mention. But— forgive the following question, Mr. Fielding—may I ask why?

FIELDING: Oh, no particular reason. It's just that there's really no point in making trouble. I'm in enough hot water as it is.

AZIZ (*touchy again*): You are worried about the indiscretion of my friends?

FIELDING (*uncomfortably*): No, no, of course not. (*meaning, "Yes, perhaps."*)

AZIZ: Indians, too, understand discretion. That is not reserved only for the British.

FIELDING: Come, come, Aziz, I wasn't insulting your friends.

AZIZ: That is good, for they are very big-hearted chaps. You know old Hamidullah, the lawyer? Or Mahmoud Ali—ah, there's a philosopher!—or the Nawab Bahadur? Perhaps you have never heard of them?

FIELDING: I've heard of them. I suppose none of you ever go to the Bridge parties?

AZIZ: As Muslims, Mr. Fielding, we do not play cards.

FIELDING: I'm sorry—it's not that kind of bridge. The Bridge is one of Turton's depressing little jokes—he means a party to bridge the gulf between East and West.

AZIZ: Ah, I see. A Bridge party. Very witty.

[FIELDING *nods*.]

No, we never go to those. My friends say to me, "What can we expect from these English? Scorn, no understanding of our customs and our civilization—social insults, you see—Better leave them alone."

FIELDING: They may very well be right, you know.

AZIZ: No, Mr. Fielding. Excuse me, I must disagree. You see, I think friendship is possible—not only possible but important. Yes, yes, I know what you will tell me—my friends tell me the same—oil and water, we do not mix. We have our political differences. You do not like our food and our customs and we try to like yours, but— (*he shrugs*) In any event, you think us backward, we find you uncouth. What to do? I say there must be friendship. Nothing will shake me in that idea. Nothing, Mr. Fielding! Nothing! I say that the friendship between two individuals is bigger than all those other things. You agree?

FIELDING: Well, I never heard of any friendships that began at those Bridge parties.

AZIZ: My friends are wise when they advise me not to go—though imagine, I might have met *you* there, Mr. Fielding. Also I am curious about the English Club where we may not enter.

FIELDING (*laughing*): You would find it excessively boring—billiards, tennis, shop talk in the smoking-room, drinks in the bar where Englishmen don't mind having a few too many since there are no Indians to observe them. It's quite deadly really.

AZIZ: Then why do you go?

FIELDING: Oh, I don't know. If I didn't I suppose people would think me peculiar, and I have found that it is simpler not to make enemies—they take up too much time.

AZIZ: Or friends either? They, too, take up time? You bring tears to my eyes, Mr. Fielding! Such a lonely life as you describe! Shall I tell you something else? This is a Persian poem that I shall have inscribed on my tomb when I die! Please listen.

"Alas without me for thousands of years
The Rose will bloom and the Spring will bloom
But those who have secretly understood my heart—
They will approach and visit the grave where I lie."

Is that not beautiful? Is it not profound philosophy? That, you see,
is what I want . . . the secret understanding of the heart!

FIELDING (*smiling*): I am not so ambitious. I only want to teach—
particularly here—I can't complicate my life with things that
would interfere with that.

AZIZ: If I were so good as you in my profession—

FIELDING: You flatter me.

AZIZ: No flattery! I assure you! I have heard your lectures.

FIELDING: Why the hell do we wear collars?

[AZIZ *works on the stud.*]

AZIZ: We wear them to pass the police.

FIELDING (*ready to laugh*): What?

AZIZ: If I'm biking in English dress . . . (*pantomiming*) starch collar,
hat with ditch—they take no notice. When I wear a fez, they cry,
"Your lamp's out." Let me put that in, Mr. Fielding. Lord Curzon
did not consider this when he asked natives of India to retain their
picturesque costumes—Hooray! Stud's gone in.—Sometimes I
shut my eyes and dream I have splendid clothes again and I'm
riding into battle behind Alamgir.[1] The Moghul Empire at its
height and Alamgir reigning at Delhi upon the Peacock Throne.
Mr. Fielding, don't you think India must have been beautiful then?

FIELDING: I do indeed. Well, you will have an opportunity to describe
it all to the two ladies who are coming to tea to meet you—I think
you know them.

AZIZ: Meet me? I know no ladies.

FIELDING: Really? Not Mrs. Moore and Miss Quested?

AZIZ: Oh yes—I remember. Mrs. Moore. An excessively aged lady.
But will you please repeat the name of her companion?

FIELDING: Miss Quested. You can tell her about the Peacock Throne
if you like. She's a Kensington intellectual. (*very gently mocking*)
She tells me she wants to know the *real* India.

---

1. **Alamgir** last of the great Moghul (Mongol) emperors of India, reigned from 1658 to 1707

AZIZ: I see.

FIELDING: She was saying the other night at the Club that she was tired of seeing picturesque Indians pass before her as a frieze,[2] that now she wanted to meet some of them.

AZIZ (*disappointed*): So this is to be a Bridge party after all.

FIELDING (*quickly*): Oh no—please forgive me. I have made Miss Quested sound a prig[3]—which is not at all what I intended. I thought it very sensible of her to want to meet Indians. If she's really going to make her life in this country.

AZIZ: Ah, now I see.

[*Significantly, for he has taken* FIELDING's *remark to mean that* MISS QUESTED *will make her life with* FIELDING *himself.*]

She is to settle here in Chandrapore altogether?

FIELDING: Well, one doesn't know yet for sure. She may be getting married here.

AZIZ (*sincerely*): I am honoured that you tell me this on such short acquaintance. I mean this most sincerely. And without doubt I will attempt to entertain her in my poor way.

FIELDING (*he hasn't caught* AZIZ's *assumption*): Well, that's very good of you. But actually, she's not the reason why I invited you this afternoon. Mrs. Moore, who has chaperoned her on this trip to India, told me that she knew you and very much wanted to see you again. She asked me particularly to invite you. So naturally, I agreed.

AZIZ (*offended that it hasn't been* FIELDING's *own idea*): Naturally. The ladies must have their wish. Though I cannot imagine why Mrs. Moore should have asked since I don't really consider that I know her. I only met her accidentally in my mosque. I had gone there one night, alone, for a moment of rest and meditation. She moved in the darkness and I thought she was a ghost. I daresay I frightened her, too, for when I saw in the moonlight that it was a European woman I shouted out "Madam, madam, madam! This is a holy place for Muslims. You must take your shoes off."

FIELDING: And did she?

---

2. **frieze** decorative part of a wall
3. **prig** smugly proper person

AZIZ (*his good humour restored by the recollection*): She couldn't. She had already taken them off and left them in the entrance in the correct way. It is remarkable, is it not, that she should have taken the trouble? So few European ladies would, especially if thinking no one is there to see.

FIELDING: Did you tell her that?

AZIZ: Oh yes. And she replied in poetry. She said, "That makes no difference. God is here." Poetry, you see. Afterwards we talked about her children and mine.

FIELDING: So you are friends after all.

AZIZ: Oh yes. I know Mrs. Moore well. She is a great friend of mine, and besides, she is an oriental.

FIELDING: How do you mean?

AZIZ: She told me she didn't understand people very well, but she knew how to like or dislike them.

FIELDING: So that's oriental. I wonder if my assistant, Godbole, would agree with that definition. He's supposed to be coming to tea today, too. We must ask him this afternoon. If he shows up, that is.

AZIZ: Why should he not show up? All Indians are not so unreliable. And for the honour of taking tea with the Principal?

FIELDING: I don't know how much of an honour it is. When I have asked him he has always found some excuse on previous occasions.

AZIZ: Ah, the good professor is no doubt too much in awe of you, Mr. Fielding.

FIELDING: More likely, he finds my food unclean and is too polite to say so. He is orthodox, you know.

AZIZ: Oh yes. Such Brahmins are very strict. All are immensely subtle. Hindu philosophy is too much for me. We poor Muslims, we rely on our heart, not so much on our intellect. The feelings of our heart will lead us to God, do you not agree?

FIELDING: Well, we are taught that God is love, but I have never—

AZIZ: You see? You see? We are brothers after all, Mr. Fielding.

FIELDING (*laughing*): My dear chap! I can't keep up with you—you make my head swim!

AZIZ (*laughing with him*): That is very good—it is the first step. Taking to another element, we will swim together and so become friends!

[*A servant enters from Stage Left and stands in the archway. Immediately behind him are* MRS. MOORE, *an elderly grey-haired woman with a rather absent manner, and* MISS QUESTED, *a thin blondish young woman in her late twenties. She has a vigorous, enquiring way about her, verging sometimes on nervousness. She is certainly intelligent and cultivated and to Western eyes not unattractive. To Indians she would seem pitifully ugly—the freckles, the colourless hair, . . . the lack of grace and feminine modesty. A beautiful woman might have troubled* AZIZ, *but because* MRS. MOORE *seemed to him so old and* MISS QUESTED *so plain, his manner to both remains easy and straightforward.*]

> FIELDING (*walking across the room to escort the women from the door*): Good afternoon, good afternoon. You had no trouble finding the way?

> QUESTED: None at all. Mr. Heaslop sent us in his carriage. He'll be coming later to take us back.

> AZIZ (*buoyantly from across the room*): Oh what a pleasure to see Mr. Heaslop later on. If he comes to fetch you, indeed you are in good hands.

[MISS QUESTED *looks at him rather startled by his tone, for he is talking about her fiancé.* FIELDING *quickly begins introductions.*]

> FIELDING: Mrs. Moore, I believe that you and Dr. Aziz have already met.

> MOORE: Yes indeed. How nice to see you again!

[AZIZ *walks to the group by the archway to shake hands.*]

> FIELDING: Miss Quested, Dr. Aziz.

[MISS QUESTED *smiles in recognition of the name*—MRS. MOORE *has mentioned the incident in the mosque. She moves with* AZIZ *to the sofa while* MRS. MOORE *finds a straight-back chair and* FIELDING *mutters instructions to the servant about tea.*]

> QUESTED: Dr. Aziz, I am especially pleased to meet you. I feel that perhaps you can help me to *understand* India.

> AZIZ: Who understands India? Not the Indians, at least.

> FIELDING: Now won't you all sit down?

> QUESTED: I heard from Mrs. Moore how kind you were to her in the mosque, and how interesting. She learned more about India in those few minutes' talk with you than in the three weeks since we landed.

AZIZ: Oh please do not mention a little thing like that. Is there anything else I may tell you about my country?

QUESTED: A disappointment we had this morning; I wonder if you could explain, of course it may be some form of Indian etiquette.

AZIZ: There is no question of etiquette. We are by nature a most informal people.

[*An astonished silence from the others greets this remark.* AZIZ *is unaware of it.* FIELDING *starts to say something but is gently interrupted.*]

MOORE: I was afraid we had blundered and given offence.

AZIZ: That is even more impossible. But may I know the facts?

QUESTED: An Indian lady and gentleman had invited us to call on them and were to send their carriage for us this morning at nine. It has never come. We waited and waited and waited.

FIELDING (*trying to smooth the matter over*): Some misunderstanding, I'm sure.

QUESTED: Oh no, it wasn't that. They even put off going to Calcutta to entertain us.

FIELDING: I wouldn't worry about it, anyway.

QUESTED (*a little heatedly*): That's exactly what everyone tells me. But if one doesn't worry, how is one ever going to *understand*?

AZIZ: I think they were ashamed of their house and that is why they did not send.

FIELDING: That's very possible.

QUESTED: I do so hate mysteries.

FIELDING: Very English of you.

QUESTED: I dislike them not because I'm English, but—from a personal point of view.

MOORE (*interrupting vaguely*): I like mysteries, but I rather dislike muddles.

FIELDING: A mystery is a muddle.

MOORE (*unemphatically*): Oh, do you think so, Mr. Fielding?

FIELDING: Well, a mystery is a high-sounding word for a muddle. Aziz and I know that India's a muddle.

MOORE: India—Oh what an alarming idea!

AZIZ (*who has been listening to this exchange in some bewilderment, moving his head from side to side as if he were at a tennis match*): There'll be no muddle when you come to visit me in my house. Mrs. Moore and everyone—I invite you all—oh please.

MOORE: That is most kind of you, Dr. Aziz. I shall be delighted.

QUESTED: I too! (*she produces a small book from her purse*) May I write down the address?

AZIZ (*horrified—they have taken a moment of politeness seriously*): How sad that my bungalow is terrible! It is near the bazaar. There is no room at all, and even that is infested with small black flies. Oh, but we will talk of something else now. See this beautiful room! See those curves at the bottom of the arches. What delicacy! It is the architecture of Question and Answer. Mrs. Moore, you are in *India*; I am not joking. Imagine—now, imagine I am some high official of the eighteenth century. This is my audience hall. I am doing justice here. A poor widow who has been robbed comes to me and I give her fifty rupees. To another, with some different complaint, I give a hundred—I should like that.

MOORE (*smiling*): Rupees don't last forever. But I agree, the modern method does seem to lack imagination—or humanity. But rupees don't last forever.

AZIZ: My rupees would last. God would give me more when He saw that I gave.

QUESTED: I had thought that our penal code was one of our more successful achievements in India. Mr. Heaslop has explained to me that there was no comprehensive system of justice for all of India before the British rule.

AZIZ: Justice? Oh, Miss Quested, you speak of something else. Yes, yes, I agree the British official can administer the law, but it takes a Prince to give the people justice. Oh, indeed yes, (*for he sees a doubtful look on* MISS QUESTED's *face*) because justice is giving, always giving, always kindness and more giving. I think we would never punish anyone.

[FIELDING *is busy serving tea.* MRS. MOORE *smiles and nods her agreement and pleasure in* AZIZ. MISS QUESTED *listens intently, trying hard to understand this foreign point of view.*]

MOORE: How different from my son's conception of being a magistrate!

QUESTED: But, Dr. Aziz—is there a satisfactory alternative to the punishment of criminals? You see, in England I served on a committee for the improvement of prison conditions and of course—

AZIZ (*interrupting buoyantly*): Poor criminal! Give him another chance! It only makes a man worse to go to prison and be corrupted. We punish no one, no one in my palace and in the evening we will give a great banquet with a nautch[4] and lovely girls shall shine on every side of the tank with fireworks in their hands, and all shall be feasting and happiness until the next day, when there shall be justice as before . . . fifty rupees, a hundred, a thousand . . . till peace comes. Ah, why didn't we live in that time? . . .

MOORE (*laughing*): But India is still beautiful, think of our mosque.

AZIZ: Mrs. Moore, do you remember our mosque?

MOORE: Of course.

AZIZ: Do you remember how we saw the moon caught in the tank of water? Trembling and bigger than the real moon? Do you remember?

MOORE: I will never forget it.

AZIZ: Do you know that the water comes down from our mosque and fills the garden in Mr. Fielding's house? A skillful arrangement of our Emperors. They loved water. Wherever they went they created fountains, gardens, hammams—

QUESTED (*producing her little notebook in which she writes down the foreign words as she comes across them*): What was that? Hammams? How do you spell that, please?

AZIZ: A hammam is a bath . . . but oh, Miss Quested, it is a beautiful luxurious bath. Imagine yourself a princess, Miss Quested, your black hair flowing down to your waist, polished and shining like the wing of a bird, face is round like the moon . . . You are surrounded by your handmaidens who rub your skin with sandalwood oil, and perfume the water of the hammam with musk, and then scatter over it rose petals for beauty. Somewhere in the garden a bul-bul[5] is singing. Oh, there is no sweeter sound than the bul-bul. You step out of your veils and into the water, and—

---

4. **nautch** entertainment by professional dancers
5. **bul-bul** songbird

[FIELDING *clears his throat noisily, half-smiling at the weird contrast between the straight-backed, unvoluptuous figure of* MISS QUESTED *and* AZIZ's *description.*]

FIELDING: Aziz, give Mrs. Moore another cup of tea, please.

AZIZ: A pleasure, a pleasure. (*he fills her cup*) And Miss Quested too.

QUESTED: Oh yes, please.

AZIZ (*he takes the pot over to her and as he pours says*): Pretend that this is sherbet you are drinking . . . the drink of those beautiful, voluptuous princesses . . .

[MISS QUESTED, *uncomfortable and alarmed by* AZIZ's *extravagance, looks up at him as he speaks, bending over her. Her hand trembles and the tea spills over her dress and the sofa. She jumps up, the cup shatters.*]

QUESTED: Oh, I am sorry . . . look what I've done . . . oh dear . . .

FIELDING: It doesn't matter a bit. (*shouts*) Ranjit!

[*The servant appears to clean up the mess.*]

QUESTED: Oh, I *am* so sorry . . . I don't know what got into me . . .

AZIZ: Miss Quested, shall I tell you what we say? We say that to spill food or drink is the sign of a generous heart, full to overflowing, you see.

[FIELDING *looks at him gratefully and makes an indication of a Muslim salaam.*[6] AZIZ *returns it, smiling.*]

QUESTED (*more at ease now*): That makes me feel better. (*to* FIELDING) Oh, I hope I haven't ruined your sofa. I am not usually so clumsy.

FIELDING: As Aziz says, not clumsiness, only generosity of spirit.

[*He is laughing.*]

QUESTED (*laughing too*): Well, at least I have learned this afternoon how to make a virtue out of an ineptitude.[7]

[GODBOLE *enters. He is middle-aged, erect, dressed in Indian clothes, a large red and yellow caste mark on his forehead. He is polite, enigmatic.*[8] *He does not shake hands, but brings the palms together in a namaskar . . . the Indian greeting.*]

---

6. **salaam** ceremonial greeting
7. **ineptitude** incompetence
8. **enigmatic** mysterious

FIELDING: Ah Godbole, I've got you here at last. You already know Aziz. Here are two new visitors to Chandrapore. Mrs. Moore, Miss Quested. My elusive assistant, Professor Godbole.

[MRS. MOORE *nods to* GODBOLE. MISS QUESTED *rather awkwardly copies* GODBOLE'S *namaskar.*]

Mrs. Moore, as I expect you know, is the mother of our City Magistrate.

AZIZ: Of Mr. Heaslop? Mrs. Moore, how can that be?

MOORE: My first husband, Ronny's father, died.

AZIZ: And Moore? Who is Moore?

MOORE: I married again. It is not considered extraordinary in England.

AZIZ: I see. I see. Well, then, Mrs. Moore we are in the same box. My wife is dead also. Now we have only our children. My children are the greatest joy to me. Yours too, Mrs. Moore?

MOORE: A joy and an anxiety.

AZIZ (*rather naughtily*): Alas for poor Mr. Fielding, he has no children! Neither the joys nor the anxieties! Does that not give you the cause for concern, Mr. Fielding?

FIELDING: Not in the least.

AZIZ: This indifference is what the Oriental will never understand. Just think—your name will die out entirely—

FIELDING: I suppose so (*laughing*)—*unless*, of course, I do get married after all.

AZIZ (*delightedly*): It is still possible! I know, I know! And allow me to wish you much happiness in advance.

GODBOLE: And I will send you up some few healthy sweets on that occasion. I will give myself that pleasure.

AZIZ: I tell you what, Mr. Fielding, we will make your visit to me a celebration . . . a celebration in advance . . . that is the best kind!

FIELDING: Nothing elaborate when we come to visit you. (*to the ladies*) Isn't that so?

QUESTED: Oh, of course. Please don't disarrange your household.

AZIZ: Not in my house—it is too dreadful!

GODBOLE: The house is but a shell. Inside, the living creature.

AZIZ: But Professor, this creature would be dead of shame. I know what! I invite you all to visit me in the Marabar Caves. When I return to Chandrapore, that is.

MOORE: You are going away, Dr. Aziz?

AZIZ: A brief visit, no more, to a relative in Calcutta. (*laughing*) He has so many daughters he needs some masculine conversation!

QUESTED: Well, when you get back, then?

AZIZ: Indeed! Please do not forget . . . we picnic in the Marabar Caves.

FIELDING: Excellent.

AZIZ: Godbole, will you join us?

GODBOLE: Oh, that is a most magnificent entertainment! But have not the ladies already visited our caves?

QUESTED: No, I've not even heard of them.

AZIZ: Not *heard* of them? The Marabar Caves in the Marabar Hills? Why they are one of the greatest wonders of the world!

QUESTED: I'm sure that someone like you, Dr. Aziz, who has seen them so often will find me foolish . . . but tell me what I should look for when I get there.

AZIZ: Unfortunately, I have never visited the caves myself. Work or private business has prevented me, and besides they are very far away.

FIELDING (*laughing*): My dear Aziz!

QUESTED: Professor Godbole, have you seen the Caves? (*he nods*) Let me ask, are they large caves?

GODBOLE: No, not large.

MOORE: Do describe them, Professor Godbole.

GODBOLE: It will be a great honour. (*longish pause*) There is an entrance in the rock . . . Which you enter . . . And through the entrance is the cave.

FIELDING: Something like the caves at Elephanta?

GODBOLE: Oh no, not at all. At Elephanta there are sculptures of Siva and Parvati. There are no sculptures at Marabar.

AZIZ: They are immensely holy, no doubt?

GODBOLE: Oh no, oh no.

FIELDING: Ornamented in some way?

GODBOLE: Oh no.

AZIZ: Why do we talk so much about the Marabar Caves? Perhaps that is our empty brag.

GODBOLE: No, I should not quite say that.

AZIZ: Then they *are* deservedly famous? Yes?

GODBOLE: Oh yes, famous with reason. And terrible . . . with reason?

QUESTED: Terrible? But how can a cave be terrible? Especially when there is nothing there?

GODBOLE: Miss Quested, pardon me, there is everything there. For in nothing, there is all.

QUESTED: I'm sorry, I'm not sure that I understand you. Is it the emptiness that is terrible?

GODBOLE: Ah, if it were a question of emptiness, then, indeed, the caves would be empty and nobody would go there. Why would they become famous, in such a case? In our religion, in Hinduism, you see, everything has two or many faces. In the terror there is also calm and comfort. The Creator is also the destroyer. Kali, Parvati, Durga, Uma are equally consorts[9] of Shiva.[10]

QUESTED: I thought you said there were no carvings there?

GODBOLE: There are none.

MOORE (*vaguely*): Adela doesn't believe in ghosts. She only believes the evidence of her eyes.

QUESTED: Well, there must be *something* to see.

GODBOLE: There is enlightenment or obscurity. Nothing to see except with the inner eye. Therefore I would advise you to choose some other environs for your picnic.

AZIZ: For *our* picnic, Godbole. Surely you will not refuse my invitation.

GODBOLE: I am honoured to accept.

QUESTED: Then, at least *you* are not afraid, Professor? I must say you have piqued my curiosity to a point where it must be satisfied. Do let us make the appointment definite.

---

9. **consorts** spouses
10. **Shiva** a principal Hindu god, the destroyer and restorer of worlds

GODBOLE: By all means. I have no doubt that you will find the Caves very beautiful.

AZIZ: Excellent. Then, Professor, describe their beauties to these ladies, please.

GODBOLE: It will be a pleasure. (*a longish pause while* GODBOLE *thinks*) However, I think I will forgo the pleasure.

FIELDING (*to break an awkward silence*): Mrs. Moore, would you like to see our College gardens? We are rather proud of them.

MOORE: Thank you. I am very fond of gardens . . . I find that they repay love in a way that human beings very often do not.

[FIELDING *looks to* MISS QUESTED *to join them.*]

QUESTED: I'll stay here if I may and talk to Professor Godbole and Dr. Aziz. This is such a rare and valuable opportunity for me.

[MRS. MOORE *and* FIELDING *leave through the garden.* MISS QUESTED *settles back on the sofa and to the scarcely concealed astonishment of the Indians, lights a cigarette. She doesn't notice their embarrassment.*]

QUESTED: Do you know, this is the very first time that I've had a chance to talk to Indians since I've been in this country? At the Club, where we usually go of an evening, people never seem to mention India or Indians. I don't know what happens to them— the Callendars, the McBrydes—

AZIZ: The Turtons and the Burtons . . .

QUESTED: Well, I'm sure they're all reasonable people in England. But somehow, when they get to India . . . they become . . . I don't know . . .

AZIZ: Unkind?

QUESTED: They become insensitive, certainly . . .

GODBOLE: They have, perhaps, lost one reality, and have not yet found another?

QUESTED (*puzzled*): That may be true . . . But the odd thing is that they don't seem to be even *interested* in India—and I feel that we can only be of some good here if we have . . . well, a very different attitude.

AZIZ: Oh, I agree . . . such as Mr. Fielding's attitude. He understands poor Indian. Godbole will bear out that fact, isn't it?

GODBOLE: Yes, yes. He makes fine principal of Government College, Chandrapore. A very impartial man.

QUESTED: Yes, I am sure he is. But you see the thing that is really worrying me . . . I mean, if I *were* to settle in India—for whatever reason . . . I mean, if I *had* a reason to stay on, what could I do? What would be the most *useful* thing for India? Is that a foolish question, Professor Godbole?

GODBOLE: Not foolish. No, no. In our ancient Sanskrit writing, *Bhagavad-gita* we are told, "Even the wise are perplexed as to what is action and what is inaction." Not at all foolish.

QUESTED: Then can you help me with the answer?

GODBOLE: Ah yes. Use and abuse are the same in the end.

QUESTED: The *same*?

GODBOLE: Without self-knowledge.

[QUESTED *shakes her head confusedly and looks enquiringly at* AZIZ.]

AZIZ (*warm and earnest. He jumps up to sit next to* MISS QUESTED *on the sofa*): In any case, why be useful, Miss Quested? Just love India. That is the greatest gift.

QUESTED (*shifting nervously deep into her corner of the sofa*): No, but I'm serious, Dr. Aziz. In England I'm used to leading an active life . . . so different from the kind of life the English wives lead out here.

GODBOLE: To love is very active. It can take all your life . . . if you accept fully all its meanings.

QUESTED (*smiling indulgently at* GODBOLE, *but looking immediately back at* AZIZ): Professor, you are probably right, but I'm not a philosopher. I need something less abstract . . .

AZIZ (*gaily*): Miss Quested, I tell you what. Think with your heart for this time, not your head. Heart! Heart, I say!

[MISS QUESTED *gets up suddenly and almost involuntarily, then she has to look for a pretext . . . she puts out her cigarette, and carefully chooses a chair across the room from* AZIZ *in which to sit.*]

QUESTED (*getting herself under control*): But . . . but that's just . . . just what I can't do. (*with spirit*) What's the point of having a brain if one doesn't use it? I intend to use mine to understand what I can about India and then to put that knowledge to some good.

AZIZ: But you'll never understand without your heart . . .

QUESTED: And I think I'll never understand with it. (*with some antagonism*) Perhaps that is the difference between Orientals and Westerners.

AZIZ: But Mrs. Moore feels . . . with her mind, too.

QUESTED: Dr. Aziz, I'm sorry. I don't mean to criticize—but I can't agree with the Oriental idea of women . . . that we mustn't use our minds. That we should be just wives and mothers . . .

GODBOLE: There is a higher ideal, perhaps?

QUESTED: Oh, Professor! Oh yes! At least, I think so. Mrs. Moore belongs to another generation . . . things were different in her day . . .

AZIZ (*coldly*): How difficult to explain this to Indians!

QUESTED (*rather nastily*): I can see that men might not wish to relinquish their privileges.

AZIZ: Where there is heart, privilege does not matter. The English have many privileges in India . . .

QUESTED: And no feelings? Is that what you are saying?

AZIZ: I have no wish to find fault.

QUESTED (*slightly heated*): But you must! You must! Civilized people can discuss things without getting heated, surely. That's what I *want*!

AZIZ: And what I want, Miss Quested, is only that you should enjoy yourself in India.

QUESTED (*getting worked up and disturbed*): Oh, picnics—and enjoyment—of course they're part of one's life . . . but my real worry is this: if I *did* stay in India, for a long time, that is . . . I might simply become another idle Englishwoman—what you call an Anglo-Indian.

GODBOLE: Oh never, Miss Quested. You would always be too thoughtful.

QUESTED: I'm told we all get thoughtless after a year. I know I can't . . . I mean, *couldn't* . . . avoid the label. What I should hope to avoid is the mentality. I feel that any modern, educated person has a duty to the community in which he lives, India, that is. So you see, enjoyment just isn't enough . . .

AZIZ: It is everything—

QUESTED (*more heated*): Life is more than frivolity . . .

AZIZ (*equally heated*): I'm talking about enjoyment . . . giving yourself to your feelings . . .

QUESTED: But Dr. Aziz—

AZIZ: Without it, Miss Quested, please understand me . . . without it, you will never love India and Indians will never love you . . .

QUESTED: Love? (*a shocked silence*) Well—I only meant that I hoped I would get along and be able to do some good.

AZIZ (*indifferently*): I see that my idea of a picnic has not pleased you. Perhaps we should think of some other, more suitable entertainment.

QUESTED (*penitent and concerned. She walks over to him*): Oh please, Dr. Aziz—please, I hope I haven't offended you. I . . . it's just that India is so big and difficult to grasp, and I have so many decisions to make . . .

AZIZ (*smiling*): I wish you good fortune with your "decision."

QUESTED: I must hold on to the best and the most rational part of me . . .

GODBOLE: We learn to protect ourselves when we learn we have something to fear.

[GODBOLE *smiles and nods. From the garden a voice is heard calling "Hallo! Hall-o!"* RONNY HEASLOP *enters from the garden, and pauses under the blue arches looking around at the room and its occupants. He is an extremely good looking man and that justifies a lot of his insensitivity to a girl like* MISS QUESTED *who hovers on the edge of intellectuality.*]

HEASLOP (*in annoyance*): Well, here you are. What's happened to Fielding? Where's my mother?

[*The Indians have stood up, but he doesn't look at them.*]

QUESTED (*coolly*): Good evening, Ronny.

HEASLOP: I want you and mother at once. There's to be polo.

QUESTED: I thought there was to be no polo.

HEASLOP: Everything's altered. Come along, and I'll tell you all about it.

AZIZ: Good evening, Mr. Heaslop.

GODBOLE: Your mother will return shortly, sir. There is but little to see in our poor college.

HEASLOP (*paying no attention to the Indians*): We must hurry, my dear. (*looks around*) Perhaps I should send a servant to find my mother.

QUESTED (*still cold*): Surely we shouldn't leave like this.

AZIZ (*with rather offensive friendliness, pats* HEASLOP *on the arm*): Come along in and join us, Mr. Heaslop; sit down until your mother turns up.

HEASLOP (*turning away*): Boy! Boy! (*a pause*) What's the matter with Fielding's servants? Have they all decided to take a holiday? I dare say they're loafing in their quarters, drinking tea . . . Boy! Boy!

[AZIZ *steps forward about to say something angrily.* GODBOLE *puts a hand on his arm and stops him.*]

GODBOLE (*gently*): Please allow us the honour, sir, of fetching Mrs. Moore and Mr. Fielding for you.

[*He leads* AZIZ *away and* MISS QUESTED *watches them until they are out of hearing.*]

QUESTED (*turning sharply to* HEASLOP): Ronny, I'm appalled . . .

HEASLOP: As well you might be. I'm appalled too, I don't know what's come over Mr. Fielding.

QUESTED: Mr. Fielding? What has *he* done?

HEASLOP: Well . . . I'm the sun-dried bureaucrat, no doubt; still I don't like to see an English girl left smoking cigarettes with two Indians.

QUESTED: This particular English girl stayed here, as she smokes, by her own wish.

HEASLOP: Yes, that's all very well in England.

QUESTED: I really can't see the difference . . . or the harm.

HEASLOP: If you can't see, you can't see . . . Can't you at least see that fellow's a bounder?[11]

QUESTED: He isn't a bounder. He just got nervous, that's all.

HEASLOP: What could have upset his precious nerves?

QUESTED (*trying to bring the disturbing ideas* AZIZ *has suggested safely down to an ordinary level*): I don't know. He was all right until you arrived. In fact he was very . . . interesting.

HEASLOP (*cheerfully*): Well, it's nothing I've said. I never even spoke to him.

QUESTED (*turning away in exasperation*): O Ronny . . . it's just impossible.

---

11. **bounder** man of unprincipled behavior, especially toward women

HEASLOP: Nothing's impossible, only difficult. Don't worry, everyone's temper gets short during this heat.

QUESTED: But this has nothing to do with the weather.

HEASLOP: Everything has something to do with the weather in India. But don't fret—after we're married you won't have to suffer through it again, I promise you. I'll pack you off to the hills every April . . . I'm not one to keep a wife grilling in the plains.

QUESTED: Really, it isn't *that*. I have a sudden . . . sort of vision of what life here would be . . . the Club in the evenings, the Hills in the hot weather.

HEASLOP: It's not a bad life as long as we do our work and keep to ourselves.

QUESTED: But that's just it—I think that part of our work is *not* keeping to ourselves.

HEASLOP: My dear, I know this country better than you. We all come out here with the honest wish to do well, not exactly mingle socially, but at least to close the gap a little. One soon finds it only leads to trouble. India isn't a drawing room. We're in India to do justice and keep the peace. Them's my sentiments.

QUESTED (*quietly*): Your sentiments are those of a god.

HEASLOP (*trying to make amends*): India likes gods.

QUESTED: And Englishmen like posing as gods.

HEASLOP: Honestly, Adela, what do you want me to do? Lose such power as I have for doing good in this country because I don't slap Indians on the back?

QUESTED: Of course not . . .

HEASLOP: Well, it's what you're asking. You don't seem to realize what my work involves—that the whole value of my job depends on reputation for utter fairness. It's the tradition of British justice. (*embarrassed*) It's not the kind of thing one goes *on* about, but I think it's a fine tradition.

QUESTED: Oh, of course . . . so do I . . . but, Ronny, why can't you be pleasant to Indians?

HEASLOP: Look, Adela, in any other country it would be different, but not in India. You'll soon find out that if I were to make friends with an Indian the gossip would be all over the bazaar in a minute.

I'd be known as the kind of official an Indian can "get round".
Don't you see how difficult and embarrassing it would be?

QUESTED: But it has to begin *somewhere* . . .

HEASLOP: If it were only my own discomfort I wouldn't mind so
much, but really, I'd be undermining all the good we've tried to do
in this wretched country—

QUESTED: But I think we could do *more* good the other way . . .

HEASLOP: Well, I haven't the choice. I'm too junior to dictate the
manners of my fellow officials . . . or myself . . . even if I wanted
to . . .

QUESTED: Even if *I* wanted you to?

HEASLOP: Adela, my dear, there is a lot I would do for you. But this
is—I dare say I sound pompous—but *this is* a matter of principle. I
can't help it if Indians don't like me . . . it's one of the hazards of
the job. The thing I've learned out here—and you will too—is
that we are better for them than they are for each other. Peace,
security, good administration, justice . . . we've brought them all
those.

QUESTED: Everything except understanding.

HEASLOP: What good will that do them?

QUESTED: I don't know.

HEASLOP: Well, there you are.

QUESTED (*with sudden passion*): But it's living in such isolation . . .

HEASLOP: Isolation? When we have all our English friends. When we
are surrounded by India and Indians?

QUESTED: Exactly.

HEASLOP (*tolerantly*): Oh, I know you want to *understand* India, get
to *know* the people and so on, but—

QUESTED (*rather desperately*): Somebody must!

HEASLOP: Of course,

[*Smiling he continues with a change of tone, wanting to get the conversation on an
affectionate level. She frowns and makes a small movement repudiating his tone.
He quickly reverts to a more impersonal manner.*]

and I've always approved of your doing good work here—as long as
you don't get *involved* . . . social work, say—but please—Adela—
please try not to be so emotional about it all.

QUESTED: *Emotional?* . . . Ronny, we must have a thorough talk.

HEASLOP (*trying to avoid the implications of this*): I'm sorry. My temper's rotten in this heat. I don't mean to lecture you and order you about . . .

QUESTED: I know—

HEASLOP: But, of course, the way those Indians let you down this morning annoyed me, and things like that keep happening—

QUESTED: It's nothing to do with them that I—

HEASLOP: I dare say, but—

QUESTED: It's something very different—it's that I think . . . I think we should . . . well, consider a bit more before we get married.

[*A long pause.*]

HEASLOP (*sad but careful*): It's all right, Adela. No need to get upset. Take all the time you want. That was the arrangement you wanted . . . that we agreed on.

QUESTED (*with a rush of gratitude*): Oh, Ronny, I keep forgetting how nice you are—and I feel so ashamed of this—muddleheadedness. It's really not like me. I *could* explain—I need—breathing space.

HEASLOP (*uncomfortably*): No, really, Adela. You've acted entirely within your rights. I don't want you worrying and feeling guilty. So take your time, and don't fret. It will work out, you'll see. You'll come round in the end.

QUESTED (*in a slightly despairing voice*): It's awful of me to have given you and your mother all this bother and still be so uncertain. (*a pause*) We've been very British over this, but I suppose that's all right.

HEASLOP (*smiling*): Since we *are* British, I suppose it is.

QUESTED: Anyhow, we mustn't quarrel, Ronny.

HEASLOP: Oh, I couldn't quarrel with you, Adela.

QUESTED: I just need a little time—

HEASLOP: Yes, yes. By all means . . . Time . . .

QUESTED: Well—(*she walks to the window and stands looking out at the garden*) Do you know the name of that green bird?

[*He comes to stand at her shoulder.*]

Up there, in the tree?

HEASLOP: Bee-eater?

QUESTED: Oh no, Ronny, it has red bars on its wings.

HEASLOP: Parrot?

QUESTED (*laughs*): Good gracious no.

HEASLOP (*dejectedly*): McBryde has an illustrated book about birds. I'll borrow it for you if you like. I'm no good at all at birds. (*a pause*) In fact, I'm useless at anything outside the job of a City Magistrate. It's a great pity.

QUESTED (*turns to him suddenly and compassionately*): Oh, so am I, Ronny. I'm . . . useless at . . . everything. I'm really awful—

[*A pause while they stare at each other. Pleadingly.*]

HEASLOP: Adela . . .

QUESTED (*sorry for him*): Ronny, I'd like to . . . tell you that I really will try to . . . work out the pattern of my life . . . here, with you.

HEASLOP (*making a move towards her which he quickly controls*): My darling . . . And I really will try to be more pleasant, if that is what you want—

QUESTED: Well, at least to Dr. Aziz because he has been (*breaks off*) . . . he has been so kind to us. He has invited us to a picnic.

HEASLOP: Us?

QUESTED: Your mother, Mr. Fielding, Professor Godbole—exactly the same party.

HEASLOP: Where on earth is this picnic to be?

QUESTED: The Marabar Caves.

HEASLOP: Well, I'm blessed. Did he descend to any details?

QUESTED (*getting heated*): If you had spoken to him, we could have arranged them.

[HEASLOP *shakes his head, laughing.*]

Have I said anything funny?

HEASLOP: I was only thinking how the worthy doctor's collar climbed up his neck.

QUESTED: I thought we were discussing the caves.

HEASLOP: So I am. Aziz was exquisitely dressed, from tie-pin to spats, but he had forgotten his back collar-stud, and there you have the Indian in a nutshell: inattention to detail; the fundamental slackness that reveals the race. Similarly to "meet" in the caves as if they were the clock at Charing Cross when they're miles from a station and each other.

QUESTED: Have you been to them?

HEASLOP: No, but I know all about them, naturally.

QUESTED: Oh, naturally!

HEASLOP: In any case, surely Fielding would never agree to an absurd scheme like that—

QUESTED: And why not?

HEASLOP: Well, he may not be quite our sort, but he has had *some* experience in this country . . .

[MRS. MOORE, FIELDING, AZIZ *and* GODBOLE *come in from the garden, sauntering along and talking pleasantly among themselves.* HEASLOP *turns at once to* MRS. MOORE.]

Mother! What is all this rubbish Adela has been telling me?

MOORE (*peaceably*): I have no idea, my dear boy.

HEASLOP: I mean this nonsense about caves and picnics. Fielding, you are included, I hear—of course you will not allow such a fantastic scheme!

FIELDING: I don't presume to make decisions for other people, Heaslop.

HEASLOP (*looking from* MISS QUESTED *to* MRS. MOORE, *ignoring the Indians*): If you are set on this ridiculous expedition then please allow me to arrange it. You can go under official auspices and that will be much better . . . and more comfortable too, without question.

[FIELDING *stands among the English, very embarrassed. He looks imploringly at* AZIZ.]

QUESTED: But Dr. Aziz has already invited us to go with him.

HEASLOP: Very kind, I'm sure. But no doubt he will understand that you will be better off in our hands.

QUESTED: But that was the whole point—we wanted to go with the Indians—we could learn something.

HEASLOP (*shouting*): Well, I consider the whole business foolish—yes, and dangerous!

MOORE (*quietly*): Dangerous, Ronny?

HEASLOP (*furious*): Yes, dangerous! In fact, Mother—Adela—I forbid it! I forbid you both! Of course I cannot speak for Mr. Fielding.

[FIELDING *makes a hopeless, awkward gesture toward* AZIZ. AZIZ *responds with the same Muslim salaam that established a rapport between them earlier. He smiles and quickly interrupts.*]

> **AZIZ:** I don't know whether you have all heard that Professor Godbole is a great authority on Indian music. Indeed, he is much admired here in the College and elsewhere. What a pity if you did not hear him. Professor, please do us the honour.
>
> **GODBOLE:** I will sing now.

[HEASLOP *takes an angry step forward and then stands still impatient and boiling.* MRS. MOORE *and* MISS QUESTED *turn towards* GODBOLE *listening politely.* GODBOLE *sings a brief Indian devotional song, while the English, with half their mind on their unresolved quarrel wait tensely. The servants appear on the edge of the verandah, the man at the waterchestnut tank stops work and straightens up. The Indians are enchanted. The English rigid and ill at ease.*]

> **FIELDING:** Thanks so much. What was the song about?
>
> **MOORE:** Yes, do tell us.
>
> **GODBOLE:** I will explain in detail. It was a religious song. I place myself in the position of a milkmaiden. I say to Shri Krishna, "Come! Come to me only." The god refuses to come. I grow humble and say: "Do not come to me only. Multiply yourself into a hundred Krishnas, and let one go to each of my hundred companions, but one, O Lord of the Universe, come to me." He refuses to come. This is repeated several times. The song is composed in a raga[12] appropriate to the present hour, which is the evening.
>
> **MOORE** (*gently*): But he comes to you in some other song, I hope?
>
> **GODBOLE:** Oh no, he refuses to come. I say to him, "come, come, come, come, come, come." (*pause*) He neglects to come.
>
> **QUESTED:** Oh dear, that sounds so unsatisfactory!
>
> **HEASLOP** (*interrupting*): Come along, Mother, Adela. We are already late for the polo. I am sure everyone will agree that you are not committed to this Marabar expedition.

---

12. **raga** melodic scale pattern

MOORE: I am committed to do nothing. Certainly not to this polo. I find I am tired and prefer to rest. Will you drop me at the bungalow first?

QUESTED: Drop me, too. I don't want to watch the polo either, I'm sure.

HEASLOP (*tired and disappointed*): Simpler to drop the polo. Well, come along, come along. (*he walks out angrily*)

MOORE: Goodbye, Mr. Fielding, and thank you so much . . . what lovely college grounds!

FIELDING: Goodbye, Mrs. Moore.

QUESTED: Goodbye. Such an interesting afternoon.

FIELDING: Goodbye.

MOORE: Goodbye, Dr. Aziz. We shall be seeing you soon again?

AZIZ: May I hope so?

QUESTED (*earnestly making amends*): Oh, please, yes, Dr. Aziz. I don't know what to say . . .

AZIZ: Say nothing, Miss Quested. You'll reconsider our picnic at the caves? I can fix the whole thing up in a jiffy. You'll see. That will be my great joy. To please you and Mr. Fielding.

QUESTED (*definitely*): I shall look forward to it. (*she looks uneasily from* AZIZ *to the path that* HEASLOP *took when he left*) Mrs. Moore! Dr. Aziz says that he is willing to arrange the picnic—what do you say?

MOORE: I say I shall be delighted. Goodbye, goodbye.

[*They both nod to* GODBOLE, *who makes a namaskar.* MISS QUESTED *responds to this. He follows them out to the garden, gently pointing out the way to the carriage.*]

GODBOLE: Goodbye—I will accompany the ladies.

FIELDING (*sinking exhausted into a chair*): Aziz, my dear chap. How am I to apologize to you?

AZIZ: No apologies are necessary between friends.

FIELDING: But you see, your other friends were right after all—oil and water.

AZIZ: You will never persuade me of that. "The secret understanding of the heart"—as I told you—I can't lose my faith in that for a moment's rudeness.

FIELDING: I'm glad.

AZIZ: I, too. Life is more interesting this way. I am only sorry for the embarrassment caused to your guests.

FIELDING: Oh, they'll survive—they may even have accomplished what they set out to do—learn something about India.

AZIZ: But still, it is unfortunate if your good ladies are caused distress.

FIELDING (*smiling at him affectionately*): You know what I should do, Aziz? I should get you a drink and then jog your elbow to make you spill it.

AZIZ (*puzzled for a moment*): I beg your pardon?

FIELDING (*sketching the gesture of a Muslim salaam and gently mimicking* AZIZ): "The sign of a generous heart, full to overflowing, you see."

AZIZ (*laughing*): You know, I invented that saying on the spur of the moment.

FIELDING: You know (*putting his arm on* AZIZ's *shoulder, laughing with him*), I know you did.

[*They are both laughing with conspiratorial pleasure as the curtain falls.*]

At the Marabar Caves, both Englishwomen are overcome by their emotional reactions to Indian mysticism. Miss Quested becomes hysterical in the caves, and Dr. Aziz is accused of assaulting her. At his trial, she becomes lucid enough to deny any wrongdoing on Aziz's part. However, despite the Englishwoman's truthfulness, Aziz does not forgive her or the British for the harm he has suffered.